TORCH GINGER

PARADISE CRIME MYSTERIES BOOK 2

TOBY NEAL

Rom. 7:20
So I find this law at work: when I want to do good, evil is right there with me.

CHAPTER ONE

Wednesday, October 20

PEOPLE SAID KAUA`I was the last of the Wild West, a jungle paradise of secretive people and strange spiritual forces. After two months, Detective Leilani Texeira just found Kaua`i slow and boring. She leaned on her hand and fiddled with the Bic ballpoints in a mug on her desk, looking for one that still worked as she contemplated a slim pile of case jackets in front of her.

Lei shuffled the pile, closed her eyes, and pulled one out. The vacation-rental burglary case had now become the project of the day. She sighed and opened the file, scanning the incident reports filed by Paradise Realty, the company managing the rentals.

"Excuse me." Lei looked up into blinking brown eyes in a chubby-cheeked face. Long brunette hair curled over shoulders bisected by a bulky leather purse, a plastic shopping bag held in one hand. "The guy at the front sent me to you, and I'd like to—I'd like to report a missing person."

The girl's round eyes blinked harder and tears seemed imminent. Lei felt familiar anxiety, a prickle along her arms that tightened her chest. She pushed the mug of pens away and pointed to the orange plastic chair alongside her desk.

"Have a seat. I'm Detective Texeira."

"Um. Hi. Kelly Waterson." Kelly clutched the bulging handbag on her lap like it held the crown jewels, setting the shopping bag at her feet.

Lei shook one of the Bics and jotted the name on a yellow legal pad.

"Name of the missing person?" Lei kept her voice brisk as blinking turned to sniffling. She pushed a box of tissues over without making eye contact.

"Jay. Jay Bennett." Kelly blew her nose and firmed her voice. "I mean, something's very wrong. He's not where he said he was."

Lei turned to her computer and her fingers rattled over the keys as she typed "Jay Bennett" into the local database. Nothing came up. No Hawaii driver's license, no outstanding warrants. She typed in Kelly's name—same result.

"Your relationship to the missing person?"

"Girlfriend."

"How long has he been gone?"

"He was supposed to call me yesterday. He's not picking up. So it's been at least twenty-four hours. I decided to fly out and surprise him. He's been camping in Hanalei." A catch in the breathy voice.

"So he has a cell phone?"

"He has a cell, but he keeps it off. He's on…a walkabout is what he's calling it. He's staying away from technology." Kelly told Lei the number, and her voice rang with pride as she said, "He hitchhiked all over the States for six months, then came to Hawaii. He's been exploring the island."

"Where are you two from?"

"Clovis, California. Not much to it, just a flat stretch of Central California nowhere. Jay wanted to see more, do more, before he started working in his dad's auto dealership."

"Any particular reason you think he's not just on a long hike or something?" Lei pulled up the Missing Persons Report screen on her computer and began filling it in. She pushed her thick curly brown hair back impatiently, bundling it into a wad and spearing it with the Bic, returning her attention to the screen.

"He thought someone was, you know, stalking him. He said he had a funny feeling about it. I decided to surprise him. I flew in from California today and drove out to where he was camping, at a park called Pine Trees. He wasn't there." She dug in the tote and brought out a man's leather wallet, plunked it on the desk. "I looked in the trash and his stuff was there. I put his clothes in this bag here—but he'd never throw his wallet away."

Uh-oh.

Lei snapped on a pair of latex gloves from a box beside the Kleenex and opened the wallet.

A driver's license: Jay Bennett, Clovis, California, age twenty-seven. A Visa credit card poked its silver edge up out of a slot, along with a Paradise Realty card with a phone number on the back. Fattening the cash area of the wallet were folded paper shapes.

Lei upended the wallet, and a crane, a turtle, a fish, a diamond, and a jumble of other origami in cursive-covered lavender paper fell out onto the desk.

"Something's happened to him! Those are my letters to him all these months. He would never throw that wallet away." Kelly stuffed a double-fisted handful of Kleenex against her mouth, shaking. Jack Jenkins, Lei's partner, blew into their cubicle with his typical energy and flung a jacket over the back of his chair. He paused, assessing the situation with the wariness of a man unexpectedly confronted by female emotion.

"Hi, Lei—I'm getting coffee."

Lei nodded and he disappeared. Lei took the real estate card out of the pile and clipped it onto the case jacket for the burglaries —there might be a connection to pursue.

Kelly seemed to pull herself together and reached into the capacious purse to pull out a man's rubber sandal, then set it on the desk.

"This is Jay's shoe. It was under the picnic table. These were on it, like this." She took three stones out of her pocket and set them on the sandal in a triangle.

Lei looked at the shoe and stones, frowned. It was creepy. They looked like they meant something, and together with the wallet, this case had just gone from odd to suspicious. She dug in the drawer of the desk for her little point-and-shoot and took a picture of the sandal with the stones on it. One was reddish, one green, and one a gray matrix with flecks of blue fire. She spread the origami shapes out and photographed them and each of the items in the wallet.

"Pine Trees is not an official campground." Lei's camera clicked. She ran past the scenic park shaded by huge ironwood trees in Hanalei nearly every morning and made it a point to call in any illegal campers. In fact, she had called in a guy sleeping under a picnic table just yesterday. "Which part of the park was he in?"

"I know it's not a real camping area. He...likes to do things his own way. He was just crashing in his sleeping bag wherever. He said he liked the picnic table near the bathrooms."

"Hm. Okay." Lei stowed the items in two evidence bags and turned back to her screen. She got a physical description: six foot two, curly blond hair, blue eyes, bearded, age twenty-seven. By the time she'd filled in the missing persons report, she was sure this was the guy she'd seen just yesterday.

Kelly produced a photo from her wallet, and Lei took it to the back room and made an enlarged color photocopy of the young man's square-cut, smiling face.

"Kelly." Returning, Lei roused the girl from a reverie as Kelly stared blankly at the fabric-covered divider, fingers wound tightly into the strap of the purse. "I wish you'd left this in the trash and called for a unit from out there. We may have blurred any prints that were on the wallet. Finding this is definitely concerning."

"Some of his stuff is still in the trash." Kelly's voice was muffled by the pile of Kleenex she pressed to her face.

Jenkins slid into his seat in their cubicle. He set a mug of inky fluid beside Lei. "Sorry I'm late. Peace offering. How can I help?"

"Ugh, if that's break room coffee, I've already had my caffeine ration for the day. This is Kelly. Her boyfriend is missing."

"I'm sorry to hear that, Kelly." Jenkins's fashionably spiked blond hair seemed to quiver with sympathy and his blue eyes were kind. Lei had no problem admitting he was better with people than she was.

The girl gave a snuffle and extended her hand to shake his. "When can you start looking for Jay?"

"Hopefully today," Lei said. "Did he ever say anything about suicide?"

Kelly's eyes went wide. "No. Of course not."

"I have to ask. I mean, he's alone, traveling. He may have been depressed, worse off than you knew. He could have thrown his stuff away and left the stones on his shoe as some kind of message."

Lei felt a squeeze in her chest as the girl considered the idea, taking it like an arrow to the heart. Kelly's eyes, which at first seemed brown, had gone foresty green—tears welling from some-where transformatively deep. Then she shook her head, so hard her curls bounced.

"No. Jay wasn't depressed. He would never do that. He said he was being stalked—maybe the shoe with the stones was a message from whoever took him."

Lei knew when to back off.

"Well, then, I just need an idea of any people he might have hung with and known." She picked up another Bic, scribbled on the pad to get the ink going.

"He mostly hung out with other people who were living in the parks. There's kind of a group of them. They move around to stay ahead of their permits, which expire every ten days. He got a little sick of them. That's part of why he was crashing in Pine Trees. But he never told me any names."

"Thanks, Kelly. Give me some contact information so we can keep in touch, okay?"

"Sure. I was supposed to go back in a few days, but I can't until I know what happened to Jay… This was just supposed to be a surprise, to see if he was ready to come home."

Lei blinked at the volume of water the girl generated as Kelly's eyes filled again. She got her number and hotel address, turned to Jenkins. "Can you sign these items into evidence? I'll walk Kelly out."

"Hang in there, Kelly." Jenkins patted the girl's shoulder and took the two bags she'd packed Jay's items into. Lei led Kelly through the beehive of modular units to the pneumatic front doors.

"Please find him," the girl said, green-brown eyes swimming again. She turned away and beeped open the doors of an electric-blue Ford Fiesta rental.

"I'll do my best." Lei reached into her pocket to rub the black worry stone she always carried as she watched Kelly drive away. She got back to their cubicle just as Jenkins returned from signing the items into evidence. He grinned at her, blue eyes alight.

"Well, this looks interesting." He rubbed his hands together. "So tired of getting all the cases nobody wants."

Lei flung herself into her office chair, did a couple spins to discharge energy. "Poor kid. God." She knocked back half of the mug of coffee and made a gagging noise. "I forget how bad this stuff is. Yeah, this case ought to be interesting, and now we get to take a drive out to the North Shore. We can also follow up on these two, J-Boy." She held up the files on the vacation rental burglaries and a noise complaint against a group located on a papaya farm in the same area.

"J-Boy? That my new handle?" Nicknames were a popular

6

Kaua`i Police Department thing. "Fine, then. I'll call you Hurricane Lei."

"That wasn't even funny when it first came out on the Big Island."

Lei scooped up the backpack she carried in lieu of a purse. That morning she'd taken a moment to whisk mascara onto tilted dark eyes, run a wand of gloss over her wide mouth. She wished she didn't have the sprinkle of cinnamon freckles across her nose —Portuguese, Hawaiian, and Japanese heritage made for a blend that was more interesting than pretty.

Now that she'd made detective, she no longer had to wear a uniform and had come up with her own—black jeans, black running shoes, and tank tops—functional clothing that looked good on a slim, athletic frame. She shrugged into the loose cotton blazer she wore to hide the Glock .40 in its shoulder holster.

"How about Sweet Leilani?" Jenkins referred to the famous Bing Crosby song. "Sweets for short." He chuckled at his own wit.

"No, dammit. Just Lei. My name is short enough."

"C'mon. It's a Kaua`i thing. I like you as Sweets. Everyone's going to crack up."

"You like cracks, I'll crack you one." She couldn't help smiling. "I'll get started on the missing person—take a run out and check the park, pick up his stuff from the rubbish."

"I'll go by the alarm company the mansions used."

"On the way back I'll check out the real estate agency that reported the burglaries. Jay Bennett's wallet had one of their cards." She tapped the item in question. "There's a phone number on the back."

"Coincidence?"

"Doubtful. C'mon—a series of robberies happen at houses managed by that company, and a missing guy leaves their card in his wallet? I'm trying the number now." She flipped the card over, punched it in, and an automated message answered. "Disconnected."

7

"That is weird. Let's meet for lunch at that noodle place and you can let me know how it goes. We'll hit the papaya farm after."

"Sounds like a plan, J-Boy."

THE TIMEKEEPER SET the jug of water down beside the Chosen. The man had curled instinctively into a ball on the floor of the cave, the collar padlocked on and tie-out cable secure. A chill from the surrounding rock must have penetrated his deeply unconscious state.

One good knock to the head usually subdued the Chosen, and this latest was no exception. Usually they were malleable and confused for some days, or stayed unconscious until their Time.

The Timekeeper tipped the man's curly blond head back and poured water into his mouth. It was always a juggling act. If he waited too long, he ran the risk of being unable to find the next Chosen. If he took them too early, he had to keep them alive, and that could be tricky.

He thought he could keep this one going long enough, but it was going to be close.

CHAPTER TWO

Y OUNG LOVERS TORN APART—THIS case pulled at her already. Lei couldn't stop her eyes from landing on her bare ring finger as it tapped the steering wheel. There was still a faint band of lighter skin marking where the engagement ring had been, and her hand tightened.

It had been raining in Hilo the day she'd taken the ring off. She remembered the patter of drops on the window, the rain reflecting the blank shock in Stevens's eyes as she put the ring in his hand and folded his fingers over it.

"I'm sorry. I'm all wrong for you, and I just can't do this."

They'd been through so much together, and even as she'd broken up with him she didn't know, couldn't say why she had to. He put the hand with the ring in his pocket, looked at her a long moment. Pain hardened his eyes into opaque blue china.

"Maybe he was right about you. You are damaged."

Her mouth had dropped open in shock—that he could hit her so low and so hard by quoting Charlie Kwon, her childhood molester. Stevens had turned and left, the door of her little house slamming hard behind him. She looked at the bare finger again, regret pulling down her mouth. He hadn't deserved how she'd ended it. She was damaged.

So what.

Everything was what it was.

But maybe now she could help another couple, do a little something for someone else in love. She pinched her arm, anchoring herself in the present moment as she'd learned in therapy so long ago.

The road, a narrow two-lane highway winding between lush banks of jungle growth, required some attention. Lei still wasn't over the thrill of owning her new Toyota truck, and she stomped on the gas just to feel the surge of power that answered. It wasn't long before she pulled into the sandy parking lot at Pine Trees Park in Hanalei.

She got out of the pickup and walked over to a picnic table that overlooked the ocean, doing a slow scan of the park. Decrepit, graffitied bathrooms and an outdoor shower occupied an open area among the towering ironwoods, a fast-growing timber brought over from Australia. Long, swaying needles shushed in the light breeze, waving over the empty expanse of lawn and beach. Behind the park, deeply shadowed valleys rose, cleft by waterfalls—a tapestry in shades of green.

No sign of anyone camping the length of the park. At midmorning on a weekday with no surf at the beach break, the area was deserted.

Lei leaned over the edge of the table, examining the sandy dirt underneath. She could see a dented shape where someone had lain —the same spot she'd seen the park crasher the day before. That must have been Jay Bennett—and this had to be where Kelly had found the slipper.

The hairs rose on the back of Lei's neck.

She scanned the ground all around but saw nothing more. She got out her little digital Nikon and photographed the area. Snapping on a pair of gloves, she peered into the nearby metal trash barrel, reaching in and pulling up a sleeping bag clearly in need of a wash. Underneath it was another slipper and a backpack. She photographed the items in the can, then hauled it all out and took it over to the picnic table, setting the items down on the tabletop and upending the backpack.

Out fell a tin of hand-rolled joints, pepper spray, matches, a bathroom kit with toothbrush, soap, comb, and a wad of cash in an inside pocket, an old-fashioned journal with a hasp, a couple of pens, canteen, and flashlight. She photographed the items on the table and the trash barrel for reference.

A chill passed over her as she zipped up the bag.

Why would Jay Bennett throw away all his worldly possessions, including enough cash and pot for at least another week of homelessness in paradise, other than suicide? If he'd been taken, what kind of perp threw away cash? And what could that slipper with the stones mean?

Lei rubbed the black stone in her pocket as she headed back to the truck.

CHAPTER THREE

LEI PULLED into the parking lot of the Paradise Realty office in Kilauea—an old plantation home restored to better than its former glory. White paint gleamed against a traditional dark green background, and a new corrugated roof contrasted in brick red. Lei went up three stairs to a wide lanai, glancing down at the file with its clipped-on card before she pulled open a screened door and stepped into the teak-floored interior.

A receptionist with a shiny tan and collagen lips looked up as Lei came in.

"Can I help you?"

"Yes. I'd like to speak with your manager regarding the break-ins at some of your rentals." Lei pulled aside her jacket to show the badge clipped to her waistband.

"Just a minute. I'll contact the owner." She pushed down an intercom button. "Ms. Wolcott, can you see a detective regarding the break-ins?"

"Of course. Send him in." The receptionist opened her mouth to correct her, and Lei shook her head, smiling. She was escorted into an interior office, decorated in what was being called the Tommy Bahama look—deep, comfortable aloha-print rattan chairs, woven mats, palmetto fans, and a gleaming desk with nothing but a Mac computer on it.

Ms. Wolcott rose from behind the desk, a regal Hawaiian woman in a short, fitted muumuu, her black hair wound into a topknot and pierced with ivory chopsticks. She came around and extended her hand to Lei.

"Oh, my mistake, Detective…?"

"Texeira, ma'am. A pleasure to meet you, and I wish it were in happier circumstances." Lei handed the woman her card.

"Me too. Believe me, I'd rather be selling you a house!" Ms. Wolcott had a warm laugh. "Call me Lehua, please. We filled out the police reports and helped our owners with the insurance claims, but we never heard another word."

"Well, after three break-ins, the patrol officers bumped your burglaries to the detective division. Do you have any theories, anything to add to the reports?"

Ms. Wolcott sat on one of the comfortable armchairs and gestured to Lei to sit as well. Lei took a notebook out of her jacket pocket.

"I have an idea. I think it might have something to do with the cleaning service, but I hope I'm wrong."

"What do you mean?" Lei uncapped her Bic.

"The service is called Island Cleaning." She got up and read a number off the screen of the Mac. "They were great for years, but recently my friend who owned the company died of cancer. Now the company's being run into the ground by her daughter, whom I've heard has a drug habit. I ended up firing Island Cleaning, and the burglaries happened right after. They still had access codes to all our houses. So now I've talked to the security company, and we've changed the locks and codes. So far, no more break-ins."

"Hmm," Lei said. "I'll give Island Cleaning a visit, see what they say. Why don't you give me contact numbers for all the rental owners, and your new cleaning service as well? You have my number if you have any further thoughts."

"Certainly." Lehua went back to her computer, printing up the list of contact information. "Now, can I sell you a house? Maybe a nice starter condo?"

Lei laughed. "Not ready for that kind of commitment yet. I'll keep you in mind if I'm ever looking."

The intercom buzzed. "Ms. Wolcott? Your son is here."

"Oh, send him in." To Lei she said, "We're having lunch."

The door opened and a tall man walked in. He glanced at Lei—and his eyes widened. "Sorry to interrupt, Mom."

"Meet Detective Texeira. She's investigating our burglaries. Detective, my son, Alika."

Lei realized her mouth had fallen open and rectified the situation. He was almost too good-looking, a tall, muscular example of the best of what happens when haole (Caucasian) and Polynesian mix to make hapa (half). Winged brows raked back from golden-brown eyes; dark hair framed a high brow, and dimples flashed.

It was all a little overwhelming.

"Good, I wanted to talk to a detective." Alika came toward her with his hand extended. "I've got some information I want to discuss."

"Hi." Lei stood. Her voice was short, and she felt her scalp prickle with embarrassment as she yanked her hand away too quickly. Handsome men made her edgy. Buying time to regroup, Lei looked down at her file, pulled out a photocopy. The Wolcotts took the two armchairs facing hers across a glossy wood coffee table.

"I was just going to show this to your mother. I wonder if you know anything about it." Lei unclipped the card from the file she'd carried in with her, held it up. "This card was found with the possessions of a young man we're looking for. Do you know him?" She slid the card and the photo of Jay across the table.

"No. Never seen him before." Alika Wolcott shook his head. His mother's curved brows drew together. She flipped the card over.

"What's this number?" She tapped the card.

"I was hoping you would know. I called it earlier and it's disconnected."

"Not any of our office phones, or any of our agents. I would recognize it. Wait a minute."

She stood up, pulled a key out on a fob clipped to a narrow pocket on her dress, unlocked a file drawer in the desk. Looked through and drew out a file, flipping it open. "I knew that looked a little familiar. That number is the old code to the security systems. We had it changed after the burglaries."

"Interesting," Lei said, her attention sharpened. She made a note on her pad—Jay Bennett was involved with the burglaries. She gathered the materials back into the folder.

"Oh!" Lehua exclaimed. "Do you want something to drink? Ice tea? Water?"

"Water would be great," Lei said. Lehua sailed out.

Lei glanced at Alika Wolcott. He'd sat back in the cushy chair, his ankle over his knee, relaxed. He wore immaculate chinos, a subdued aloha shirt, slip-on loafers—the Hawaii business-casual uniform. He inspected her equally, lively curiosity in his eyes.

"You aren't what I expected in a detective."

"Oh? Well, I didn't expect you at all." That sounded all wrong —she knew it as she said it.

He shrugged. "Fair enough."

"So you had some information you wanted to discuss?"

"Yes. It's about Island Cleaning."

"Your mother told me she suspects they may have had something to do with the burglaries."

"I agree. Not only that, I'm concerned about Lisa Nakamoto, the owner."

"The druggie?"

Something flashed in his eyes, quickly suppressed. "Where did you hear that?"

"I'm a detective. We have sources." She wasn't about to tell him his mother had been that source.

"Well, that's not a fair statement. Lisa may be caught up in something. I'm worried about her."

"What kind of something?" Lei pretended to take a note.

"Something related to drug production. But she wasn't that kind of person."

"Addiction makes good people do bad things."

"It's not that simple." His eyes narrowed, defensive. Lei did a relaxation breath—in through the nose, out through the mouth. Then another.

"Let's start over," she said. "What would you like me to do about your friend?"

"Locate her. See what's going on."

"I can try, since it relates to this investigation."

"Here's her number." He grabbed a Post-it off his mother's desk, scrolled through the contacts on his phone, and jotted the number just as Lehua came back in, carrying a glass of ice water.

"Thank you." Lei took a sip of water. Alika handed her the Post-it, his fingers brushing hers, and an unexpected awareness rippled through her. Spooked, she set down the glass and stood up. Charlie Kwon had ruined her ability to respond normally to an attractive man, and knowing that didn't seem to help.

"I have a couple of leads to follow up on here. Anything else?"

"Well, yeah," said Alika. "I've had a break-in at my model home. I'd like you to add it to the investigation."

"Okay. Tell me more." She decided not to sit back down and flipped open her notebook.

He gave a phone number and address outside of Kapa`a.

"I'll give you a call and stop by to inventory what's missing."

"It was great to meet you." Lehua came around from behind her computer, pressed a small square of tapa cloth into Lei's hand. "This is someone I think could be helpful."

Lei glanced down at the hand-printed card on native fiber

cloth. Esther Ka`awai and a phone number was all that was written there.

"Who's this?"

"A local resource. I think you might need her help."

Lei frowned. "Okay. I'm looking for any and all leads."

Lehua Wolcott just smiled, enigmatic, and gave a little wave as Lei headed for the door. Alika followed her out to the truck. She got in and rolled down the window.

"Island Cleaning cleaned my house. Or I should say, 'houses.'" He leaned against the vehicle so his arm bracketed the window.

She nodded. "Go on."

"I'm a developer. Island Cleaning had the contract to do all my construction cleans after a house was finished, and periodic cleans while they were on the market. I noticed the same thing my mother did—the work wasn't being kept up, they missed appointments, and so on. I called Lisa one day to tell her to get her crew to shape up; she seemed really upset, crying, like she was in trouble. She seemed to want to tell me something, but she wouldn't."

"Probably thought she could get somewhere with you by playing the damsel in distress."

"Hmm. So you admit some women might find me interesting."

"No. She just knew a sucker when she saw one."

They stared at each other for a long moment. He smiled. The charm of it lit his face like lightning.

"You're not that into me, are you?"

"That would be a yes. Or is it no? Now you're trying to trip me up." She smiled, because she couldn't help it.

"You have a dimple." He touched a finger to her cheek. "Right here."

"Hey." She jerked her face away and turned the key. The truck roared into life.

He grew serious and spoke quickly. "I mean it. I'm worried about Lisa. I think she might be in danger, being forced to be involved with these break-ins somehow."

"Who do you think is behind it?"

"I don't know. Maybe her boyfriend, Darrell Hines. He's an icehead time-share salesman, got her into using."

"Right now all I'm working on is the burglaries. You'd do better to call Detective Furukawa—he's in charge of drug investigations—with this 'tip,' but I'll pass it on." Lei felt the frustration of the limitations put on her. Furukawa, aka, "Fury," wanted any and all information on the drug trade routed through him.

"You left your card with my mother, right? I might want to call you." Alika's golden-brown gaze was intent.

"Okay. Bye then."

Lei cut her eyes away and kept her voice cool. She pulled out and drove sedately down the road, flicking a glance to the rearview mirror. He was still standing there, watching her, jingling something in his pocket like a man making a decision. She glanced at her phone on the seat as if it might ring, caught herself, and turned up the radio to blast her thoughts away. She headed for the nearby noodle house for lunch, speed-dialing Jenkins to join her.

THE NOODLE SHACK was another old plantation house, unrestored this time but surrounded by lush plumeria trees. The worn, pock-marked floor, sagging screens, and battered wooden counter belied the delicious Asian noodles the place specialized in. Lei climbed up onto one of the worn vinyl stools at the long counter and ordered a saimin, Jenkins joining her.

She scooped the fragrant noodles out of the deep plastic bowl with her chopsticks and spoon. Jenkins gave up on the chopsticks, never having mastered them in his short year in Hawaii, and wrestled the noodles into a squared-off traditional spoon with a fork. When they'd both made some progress, Lei settled back a bit, wiped her mouth.

"So interesting about the missing guy. I found his stuff. All his stuff." She filled Jenkins in on her discovery. "And the real estate owner ID'd the number on the back of the card as the old code for the vacation rentals that were hit."

"So he was involved. Foul play or suicide?"

"Don't know. I'm going to read through the journal and letters, see what I can pick up about his state of mind. Weirdest thing about this was the shoe with the stones the girlfriend brought in. Can't help thinking it was some sort of message, and I want to check the missing persons database when we get back to the station, see if there have been any other disappearances. How's the alarm company on the burglary case?" Lei took a sip of Diet Coke.

"Small-time outfit." Jenkins chased a strip of egg around with his spoon, gave up and slurped the broth by picking up the bowl. He set it down. "They say they changed the codes on all the houses for Paradise Realty, and nothing's happened since they did. The security systems were turned off by someone who had the codes at the time of the burglaries."

"Yeah. Lehua Wolcott at the realty company suspects Island Cleaning, who took care of the homes. She believes Lisa Nakamoto, the owner, has a drug problem. Alika Wolcott, her son, was worried about her too, said he can't get ahold of her." Lei pushed her notebook over to Jenkins as she took her last bite. "Now we have to see if there's some sort of connection between Island Cleaning, Lisa Nakamoto, and Jay Bennett."

Jenkins perused her notes. "Hm. I wonder if the 'ice' investigation the Lihue detectives are working on is going to end up overlapping with this one. They've been saying there's enough traffic to show we've got a major producer somewhere on island."

"Well, let's drop in on Island Cleaning and see whether or not they're really clean."

Jenkins rolled his eyes, but they hurried to settle the bill and get on the road. Lei, used to working with her older, more sedate partner, Pono, on the Big Island, was still sometimes surprised by Jenkins's willingness to jump in with whatever her latest idea was.

It gave her pause to realize she was the more seasoned of the two of them.

They pulled their cars up twenty minutes later at a shabby false-fronted storefront on a side street of Kapa`a, in the area that hadn't been face-lifted for tourist foot traffic. Lei got out of the truck and went to look in the locked glass door, but couldn't see through the peeling, mirrored windows. The Island Cleaning sign above the building, of the plastic illuminated variety, was turned off.

Jenkins knocked once, twice, three times, while Lei walked to the side of the building and looked down the narrow alley. Three aluminum trash cans sat on the cracked asphalt outside of what must have been the back entrance. She gestured, and he hurried after her. Weeds pushed up through the cracked cement around their feet as they listened for several long moments at the rusting metal back door.

Jenkins shook his head. "No one here."

One of the old-fashioned galvanized lids had blown off. Several empty Sudafed boxes had her gesturing Jenkins over to where sealed black plastic bags bulged with bulky garbage. Lei ripped a bag open; it was filled with empty muriatic acid and yellow HEET gas-line antifreeze bottles. What would they need gas antifreeze for in Hawaii?

Only one reason.

She looked at Jenkins wordlessly, and they opened the rest of the trash cans. More empty blister packs and bottles of ammonia cleaning agent filled the other bags.

Lei speed-dialed Fury Furukawa while Jenkins went to the opening of the alley to keep a lookout.

"Island Cleaning in Kapa'a," she said when Fury answered. "Possible meth lab. We have discarded production supplies. Come over and check it out."

She and her partner drove around the block to park where they could keep the building under surveillance until Furukawa and the senior detectives arrived. It didn't take long. Fury drove a tricked-out GTO, black with a silver flake and a lightning bolt down the roof. Kenzo and Henriques came together in something only slightly less flashy, a yellow Camaro.

Real subtle and low key, Jenkins observed sourly via text message. The Lihue detectives had been hazing Jenkins for months before Lei got to Kaua'i; now the rivalry continued as the more experienced detectives blocked them from interesting cases.

The radio crackled into life. "Come in Ginger 4 and 5, this is Hilltop 2." Fury's call sign.

"Ginger 4 here," Lei answered.

"Looks empty," Fury said.

"Check trash cans in alley—contents consistent with meth production."

"Copy that."

Arizumi, aka Flea, a very tall Japanese and Fury's partner, got out of the Mustang and sauntered into the alley. He looked into the first can, prodded about. Looked back to the cars and nodded.

The radio crackled again. "We're going to surveil this building and put in for a warrant on the Drug Enforcement Agency fast track." Fury referred to the quick warrant procedure used for suspected drug production. "I'm gonna leave the boys here, hope one of the iceheads comes back. Let's debrief at the station."

"Copy that." She hung up the radio and drove by the other vehicles, giving a little finger wave. It felt damn good to beat the arrogant veteran detectives to a major break, and it looked like she was going to get to work a real case. Finally.

"Thanks, Jay Bennett," she whispered. "I'm gonna find you no matter what."

CHAPTER FOUR

JENKINS STOLE a stale doughnut from the pink box on the conference table as short, muscular Detective Sergeant "Fury" Furukawa folded his arms and gave Lei a good stare out of hard brown eyes. Flea, his sidekick, collapsed his angular length into one of the chairs around the Formica table. The industrial-gray walls were lined with whiteboards on one side, citations on another, and inspirational posters touting connections and teamwork in between. Lei wasn't feeling either from Furukawa.

"I told you to bump any and all information relating to narcotics to me and my team."

"Obviously we didn't know we were going to find a meth lab, Sergeant. We're working our burglary case and went there to look for Lisa Nakamoto, the owner of the company." Lei filled in the content of the interview with Alika and Lehua Wolcott. "They seemed to think the cleaning company was responsible and that Lisa is in the thick of it. Seems like we should find her, bring her in for an interview at least."

"Okay. We'll take it from here."

"What about finding and interviewing Lisa?"

"I said we'll take it from here."

"But this relates to our burglaries. Let us look for her today."

"She's now a suspect in a meth production lab. Don't you think that's bigger than a burglary job she probably pulled to get cash for her operation? Like I said, we'll take it from here. Find another case to work on, and we'll let you know when we bring Nakamoto in. I'll let you question her."

Jenkins must have seen the fire in Lei's eyes because he put his hand on her arm, squeezed.

"You got it, Sergeant. We're just glad we had a good lead." He hustled Lei out and back to their cubicle. Lei flung herself into her office chair and did a few spins.

"I can't stand his attitude. I'm burnt on this whole thing. Just when a case gets interesting…"

"Wasn't it you who said we were paying dues?" Jenkins asked. "We just have to keep showing up and doing good work. They'll trust us eventually."

"Yeah, well, at least we get to keep working the Jay Bennett thing, even if the case crosses with Fury's. I think I'll get started reviewing Bennett's journal and letters."

"Want some company?"

"No, thanks. I need to clear my head. I'm going to take them back to the evidence room and work on them there. Can you do some searches for missing persons? Maybe go back five years or so?"

"Why? What're you thinking?"

"I don't know. Just something my gut is telling me. I mean, Bennett could be a suicide or someone related to this burglary grabbed him, or it could be something else. I'll do it if you don't want to."

"Okay, Sweets, since you asked nice."

"Just Lei. Please." She poked him in the shoulder. "And thanks for helping me keep quiet in there. I feel like Fury's looking for an excuse to make trouble for me."

"He's an ass. Besides, what are partners for?"

LEI HANDED each item from Jay Bennett's backpack over to
Clarice, the evidence clerk. Clarice Okamoto took her job seriously, squinting through rhinestone cat's-eye glasses at her
computer screen as she listed the items Lei described on the inventory sheet and signed them in. Lei loaded everything but the journal, folded letters, stones, and slipper into the box Jenkins had
started and carried it back into the climate-controlled little room.

She put the box away on one of the shelves and switched on
the overhead light to study the remaining items at the little steel
table. She looked into the depths of the room stacked high with the
debris of crime, and a sudden wave of claustrophobia had her
putting her hand into her pocket, touching the smooth black stone
and taking a deep breath in through her nose, out through her
mouth, as she had learned in therapy. She still needed to use those
tools, though the intensity of her posttraumatic stress symptoms
had abated a good deal since the Big Island.

Still, sometimes Lei really missed her shrink.

She'd done therapy for a year with the unconventional Dr.
Wilson, a psychologist who worked with the Big Island PD after
the case she'd worked on activated suppressed memories from her
childhood. Lei hadn't had the time or the motivation to find anyone
new on Kaua`i.

It wasn't protocol, but it couldn't hurt to study the items somewhere comfortable. She shoved them into a plastic ziplock and
pushed her way out of the close space.

"Working at my desk," she said to Clarice, and painstakingly
signed out the items in question. She hustled out of the building
and headed for home.

Evening was turning Hanalei golden as Lei drove around the
narrow curve of road descending into the valley. She never failed
to catch her breath over the postcard-worthy view: a rugged green
triptych of mountains bisected by waterfalls rising steeply above a

25

lush green patchwork quilt of taro fields, the shiny dark snake of Hanalei River winding through it.

Keiki, her big police-trained Rottweiler, greeted Lei ecstatically with much happy butt waggling and greeting woofs as she pulled up at the little cottage on the river toward the back of the valley. Lei unlatched the gate and climbed the sagging steps onto the painted porch of the square, tin-roofed cottage, a relic of a time when such cottages housed entire families. She patted the dog, giving her a chest rub.

"Glad I've got you keeping an eye on things, girl." Keiki pressed her broad forehead against Lei's leg in reply. Lei jiggled the key in the lock. The cottage was so old it was difficult to secure. She'd put sturdy hasps on all the windows and double locks on the doors. Still, it was frighteningly easy to break into—the wood splintery and aged.

Above all, Lei needed to feel safe in her home. Though isolated on the long one-lane road, the landlady's family lived in an adjacent house and anyone trying to stake out her place would be obvious. The cottage had what she needed: a wire-fenced yard that went all the way around the house, so no one could approach without Keiki sounding the alarm.

Unless, of course, Keiki was out of commission. She shuddered at the memory of her dog's injuries last year in the course of a bizarre conspiracy centered around Lei's family, a case that had broken open memories from her past.

Lei fixed herself a glass of pale chardonnay and a bowl of carrot sticks, taking them out onto the back porch with the journal and letters from Jay's backpack. She took a minute to enjoy the view: a lush flowering tree shaded the fenced yard, just big enough for Keiki to run around in. A thick lawn rolled down to the shiny green skin of the river, snaking between banks of buffalo grass. On the opposite bank, a raft of hau bush dropped bright yellow, cup-shaped blossoms into the water, spinning in invisible currents.

Her landlady, an elderly widowed Filipino lady who lived

nearby with her extended family, said it was a good thing the river-
bank had that steep slant to it "cuz da river she flood plenny every
year."

The metal hasp on the journal was locked, but it was a simple
mechanism. Lei poked around with a paper clip until it gave. The
pages were filled with flowing, elegant script, not quite what she'd
expected.

JULY 1

The beginning of my voyage. I put here my hopes, my dreams,
my discoveries. I've always wanted to do this, just shake the dust
of that boring little town off my feet, the idea that success is
wearing a suit and selling cars or houses, pimping that metholog-
ical American dream.

IT APPEARED that Jay Bennett had left Clovis with the clothes on
his back, his sleeping bag, and a dream. He'd hitchhiked and
panhandled across the state. The entries were spotty but cogent,
revealing intelligence and a reflective nature. She flipped through
the journal to where he'd arrived on Kaua`i, only six weeks ago. It
was now near the end of October:

September 16

The air here is soft. It touches the skin like walking through a
cloud. I can feel my pores opening. Everywhere is color, and if
color were sound the world would be filled with music. People are
generous. Most of them will tell me something helpful, like where
the post office is, or what kind of food malasadas are (Portuguese).
I rotate between the parks on the North Shore so the cops don't
kick me out for not having a camping permit...

The last entry was from the day before yesterday, marked by a punch-holed Frequent Smoothie Shopper card from the Health Guardian, a natural foods store in Kapa`a.

October 19

I'm getting letters from Kelly through the general delivery. I hate it when they come; but I love it too. I can't stop myself from reading them again and again. I've folded each one in a special way so I can remember which one it is. I have the time to do things like that.

Her voice is like a foghorn echoing across the miles, calling my name and warning me away at the same time. I know if I listen to it I'll go back to that stifling little town with its box stores and exhaust fumes, Mom and Dad trying to get me back into the dealership—everyone relieved Jay's "hippie phase" is over.

Sometimes, like tonight, when I'm lonely and all I have to eat is a can of cold beans and there's no one to share the glory of Hanalei Bay with—the moon kissing the water full of stars—I think I'd better just go home.

I could bring Kelly here for our honeymoon and stop looking for what I'm beginning to wonder if I'll ever find.

Lei found herself blinking back tears.

She closed the journal, looked up and out toward the bay where Jay Bennett had last been seen. His writing was vivid and alive. She felt like she knew him already, and this last entry sure didn't seem like a suicide note.

She couldn't get over the dread seeping into her, a profound conviction that he was in serious danger if not dead already. Sunset stained the sky behind the sculpted outline of Bali Hai Ridge in the far distance as a few hau bush blossoms spun lazily in the current of the river. A mosquito bit her, a surprising little sting, breaking the spell. She smacked it and went into the house.

She called Jenkins while pulling a couple of burritos out of the freezer.

"Yo."

"J-Boy, lose the mainland slang. Listen, did you pull anything together on the missing persons? I'm getting a really bad feeling about Jay Bennett."

She peeled the plastic off the burritos and plunked them into a glass dish, splashed salsa over them, and put the dish in the microwave for three minutes.

"Yeah. I printed up a bunch of the reports, the last five years of disappearances. There've been a lot, when you consider our remote location and only sixty-five thousand year-round residents on the whole island."

"Well, I read the guy's journal and I don't think he's a suicide."

Lei took a sip of her chardonnay and sat down at the little Formica table. Keiki padded in and flopped theatrically at her feet, exposing her belly for a rub. Lei used her toe to scratch the dog's tummy. The last rays of the sunset slanted through the window and caught in her wineglass. She spun it between her thumb and forefinger, watching the ball of light bounce around in the golden liquid.

"Anyway, he seems like…well, a sensitive a guy, a thinker. Not the druggie I initially took him for. More like a seeker."

"Frickin' hippies," grumbled Jenkins. "Finding themselves on the public dole."

"You'll get no argument from me about hippies on welfare, but I think this guy had some family money; didn't seem that type. Bennett had a girl and a family trying to get him to come home, and he was basically deciding to go back. I haven't read the girlfriend's letters yet."

"I did printouts on the last five years of missing persons." He yawned. "How about I give them to you tomorrow?"

"Guess that'll have to do. See you." She closed her phone. The microwave dinged—her dinner was ready.

Lei took the letters out of the ziplock bag after she ate. Each one was folded carefully, some in origami shapes. She opened the topmost one, careful to preserve the creases so she could refold it.

Dear Jay,

I'm getting on with my life like you told me to. I go to work in the mornings, and I walk Chester, and I have dinner with my parents on the weekend, and I talk to my girlfriends on the phone.

You told me to do all that.

And I'm trying not to miss you... But I know I have a distant look in my eye that can't help looking for you and a distracted air about me because one ear is always cocked for your voice.

I hate myself for it, and I hate you for making me that way, and nothing about any of it changes the fact that I love you and miss you. Don't be surprised if I just show up someday and do something about it.

Kelly

Lei sucked in a shuddering breath as her eyes fell on the naked ring finger of the hand holding the letter. Her heart squeezed as she pictured Stevens laughing, blue eyes crinkled, head thrown back. Stevens reaching for her, lifting her so their faces were the same height, kissing her. Stevens asleep with Keiki, curled around the dog on the couch.

On the day he'd asked her to marry him, they'd been on one of their long, rambling drives, exploring the far corners of the Big Island, and they'd come to the farthest point south in the entire United States—the long empty sweep of windswept grass and rugged lava beach called South Point.

Stevens had spread a blanket in the lee of a lava outcrop, and they'd finished deli sandwiches and bottled lemonade she'd packed. Keiki had gnawed a beef bone, and Lei's head had been pillowed on Stevens's thigh as she watched the lazy turn of one of the vast white windmills that marked the rusting line of an abandoned wind farm stretching for miles on the wide-open bluff. She'd sighed with contentment.

"Thanks, Michael. This is so nice."

She'd extended her hand up to touch his face, and he'd dropped the ring into her palm. She'd gasped as diamonds kindled into flame in the rays of the setting sun.

"Marry me."

She'd slipped the ring on her finger in answer and reached up to draw him down into a long kiss that said all she'd never been good at putting into words.

Abruptly she refolded the letter. What could it possibly tell her about this case, about what had happened to Jay Bennett?

Nothing.

Maybe Jay had taken a long swim to nowhere—but Lei didn't believe it. Jay Bennett was going to go home to Kelly and bring her to Kaua`i for their honeymoon. There was also a good chance the circular currents in the bay would have washed him in and he'd have been found by now.

Jay Bennett was gone, but he wasn't a suicide. And what the hell did that shoe with the three stones mean? She should take another look at those stones. There had been something unusual about them.

Lei refolded the letters, stacked them, put them in a ziplock bag, and stowed it and the journal in her backpack to take back to Evidence tomorrow morning. She dug out the slipper and the three stones and set them on the table, turning on a powerful overhead lamp.

Shoes are universal, anonymous, and yet intensely personal. She picked up the worn slipper. It had once been a good brand, with a nylon webbing strap and a built-up area that would have supported Jay's instep. It was worn now, the brand name no longer discernible—but his footprint was. The slipper carried the deeply impressed outline of his toes and extra heel wear that indicated he didn't always pick up his feet when he walked.

Lei picked up the closest stone, a reddish opaque round with translucent spots and patches of black. She knew it wasn't local. The next one was more jagged, pale green with crystalline white striations. The last was a round cabochon of some type of opal with blue fire caught in its matrix. She needed to find out what the stones meant, what type they were. She scooped the stones into a smaller ziplock.

Lei fingered the dog-eared green Frequent Smoothie card with its multiple punch holes—the next place to look for Jay Bennett.

CHAPTER FIVE

Thursday, October 21

LEI STARTED her day by driving to the little store in the middle of Kapa`a, a freestanding purple building called the Health Guardian. She'd driven by it a dozen times, always noticing the tables outside filled with earthy-crunchy types drinking green shakes and eating salads.

Inside the weathered building the smells hit her first—powerful scents of rosemary, garlic, and sage. She looked up and, sure enough, skeins of garlic and bundles of herbs hung from the rafters. Low shelves displayed what Lei thought of as "hippie food"—boxes of quinoa, bags of lentils, bins of granola.

Lei went straight to the counter, where a tall, cadaverous man was working an old-fashioned register. She waited behind the last customer, taking in the atmosphere.

"Help you?" Hooded blue eyes looked at her warily from a seamed face. A ponytail drew graying hair back from a forehead bisected by a bandanna.

"Yes." She opened her jacket and showed her badge. "I'm

investigating a missing person—this man." She pushed the photo of Jay Bennett over to him.

He tapped the photo. "How long has he been missing?"

"Not long. He disappeared a few days ago."

"I've seen him—he picked up food here."

"Can I talk to you privately for a few minutes?"

He looked at her a long moment, then at Jay's photo.

"Okay." He waved over a young man to cover the register. "Come back to my office."

He led her through a thick curtain of clattering bamboo beads and cotton fabric. The room in back held a lounger, a stereo, storage racks, and a computer workstation.

"Sound carries in here." He shut an inner door and sat in the lounger, gesturing her to the couch. Lei sat down. She took out Jay Bennett's photo and reached in her pocket to bring out the three stones and place them on the table. The aging hippie rubbed his knuckles as if they hurt him. He cleared his throat.

"I don't believe I know your name," he said with an old-fashioned formality.

"Detective Lei Teixeira." She extended her hand. He shook it.

"Jazz Haddock. People call me the Guardian, not only because I look after their health but because I look out for our alternative community."

"So how well did you know Jay?"

"Not well. I knew he was camping around. He'd shop here."

"When did you last see him?"

"Last week. He came in a couple times a week, liked the smoothies."

"How'd he pay?"

"Cash."

"He ever say anything about someone stalking him?"

"No." Haddock cracked his knuckles. "Did he say that?"

"Yeah. Apparently he thought he was being followed. Told his girlfriend about it. You have any ideas about that?"

Haddock's eyes skittered around the room, coming to rest on the bookshelf. "Maybe."

"What do you mean, maybe?"

"Maybe I know something." He folded his seamed lips together.

"You gonna tell me what it is?"

"Maybe."

She decided to let it go for the moment. "Did he ever meet anyone here?"

"Not that I saw. This is about more than Jay Bennett, isn't it? It's about all the other disappearances too."

"What disappearances?" Lei rocked back in astonishment, suddenly wishing she'd gone to the station to see what Jenkins had been able to pull up. She'd left a message on his phone that she was going to the Health Guardian first.

"Yes. I've been watching it happen for years." Haddock's chambray eyes glistened as he looked at her. "I've written letters to the editor. I've called the police department every spring and fall, but I've always been ignored."

Lei dug in her jacket pocket for her notebook. "I'm going to have to corroborate that, Mr. Haddock."

"Call me Jazz," he said. "I warn them too." He gestured back toward the café area. "I've posted pictures of the missing; I tell people they're in danger if they're camping alone. But no one listens… He always finds a way to take another."

"Who's 'he'?" Lei made notes as fast as she could write.

"I don't know, of course. Not that the police would listen to me if I did. I've tried everything I could short of hiring my own detective to find out where they disappear to."

"I'm working on it now—and I'm sorry no one listened to you."

"It's been going on for at least five years." Jazz stood up, paced. "But I'm the wrong color to be heard here; the hippies are 'undesirables' in the community, and they came here to escape so it takes a long time for anyone to miss them—sometimes no one ever does."

He got a binder off the shelf and handed it to her.

She opened it. It was filled with clippings about missing people from the island. She closed it again, overwhelmed. "Can I take this? Look it over?"

"Sure, if it will help. I think he's doing something careful with the bodies so they're never found."

"Where are you getting this? How do you know they didn't just leave Kaua`i?"

"Too many stories to tell." Haddock continued to pace. He seemed ambivalent about how much to tell her. Lei's stomach churned and the odd smells of the store were making her light-headed. She found her hand slipping into her pocket to rub the black worry stone.

"You say 'he.' What makes you think it's not...a group? Or related to drugs or something?"

"I think I might have heard something about that," he said with a degree of confidence she found chilling. "I've been involved with TruthWay since we got here, and we keep an ear out for what all the groups are doing. It's mostly adult males that are taken—young and fairly fit. They're heavy and strong. Takes some muscle to deal with them, I would think."

"What's TruthWay?"

"We're a religious group. We've been called a cult before, but only by the unenlightened."

Lei wrote truthway hard in the notebook, underlining it. "What about a possible drug connection?"

"Lots of people smoke a little grass—myself excepted, of course." His chambray eyes dared a twinkle. "Jay looked like a guy who liked to burn a little now and again, but I didn't know him well enough to say. That's not the kind of thing that gets you disappeared around here."

"Then what is?"

He threw his hands up. "No damn idea. All I know is, it keeps happening."

"What do you know about burglaries in the area?"

"There's always some. Break-ins on rich people's houses or tourist cars mostly. Meth or heroin addicts trying to support a habit. But this is Kaua`i. It's a small island. Anything goes on, somebody knows something."

"You've put so much thought and care into this." She tapped the binder.

"Just don't ever make me have to speak to that prick Fernandez again," Jazz spat. "Bastard busted me for possession a while back, and he's never listened to anything I said since. Go ahead and look at the binder, and call me after you do."

"Thanks so much."

He held the beaded curtain aside. "Need anything from the store? I've got a lot of great fresh tomatoes right now. Organic."

"Sure. Show me where things are in this place. I've never shopped in a health food store before."

Lei left with a couple of string bags filled with fresh produce, pasta, and a chicken, and the binder filled with missing people. She called Jenkins as she pulled out.

"J-Boy, meet me for lunch at the usual place. Got a lot to bring you up to speed on."

"Sure you want to do that? We could eat here."

"We need privacy. And bring the printouts on the missing persons."

A long pause as Jenkins digested this.

"Okay. See you there."

Lei parked in front of the little hole-in-the-wall Mexican restaurant that was their favorite lunch place. She brushed through the swinging half doors and strode across the worn plank floor to her favorite table, in the corner facing the door.

"Hey, Ginger." Anuhea, the petite Filipino waitress, set the slightly greasy laminated menu in front of her with a smile. "Jack coming?"

"Sure is—he's going by J-Boy now. Ice tea, please, and we don't need menus."

"Coming right up." Anu sashayed off.

Lei took out the thick binder. Suspect number one in this whole thing needed to be the enigmatic Jazz Haddock, a man who called himself the Guardian and seemed to know way more than he should about what was going on. She took out her notebook, flipped to a new page, and began jotting down everything she could remember about Haddock.

The doors creaked open and Jenkins slipped into the plastic chair across from her, a manila folder in his hands.

"Hey. I struck gold at the health food store." Lei tapped the binder.

Jenkins laughed. Lei saw Anu's appreciative eye on him from across the room.

"That's gotta be a first. Lei in a health food store, let alone 'striking gold.' What did you do, find a clue in the bag of bean sprouts?"

She filled him in on her meeting with Jazz Haddock.

He gave a low whistle. "Interesting."

"I want to see those missing persons reports."

Jenkins slid a stack of photocopied papers out of a manila envelope. "It's kind of scary actually. There are a lot more than I would have expected on an island this size. I went back as far as 2000 and there are sixteen. Seems more frequent from 2005 to now."

Jenkins looked through the binder as Lei organized the reports chronologically.

Next she sorted them according to age, race, and gender, looking for trends. There did not appear to be too many commonalities other than the majority were Caucasian and of no fixed address. The easiest people to 'disappear' would be those like Jay

Bennett—young, transitory, perhaps ending up on Kaua`i as part of a larger picture of leaving home far behind.

There were some notable exceptions: a few women apparently fleeing abusive husbands, some wandering Alzheimer patients, a lost hiker in Kokee whose body was later found. She removed those and set them aside.

Their lunch arrived and she ate automatically, still scanning, as Jenkins flirted with Anuhea.

"Most of the disappearances seem to be in May and October once I took out the 'outliers.'" She laid the May/October sheets together by year, and the hairs rose all over her body as she looked at the faces lying across the table, stretching in an unbroken line of pairs back to 2005. "Something's definitely going on with this."

Jenkins peered over. "Wow. I didn't put that together last night. I was pretty tired. Plus you have those ones that don't fit the pattern." He gestured to the outlier pile.

"Yeah, but once you account for those as more naturally occurring situations, it begins to look like someone might be preying on the transient community."

The timing sparked something in her memory—something about October and May/June.

"I gotta get my laptop." Lei jumped up and went to the truck, fetching her laptop and turning it on.

"We should be back at the station for this. Wouldn't want anyone to pick up on it." Jenkins gave a worried glance at Anu, who was wiping down a nearby table.

"I know, but I don't want anyone there to pick up on this either and snake us out of our case before we talk to Captain Fernandez. Just make sure no one sees anything." Jenkins restacked the sorted printouts, slid them into the envelope, and set the binder on them. Lei's computer sang a "done waking up" song to her, and she logged onto the wireless hotspot that made the restaurant a favorite haunt, hit Google, and did a general search: "Celebrations in October."

There were harvests, Halloween, Homecoming Football Games, Octoberfest, and the ancient celebration of Samhain.

She searched under the same phrase for May and came up with May Day, maypoles, Cinco de Mayo, and the spring celebration of Beltane.

She'd known there was something significant about May and October—the ancient rituals in Europe of planting and harvest. But what did that have to do with Hawaii, which had never had to follow that seasonal calendar, let alone those old fertility rituals? Hawaii had its own calendar, its own lore. She dumped the photocopied pages back out, looking at the pairs, analyzing the demographics.

"I want to see if there are any trends. Got a highlighter?" Jenkins procured one from Anu, and Lei made hash marks under headings on her notebook as she had Jenkins sort the sheets: Male, Female, Caucasian, Other Race, Under 30, 30–50, 50–70. Most of the victims in her impromptu Venn diagram ended up in the Male Caucasian Under 30 category.

She sat back, highlighter in hand.

"So who is Male Caucasian Under Thirty? Transient hippie guys like Jay Bennett. Or young surfers camping on the beach."

"There are only three females, one under thirty, two thirty to fifty. Why not more females?"

"I don't know, but it could be because women seldom travel and camp alone."

"So what's the connection between these missing people and May and October, and why?" Jenkins had the line between his brows that meant he was worried, and Lei was wide-awake now, nerves jangled by the implications.

"Let's check the binder Jazz gave me, see how many of our missing persons are in here." She pulled the binder over and flipped it open. "Haddock is the owner of the health food store. Calls himself the 'Guardian of the alternative lifestyle community.'"

"Let's do background on him as soon as we get back. Always suspect anyone volunteering information." Jenkins repeated the lesson drilled into them both by Sergeant Furukawa.

"I know." Lei slapped the binder shut as Anu came by and refilled their water glasses. She didn't have to imagine the extra swing Anu put into her hips as she walked by Jenkins. "Whatever else he is, Jazz Haddock has it in for the captain. He said the cap had busted him and that he wouldn't listen all the times Jazz has tried to get a case open on the missing persons."

Jenkins whistled again.

"Maybe this isn't the best place for us to talk, but I don't want it getting around the station either. And who knows? It could be the captain has been turning a blind eye. I don't know him well enough to tell." Lei checked off all the names Jenkins had printed up against the binder; they matched.

"I can't see him being that blind or that bought off. Still, when you look at the pattern, it makes you wonder."

Anu dropped the check at Jenkins's elbow.

"Thanks." Jenkins winked at her. "You're the best."

"I sure am," she purred, and trailed smooth oval fingernails across his shoulder as she walked away. Jenkins's neck flushed.

"Let's get back to the station. You can get your heart rate back down running background on Haddock while I talk to Captain Fernandez."

"Think you're putting me on desk duty that easy?" Jenkins threw a couple of bills on the table and followed Lei through the swinging doors. "Think again, partner."

THE TIMEKEEPER PADDED across the cave to check on the Chosen, the headlight-style flashlight barely piercing the smothering dark of the cave. The man was sitting up, the padlocked collar around his neck securely attached to the tie-out cable, his legs drawn up tight against nakedness and chill.

"Why am I here?" His voice jarred the Timekeeper. He never liked it when they talked to him. "What are you doing with me?"

The Timekeeper carried two buckets. One was covered with a lid for bathroom use; the other held an assortment of food and a gallon jug of water. He set them within reach and walked away.

"Why am I here?" the Chosen called after him. "For God's sake, leave me a light at least!"

The Timekeeper went back out to the quarter horse he'd ridden to the cave and dug the duct tape out of the saddlebag. Chances were slight the man's calls for help would attract anyone in this remote area, and the entrance of the cave was all but invisible. Still, it wasn't good to take chances, and the Timekeeper didn't like to hear anyone in his special place but the Voices. He carried the tape back into the cave and silenced the Chosen with it.

He didn't leave a light, either.

CHAPTER SIX

THE CAPTAIN WAVED Lei and Jenkins in, then shut the door of his office. Fernandez cut an immaculate figure, hawklike features framed in well-tended silver hair. Lei stifled her apprehension. She'd been in his office only once, for her transfer interview a few months before.

"What's so urgent?" The captain gestured to the supplicant chairs in front of his desk.

"Something big." Lei placed the file on his desk as they sat.

He pulled the folder over and leafed through it. "What's all this?'

"I stumbled onto this missing persons pattern with the disappearance of a guy named Jay Bennett, who was beaching it at Pine Trees. Got a visit yesterday morning from his girlfriend from California that he hadn't called in when scheduled, and she'd found his wallet and some other stuff it's unlikely he'd voluntarily leave behind. I went out that afternoon to check the area and canvass and found more of the guy's possessions in a trash barrel. The girl who reported him missing also turned in these." She took the stones out, set them on the desk. "They were left on one of his shoes in a triangle pattern. Someone threw away all Jay Bennett's possessions. Either he was snatched or it was a suicide, but after I examined some of what he left behind, I don't think it was suicide. So I had Jenkins do an MP search. These are what came up, back to 2005, when a regular pattern of disappearances emerges."

She paused. The captain was looking at the pairs, held together with paper clips. All the outliers were clipped together in another pile.

"Hmm, this is interesting." The captain stroked the neat goatee on his chin. "I remember a lot of these cases. The ones you've set aside in pairs did stand out in that they were transient and traveling alone. Seemed unrelated at the time."

"Any bodies ever recovered?" she asked.

"When we find a John Doe we try to match them to Missing Persons as much as possible. That automatically takes them out of the MP database, so no."

"So…don't you think that's odd? So many disappearances without a trace, at the same time of year, going back so far?" Lei could feel Jenkins vibrating with excitement beside her.

A long pause, then Fernandez nodded. "It's strange when put together this way, but given the demographic of the missing, not a definitive pattern. In other words, there could be a lot of explanations."

"Captain, I beg to differ. That's ten people missing in the last five years, regular as clockwork in May and October. I want to show you this."

She lifted the binder off her lap and passed it to him. "Apparently Jenkins and I aren't the only ones to think this is a pattern."

"Where did you get this?" Fernandez put a pair of gold-rimmed reading glasses on his nose and leaned in to examine the binder.

"Health food store owner. Jazz Haddock."

Fernandez set the glasses aside with a snort. "Man's a pothead. Got a screw loose from too much drugs."

"Doesn't mean he isn't just handing himself to me as a suspect." Lei held eye contact with the captain. "I think he bears

more investigation, sir. He seems to know too much about this."
She wasn't above playing on the captain's biases to get the investigation to move ahead.

Fernandez picked up the binder in one hand, the stack of printouts in the other.

"All right. You can work in some canvassing at the parks on this latest missing person, see what you can pick up—but until we get something harder, something indicating foul play, your priority's the mansion burglaries."

"About that, sir. That's what led us to the Island Cleaning meth factory," Jenkins said. "We think our lead suspect, Lisa Nakamoto, was behind the burglary jobs, and when we went out to her business we found evidence looking like meth production. Sergeant Furukawa wants us to wait until he brings Nakamoto in to do anything more."

"Didn't know it was your investigation that led to the Island Cleaning raid." A long pause. Apparently Fury had taken credit for their discovery and they'd already raided the building. Lei felt a surge of frustration but bit her tongue.

Captain Fernandez stroked his beard some more. "Okay, wait on that one until the narco team brings in Nakamoto. You can move ahead with pursuing this, but keep it under wraps for now."

"Of course." She collected the folder. "I'll keep you posted."

Lei hurried back to the workstation, tense and energized. Jenkins followed as she started a new case file online, titling it "May/October Missing Persons," while Jenkins got a case jacket going, filing duplicates of the missing persons photos with a two-hole punch.

"We're on a roll now." Jenkins rubbed his hands together gleefully and slapped them down on his thighs. "What next?"

"Let's get out and do some canvassing, start at the south side of the island and work our way back through the parks to Ke`e Beach, the beginning of the Na Pali cliffs. This time of year more of the park dwellers will be on the dry side of the island."

Lei put the file with pictures of the pairs of missing into her backpack, Jay Bennett's on top.

"Sounds good." They got to the parking lot and flipped a coin for which car to take. Jenkins won, so they got into the Subaru.

"It's pretty unbelievable that so many people have disappeared without anyone in KPD putting the pieces together."

Lei shook her head—conflicted. Jenkins criticizing the way locals did business wasn't something she wanted to hear; but she couldn't help agreeing that the law enforcement community had missed what was happening. If it had been local teenagers disappearing, the community would have been up in arms. Still, part of her understood resentment toward these outsiders, whose biggest contribution to the area was increased drug sales and overflowing toilets in the parks.

"We're dealing with it now," she said shortly.

Her cell rang.

"Texeira."

"It's Alika Wolcott. This an okay time?"

She glanced over at Jenkins. "Shoot. What's up?"

"I wondered when you were coming by to check out my burglary."

"Oh crap. I totally forgot."

"Way to make me feel special." Flirtatious, slightly mocking tone.

"There's a big case. It's taken over everything, and I completely spaced it. I can send a unit to take your statement."

"I'd rather you came yourself."

Lei paused, chewing her lip. Jenkins glanced at her, cocked an eyebrow.

"Okay. I guess I can swing by on my way home from work, but it's going to be later, a lot later."

"No problem. You got the address?"

"Yeah. You gave it to me at the office."

"Bring a swimsuit."

"What?"

"Bring a swimsuit. I want to show you my new pool."

"This is business," Lei said frostily. "I'll come and take a statement and an inventory, see what I can see. That's all."

"I hope you'll change your mind when you see the pool. Later, then." He wisely hung up before she could.

"Who was that?"

"Dude I met at Paradise Realty. Wants me to check out a break-in at his place." Her scalp flushed with annoyance and something else.

"He hitting on you?"

"Trying. Wants me to come swimming in his pool."

Jenkins laughed. "He obviously doesn't know who he's up against, Sweets."

"Hey. I like guys as much as the next girl. Just not slick developer dudes with pools."

"Right. Tell that to the working slobs who've tried to ask you out."

Lei ducked her head. "I'm getting over a relationship. 'Nuff said."

"Okay, if you say so." Jenkins concentrated on the road and Lei leafed through the folder of missing persons photos they planned to show around. They drove on in silence, out past Lihue and Waimea to the park called Polihale, which marked the southern end of the Na Pali Coast.

Polihale was in the lee of precipitous mountains that blocked rainfall, so it was as dry as the opposite side of the island was green and lush. A mile-long stretch of windswept beach culminating in rugged red cliffs, Polihale was the wintering ground of the peripatetic homeless community.

They parked the Subaru and got out. Hot wind tugged at Lei's curls, and she bundled them back with a rubber band, taking off her jacket and draping it over the seat. She slipped her gun and her badge into her pants pockets; Jenkins did the same. No sense advertising they were cops—the park dwellers would pick up on that soon enough.

Locking the car, they set off across the dunes. Kiawe trees, brought in by missionaries centuries ago, strewed the path with thorny, brittle twigs.

"Good thing we're not barefoot," Jenkins said.

"Think that's the idea." Lei referred to the rumor that the missionaries had brought the trees in to force Hawaiians to wear shoes. She tipped her head back to look at one of the gnarled trees, slanting sideways from the prevailing wind direction. "Annoying as the thorns are, without the kiawe we wouldn't have any shade at all out here."

Over the rise of the first dune the park appeared—a series of desolate cement pavilions with built-in barbeques and chained-down picnic tables. Graffiti covered everything, and the metal oil-barrel trash cans were overflowing. Jenkins made a little disapproving sound and Lei surveyed the area with her hands on her hips.

Clustered beneath the rise of another dune were a group of tents. She pointed. "Over there."

They struggled a bit though the shifting dunes, the wind-blown sand stinging like needles. The tent village had made the most of the landscape—huddled in a hollow and sheltered by several large kiawes, the area was pleasantly warm and still. On a carpet scrap in front of one of the tents a young mother changed a baby's diaper. She shaded her face to look at them, and called to someone inside a nearby tent.

They slithered down the embankment into the cuplike hollow.

"Hey. We're looking for some missing people and wondered if you could take a look at some pictures." Lei indicated the file folder of photos.

"Sure," the woman said. She wore a paisley smock, strings of puka shells, and her blondish hair was in waist-length dreads. The nut-brown baby burbled a greeting, waving both hands.

A lean, muscular man emerged from the nearest tent, standing upright in a patterned brown sarong. Thick sun-streaked hair brushed his shoulders, his skin gleamed with oil, and if Lei wasn't mistaken, he wasn't wearing anything but the sarong.

"Hey," he said. "I'd like to take a look at those pictures."

"Sure." Something about his narrowed eyes and arrogant physical stance put Lei on alert, but she kept her voice and demeanor relaxed, her eyes down. She handed over the file of printed color pictures.

As they stood there, the occupants of five tents emerged one by one. They ranged in age from an older couple in their sixties to several young people. They clustered around Sarong, looking at the photos of the missing.

The older man pointed to one of the pictures with a knobbed forefinger.

"I knew her. She was a nice girl." He was missing several teeth, so the words were slurred, but there was no mistaking the snap of intelligence in his eyes.

Lei took the picture out of the pile. He'd pointed to Tracy Enders, age twenty-six, disappeared in October of 2008.

"When did you see her last?"

"Ha`ena," he said. "We switch parks when our permits expire. Tracy didn't like Polihale as much, but the rain started early that year and so we were packing up to hitchhike out here, get away from the rain. When we went to leave, Tracy's tent was still up but she was gone. We looked around, called for her, figured she'd hitched into town or something." He shrugged.

"Did you find anything unusual at her tent? Anything out of the ordinary?"

"No. I knew something was wrong, though, when we went back after the ten days on our permit was up and her tent was still there. It was ticketed though—and then the park guys took it down eventually."

The young woman with the baby piped up.

"I knew this guy." She pointed to Jay Bennett's photo. "Camped with him out at Ha`ena; he even came to the papaya farm a few times. Nice guy. What happened to him?"

"We don't know." Lei belatedly remembered she and Jenkins had meant to go by a papaya farm where a noise complaint had been reported. In the excitement of following up on the Island Cleaning lead, it hadn't seemed important.

"All these people are missing?" Sarong asked, dark eyes piercing.

"Yeah. We want to know where they might have ended up."

"I can guess." He smiled, a wolfish display of extra-long canines that hadn't seen a toothbrush in a while. "Suicides. Lotta people come here to disappear, find it lonelier and harder than they thought paradise should be."

"We're considering all angles," Jenkins said.

The older woman spoke up, pushing long white braids behind her shoulders. "What Tiger is saying is that some things go on here, it's better not to look into too much. Better to camp with friends and watch out for each other."

"That's right. For your own safety, stick together," Lei said. "Can you look through these again?"

The file made the rounds. The old man handed them back.

"I hope you find them."

Jenkins collected names. Lei doubted there was a single real one in the list he earnestly wrote down in the spiral notebook he carried, and the address had to be listed as "Local Parks" as the little colony made no bones about their lack of address.

Done interviewing, Lei and Jenkins trudged the length of the sun-scoured park and found no one else.

"Real tourist attraction, this." Jenkins, back at the Subaru, dumped sand out of his shoes.

"Yeah, the hidden Hawaii no one misses seeing." Lei took a pull off her water bottle. "Something about the way they live is kinda appealing…No responsibility, just enjoying the outdoors all day."

"Those tents were hotter than hell and the shower didn't look like it worked," Jenkins said. "I'd rather go to work and be able to get in a comfy bed at night."

"Yeah, I guess." She looked back as they pulled away. The man they called Tiger looked down at them from the top of the dune, his brown sarong somehow blending with the sand, muscled torso gleaming. He did remind her of a big cat, watchful eyes on the car as they pulled away.

"Let's run that guy they called Tiger," she said, pulling the Toughbook computer out of its custom fold-down support arm in the glove box. "I like him for something. Not sure what, but he's got a smell about him."

"Yeah, BO," Jenkins said. "He said his name was Jim Jones."

The name reminded Lei of something, but she wasn't sure what. She punched in the name. No matches on Kaua'i. Expanded the search. Came up with a few hits on the other islands, but no one matching his description.

Suddenly, she remembered the name.

"Jim Jones is the cult leader who made his people drink the Kool-Aid!" she exclaimed. "He's sending us a message, all right. Turn around. I want to bring him in!"

CHAPTER SEVEN

J ENKINS CRANKED A TURN, and they hauled ass back to the park. This time Jenkins drove the all-wheel drive as far as he could up onto the sucking sand while Lei radioed that they were bringing someone in for questioning.

Lei hit the dune at a run, her cuffs in her back pocket, baton in hand, gun in sight in the holster, badge clipped to her belt. Jenkins was right beside her as they ran into the little tent village.

It was deserted.

The tents were empty, belongings neatly stacked inside, but the campers were gone.

Lei hurried through, checking, then ran to the top of the nearest dune. She looked in all directions. Nothing but sand and sparkling ocean as far as the eye could see.

"Can we search these tents for ID, substances?" Jenkins asked, peering into the one Tiger had come out of.

"I think they are considered temporary dwellings, so we'd need probable cause."

"I think I see some probable drugs in here," Jenkins said mockingly, and unzipped the tent.

They ended up rifling through the belongings in all the tents.

The total lack of anything personal was notable—left behind were sleeping bags, food in plastic Tupperware, toiletries, even a small kitten. But no personal items, not so much as a photograph.

They rezipped the tents but made no effort to conceal their search—after all, it was evident the group had anticipated it. Lei made sure the kitten's water dish was full. She frowned.

"How did they do it? Where did they go?"

She surveyed the area again. Dunes, clumps of dry bushes, a few twisted kiawe trees, the barren pavilions. She and Jenkins tramped the length of the park and banged the bushes with sticks, getting hotter and more frustrated by the minute. There was nowhere to hide. And yet they were gone, vanished. "Jim Jones" was taunting them from some hideout; Lei was sure of it.

They went back to the Subaru, emptied their shoes again, drained their water bottles, and radioed in defeat.

Back at the station, evening was encroaching with a cooling of the light. They booted up computers in their workstation to enter notes.

"Seems like they must have something to hide. Like they were prepared to get made."

"I think that's exactly what they're prepared for," Lei said. "They're more than just a random group of campers. I think they might be some kind of cult, and 'Jim Jones' is their leader."

They put out a Be On Lookout—a BOLO—on one mixed-race male, mid-thirties, approximately six foot, wearing a sarong and going by "Tiger" or "Jim Jones." Lei had little hope it would yield anything; the guy could disappear if he wanted to, which reminded her why this case wasn't simple.

So many of these people wanted to disappear—that's what they came to Kaua`i for.

She drove homeward distracted, mulling over the case, and halfway home turned into the subdivision on the bluffs overlooking the ocean where Alika's development was going up. She drove around gracefully curving roads studded with full-sized transplanted coconut trees and pulled into the driveway of a huge Mediterranean-style mansion. Its gracious edifice was punctuated by wrought-iron railings and red tile roofs on multiple levels. The house appeared finished, though the lawn wasn't yet filled in; roped off with plastic tape, sprinklers whirled over thin shoots of grass.

She rang the bell, a chiming song deep inside the house. Alika came to open the massive double door with its beveled glass insets. He had nothing on but a great physique and a pair of swim trunks.

"Thought I told you this was business."

"I was planning to take a swim in the pool. It's out back." He gestured. Her scalp prickled with embarrassment—she'd overreacted.

"You said you had a burglary?" She held up the little Nikon and a clipboard with incident report forms attached.

"Upstairs, and the garage. It's for real, in case you thought I lured you here on false pretenses. But maybe after you investigate you'd like to take a swim too?"

The idea sounded wonderful. Lei felt sticky from tackling the Polihale dunes, but she shook her head.

"Think I'll pass. Where's the supposed crime scene?"

"Follow me." He preceded her up a curving staircase trimmed in native hardwood koa and led Lei into an office off the landing.

"I bought some nice furniture for showing the house. Leather couches, a flat-screen TV. Everything is still here but the TV." He gestured to the leather couches, still partly covered in plastic bubble wrap. "It looks to me like they decided not to take them."

Lei pulled out the Nikon and took some pictures, began filling out the form.

"Any damage? How did they get in?"

"Don't know how they got in. Kinda like those other burglaries that way. I don't have the house alarmed yet, but nothing was broken into. It seems like the burglars unlocked the door, took what they wanted, and locked up again."

"Anything else?"

Alika was standing a hair too close. She couldn't help feeling the heat from his near-naked body and pick up his scent—a subtle hint of clove and cut grass.

"Yeah. They took some supplies I was storing in the garage downstairs."

"I better see that; then you can put in a claim with your insurance."

He led her back downstairs. She looked out the sliding-glass doors off the living room to the patio, where a cobalt-tiled pool shimmered.

"Wow. The pool really is gorgeous."

"I'm kind of proud of it." His voice warmed. "I wanted it to go with the Mediterranean feeling of the house, so I used Portuguese tiles." He led her over to the sliders, pushed one open. The pool area was surrounded by a redwood fence that cut the wind. Areca palms bent gracefully over smoothly groomed grass, and oversized terra-cotta planters bloomed with bright red geraniums. The pool was set among them like a giant lapis lazuli.

"Oh—that looks so good," Lei said longingly.

"Well, let's go swimming. The garage isn't going anywhere."

She paused, considering. She felt suddenly intolerably hot and itchy from the day.

"Okay. Let me get my suit."

She went back out to the truck, dug the brand-new bikini out from behind her seat. The tags still dangled as she hadn't had time to wear it, and she eyed the scraps of yellow material apprehensively. A fast-talking saleslady had gotten her to try it on when she went in for her annual black tank suit and wouldn't take no for an answer once she saw it on Lei, giving too deep a discount to turn down. Lei put it behind her back as she returned to the house and Alika.

"Where can I change?"

"Through there, guest bath." He pointed.

Lei walked through the house and into the elegant bathroom, where she reached over to the sink and splashed water on her face. She peeled off smelly clothes, avoiding looking at herself until she had the suit on.

It really was amazing. The halter top was just ruched enough to give her a little more fullness up top, and the high-cut bottom with a gold ring at the hip emphasized her long, toned legs. The yellow highlighted her tan, and tiny brown polka-dots subtly mimicked her freckles.

She'd never looked better.

She shook her hair out of its wadded ponytail, ran her wetted fingers through so her curls reared up like a lion's mane, and decided there was nothing to do but knock his proverbial socks off.

She strode out of the bathroom like a model working the ramp. Alika was already in the pool, and she got the pleasure of seeing his mouth drop open before she executed a smooth dive in and came up next to him, gasping.

"The water feels great."

"Yeah," he said, his eyes alight with appreciation. She pretended not to notice and went into a tidy overhand crawl, doing ten laps before she took a break at the shallow end.

He was still lapping the pool with a smooth, powerful backhand. The cobalt tile made the water look clear as sapphire, and with the sunset gilding the gracious plantings, catching the splashing water shooting off his arms, it was a scene out of a fantasy.

He pulled up beside her, blowing water off his lips, drawing her eyes to their well-cut form.

"I could get used to this," Lei said.

"I hope you will." His dark eyes were serious as he moved in on her. She moved away, keeping several feet between them.

"Ha-ha. I bet you say that to all your pickups."

"I told you. You got me wrong. But I can see I'm just gonna have to put in the time and prove it to you."

"You don't have to prove anything to me."

"Yes, I do. You think I'm this big playboy. I'm a little bit of a player, yeah. But mostly I work. I don't have time for any 'relationships.' I haven't wanted to get to know someone in...well, a while. You interest me. On all levels." He was turned away from her, addressing his remarks out into the shimmering air in front of them, so Lei was able to tolerate the intimacy of what he was saying.

She floated into the warm water surrounding him, put her lips near his ear. "I like you too."

Then she moved away, breaking into another set of laps. He seemed to chase her, and back and forth they went.

Purple darkness spread from above, stars filling the sky like night-blooming jasmine. The pool went dark as a well. Lei got out, wrapped herself in a towel from the cabana. Alika stayed in the pool, his arms draped along the tiled edge, his head thrown back, eyes closed.

"Wanna show me the rest of your burglary?"

"Sure I can't show you my etchings upstairs?" Teasing in his voice.

"Not tonight, but I'm sure they're...unforgettable. I really do have to get going."

He sighed with exaggerated disappointment, getting her to smile, and hoisted himself lightly out of the pool, belting on one of the terry cloth robes. He handed her another and they padded through the Mexican tiled kitchen to the garage.

He flicked on powerful overhead lights. The garage was in disarray. He pointed out buckets partly full of paint left behind while full ones were gone, empty pallets where supplies would have been, and the area where a truckbox of expensive construction tools had been. Only a rolled carpet remained.

Lei photographed the scene. "Your insurance should cover this."

"Yeah, but that's not the point. I don't like the idea that someone's got access to my place. I've changed the locks and alarm codes, but too late already."

"I thought this was a model home."

"It is. But I'm going to live in it—might as well. I always pick one of the houses and live in it while it's on the market. Actually helps it sell."

"Nice to be able to live like this."

"It's a gamble." He shrugged. "With the economy what it is, I could be in this one awhile."

Lei couldn't muster any sympathy so didn't try, finishing with the photos.

"Okay. I'll open a new report for you tomorrow, and if you need copies for the insurance company I'll send them to your e-mail."

"Think this could have anything to do with Lisa and her problems?"

"I know she was your friend, but we haven't been able to find her and we want to question her anyway. I'd say she's definitely a possibility as one of the burglars. She could have taken a key from you, had it copied. Maybe she thinks you can afford it."

He cleared his throat. "She had a key. I'd told her she could use the pool."

"Did you change the locks?"

"Yeah. Yesterday."

"So when exactly did you notice the stuff was missing?" She picked up the clipboard again, noted Lisa Nakamoto as a possibility.

"Two days ago. Can't believe she'd do that to me." He shook his head, and gave the e-mail info to her for the insurance claim. They went back into the kitchen, where Lei picked up her dirty clothes, wrinkling her nose.

"Ugh. I don't want to get back into these. Can I borrow the robe?"

"Only if you bring it back and use it again," Alika said. "In fact, I've got something coming up I think you'd enjoy."

"What kind of something?"

"An event. I need a date. Interested?"

"What kind of event?" Lei kept her eyes on the incident report, trying not to notice her heart had sped up.

"An event. You know, music, food, you wearing something tight and silky. Maybe some heels…"

"Wait a minute. Really? You're asking me out."

"My God, woman, you aren't making it easy." Alika's deeply injured tone made her smile. He went on. "It's a ball to benefit the National Bird Refuge at Kilauea. They have a lot of outreach programs to schools and so on that rely on donations. It's at the Princeville Hotel."

Lei had driven by the hotel's magnificent edifice and speculated on the view it must have, perched on the cliff overlooking the entire Hanalei Bay. She did want to see that. And the Bird Refuge sounded like a good cause. The feeling of attraction-apprehension he elicited rose up in her again.

"When is it?"

"Tomorrow night, which as you know is Friday night."

"That's pretty soon," she hedged.

"I figure, strike while the iron is hot. And the iron is hot."

A blush prickled up her neck. She decided to shut this down.

"I don't know why you're bothering with me, Alika. I can tell I'm not your type—heels? Come on. And you're definitely not my type."

"I like you, hard as it is for you to believe. Plus I want to see what you look like in a dress."

"Do I get to see what you look like in a dress?"

"It's not entirely out of the question, if you're into that."

Lei couldn't help laughing. "Naughty!" she exclaimed.

"Ah. Everyone eventually discovers my middle name. We could have some fun. You aren't entirely opposed to fun, are you?"

"Not entirely."

"Okay then. I'll pick you up at seven."

"No. I'll drive myself and meet you."

Long pause.

"Don't you trust me? I won't drink more than a glass or two of champagne. I promise."

"No. I'll drive myself, or no deal."

He threw up his hands in mock surrender, teeth flashing in the dim light.

"I'll meet you then, at the portico at seven p.m. I'll be the man looking insecure, with a red rose in his teeth."

"Okay. But you gotta behave. I get snappy when I'm embarrassed."

"Imagine that."

When she pulled the truck out, he was still standing in the driveway, his hands in the pockets of the robe, watching her go.

CHAPTER EIGHT

LEI WAS PUTTING away the natural food groceries from the health food store, still in the cotton robe and bikini, when Keiki burst into Intruder Alert barking.

No one dropped in on her out here. She slipped the Glock out of the holster hung over the back of the kitchen chair and slid it into the roomy pocket of the robe, tightened the belt, and went to the front door. A tall curly-haired man, backlit by the headlights of a taxicab, stood near the chain-link gate.

Keiki let him know Lei was well guarded.

"Lei?"

"Yes?" Her hand curled around the reassuring pebbled grip of the Glock in her pocket. That cool weight had come to feel like an extension of her hand.

"Lei, it's me, Wayne. Your dad."

She switched on the porch light.

Her father stood behind the crisscrossed wire in creased dark jeans and a plain white T-shirt with a small duffel in his hand—post-prison issue. Light gleamed off his silver-shot hair and craggy features. She couldn't see into the shadowed hollows of his eyes.

Her thoughts flew away in shock. She hadn't seen him in

months, since she'd visited him at Halawa Prison, a brief reconciliation never consolidated beyond a few phone calls and letters.

"Hey, Dad. What're you doing here?" She was aware of the rattling idle of the taxicab's engine, the harsh glare of its lights, the total awkwardness of the situation. She came down the steps to the gate.

"I got out," he said simply. "I heard you moved, so I came here."

"Aren't you supposed to stay on the island your parole officer assigns you? Isn't there a halfway house you're supposed to go to?"

"Yeah." A flush of embarrassment marked red flags on his high cheekbones. "But there's no room for me there yet. A condition of my probation is that I'm on the same island as my daughter, the police detective. Congratulations on the promotion, by the way."

"Thanks." Lei stared at him hard. "But you should have told me, called me, something. You can't just show up here, at my home, and expect me to—I don't know what."

"I'm sorry. I can come another time."

"No." She gestured impatiently to the cab, waving it off. "Come in. We'll figure something out."

Her heart thudded, nervous energy making her hands sweat. That visit last year had been the first and only time she'd seen him in twenty years, and she felt like she hardly knew him. Lei turned and gestured to Keiki. "Sit."

Wayne extended his hand, fingers down, for the dog to sniff, and Lei patted the big square head. "This is my girl, Keiki. I told you about her."

"She's beautiful."

They both looked down; Lei took some relaxation breaths as they patted the dog. Keiki dropped to the ground for a tummy rub, milking the attention.

Lei cleared her throat.

"I'm just getting some dinner on. It's not much, but you can join me. Do you have somewhere to spend the night?"

"I got nowhere to go. I got off the plane and just came. I wanted to see you."

"All right." Lei sucked in another breath, blew it out. "You can stay at my place tonight."

"You don't have to do that. I can stay at a motel. But I'd like to join you for dinner."

"Okay. We'll start with that."

She led the way up the weathered wood steps onto the porch, through the front door into the modest little cottage. He set his bag down inside, looking around the spare living room with its sofa, coffee table, and ancient television.

"It's so good to see you." For the first time, he smiled, a grin that must have been devastating when he was younger and still dazzled.

"It's good to see you too." Lei was surprised to find it true. "Come and join me for a really unimpressive dinner."

After they cleared the remains of two Lean Cuisines into the trash, Lei gestured to the back door. "I like to sit out here and look at the river at night. Come check it out."

They sat side by side on the top step of the back porch. Patchy moonlight gilded the smooth-skinned river as it wended between black jungled banks. Lei cleared her throat.

"I'd like you to stay. It's a chance for us to catch up a bit."

"You sure? I know I should have called... I just couldn't find the words."

"Yeah, I'm sure. You have anyone you have to check in with?"

"My reintegration specialist—a fancy name for a parole officer. I'm supposed to let him know I'm with you. He's working on getting me into a halfway house—pardon me, a restoration center. I'm supposed to get ready for a job." He gave a short bark of laughter.

"Well, why don't you make the call while I'm in the shower? I've got to get out of this suit."

"Sounds good." His voice was reluctant. Lei refused to feel sorry for him—he'd just landed on her doorstep after being out of her life for twenty years.

Wayne had gone to prison for dealing when she was five, leaving her with a drug-addicted mother who eventually overdosed when she was nine. That had left her in the care of his sister, Rosario, to be raised in California. Aunty Rosario had kept her father's letters from Lei until last year, after which Lei decided to visit her father in prison.

She got up, fetched her cell phone, and handed it to him.

"I don't have a land line," she said. "I'll be out in fifteen minutes or so."

A short time later she came out of the bathroom, squeezing her hair with a towel, a loose tee over sweatpants enfolding her in cozy comfort. Her father came in from the porch with the phone.

"Done. The fancy name parole officer thinks it'll take a few days, though. Can I stay with you until then?"

"What's his name? I'll call and verify."

"Okay." He handed her the phone as he went past her into the living room. She looked at the Numbers Dialed and called the most recent one.

"Hello, Corrections Aftercare Solutions. This is Aaron Spellman."

"Corrections Aftercare Solutions, that's a new one," Lei said. "Is this the parole officer for Wayne Texeira?"

"It sure is. Is this the daughter?"

"Detective Leilani Texeira. Badge number 2367."

"Thanks for getting back to me, Detective. I told your father you would have to call in."

"I know. What's the situation on the halfway house?"

"Kauai Restoration Center is what we call it. Well, it's full right now. I'm trying to get a space for him in the dorm across the street;

it's cheap but clean, and he can go to the meetings with the social worker and job skills classes easily, on foot."

"How soon?"

"Not sure, but I'm working on it as fast as I can. Can't squeeze blood out of a turnip, as we say here on the Mainland." He had a humorless chuckle that abraded her nerves.

"What are the alternatives?"

"Well, I need for you to be responsible for him until he gets into the program. Can you do that?"

Lei blew out a breath. She'd wanted to get to know her father a little more; now it looked like it was going to be a crash course in togetherness.

And if so, there was something she had to tell her father. Finding a way to do it was going to be the tricky part.

"Okay. Call me back at this number as soon as you have something."

She went back out on the porch, and a few minutes later Wayne rejoined her.

"Appreciate you having me. I wish things were different, that I was doing something for you."

"It is what it is." That phrase had carried her a long way.

"Your mother and I had some happy times when you were little," Wayne said. A candle Lei had set in an empty mayonnaise jar gleamed on his silver-streaked curls. "She loved to dance, that girl. You know, your grandparents on Oahu—strict Japanese. They weren't happy when she fell in love with a paniolo. A cowboy wasn't what they had in mind for their girl."

Lei had never heard much of anything about her grandparents, the Matsumotos, and Rosario and Wayne's parents had died before she was born. She turned toward him, eager to hear more.

"We met at a rodeo. I was doing calf roping. She was with friends, sitting in the bleachers. She was wearing a white dress, probably not the best choice for a rodeo, and she had on a red straw cowboy hat." He sighed. Lei almost held her breath, seeing her petite young mother through his eyes. "I brought her a shave ice, and it spilled on that dress. She gave me her number and the rest is history."

"So my grandparents. They didn't approve?"

"Turns out they were right." He sighed again. "They wanted her to date a Japanese boy. I was too Portagee, too Hawaiian." The racial and cultural lines of the islands often were hard to understand for outsiders, but like elsewhere, people tended to stay in their groups.

"So why…didn't they ever look for me?"

"I don't know. We can look them up if you want."

"No. If they didn't care enough to find me after Mom died, I don't want to know them either." Her words came out more forcefully than she meant them to.

The rain pattered gently on the roof, and patchy moonlight glimmered on the swollen chocolate river as the clouds thinned and parted in a restless wind, revealing a mercury drop of moon.

"I'm sorry," he said.

"It's okay. I see a lot of how people treat their families in my job and it isn't pretty most of the time. I'm used to it now. So where did you get married?"

"We eloped. We were only eighteen. Got married at the county courthouse. Maylene had on that same white dress, and carried an armful of wild orchids I'd picked for her."

He went on with a few more stories from when Lei was little, before he was arrested and her mother went down into the darkness of her addiction. They'd been a happy family once. In the flickering light of candles, Lei was almost able to forget all that came after he was taken away.

CHAPTER NINE

Friday, October 22

THE SMELL of coffee woke Lei. She propped herself up, pushing curls out of her face as she peered at the clock on the nightstand—and groaned when she saw the time. No time for a jog this morning. She flung her covers back and belted on her old kimono. The sight of that robe always reminded her of Stevens—of all the times he'd taken it off her, or taken her with it on... She hated to be reminded, but she couldn't bear to part with it—a familiar tug-of-war.

She went out into the kitchen and glimpsed the silver-streaked, curly top of Wayne's head through the screen door leading into the backyard. A mug of coffee, already dosed with cream, waited by the pot. She picked it up, pushed the screen door open, and sat down next to her father on the top step.

Keiki nosed through the grass of the yard below, snuffling in the dew. The river flowed past, a great shiny-skinned eel, rippling with hidden power. Golden hau blossoms swirled in the current—it must have been raining somewhere in the mountains. She looked up at massed gray clouds hanging over the green peaks in the distance.

"Sleep well?" Lei took a sip of her coffee. Delicious.

"Pretty good. It's so quiet here," Wayne said. Her mind flashed to the constant clangor of prison—even at night it would be filled with sound, most of it that of human misery.

"The prison coffee is terrible." He looked at the mug of coffee in his hands. "It would either be burned, like it had cooked for hours, or it was pale as tea, like they just took the burned stuff and threw water in and served it again. I got used to it, so now this tastes funny to me."

"Quiet and good coffee will grow on you quickly—don't worry. Why don't you just kick back today? Keiki needs a walk, if you don't mind."

"Sure, whatever I can do."

JENKINS HAD SAVED her a seat for roll call. She slid into it, barely on time, as the captain monotoned about departmental business and the week's priority cases, none of which they were involved with. Several of the Island Cleaning employees had been rounded up, but Lisa Nakamoto was still in the wind.

The captain didn't mention Lei's new missing persons case.

Back at the cubicle, Lei found a stack of pink message slips marking calls from Kelly Waterson and Norville Bennett, probably Jay's father. Lei's stomach clenched. Best thing to do was something for the case—she didn't have anything to tell them, and for now that justified not returning their calls.

She taped white paper over a cork board, then took a Sharpie marker and began a timeline that started with the approximate date of Jay Bennett's disappearance, October 19, and Kelly's visit that began the case the morning of October 21.

She added a branch for when she found Jay's personal items

and opened the missing persons case on him, and followed that with the visit to the Health Guardian, confirmation of multiple missing, and the trip out to Polihale that had resulted in discovery of the mysterious park dwellers led by "Jim Jones."

That was as far as she could go. She propped the board up and stood back from it.

Jenkins blew in. He'd been "talking story" in the conference room.

"More canvassing today? The parks might be more crowded since it's Friday."

Friday. Lei remembered she was going with Alika to an event tonight. She had only one dress, and it wore memories. She would have to find time today to grab something new.

"Yeah, we can go back to Polihale and make our way this direction. I just wanted to work up a board, look at a few things first."

She pinned Jay's blown-up picture to the board. Jenkins booted up his computer as she fetched the binder Jazz Haddock had put together and sat down with it.

"Too much of a coincidence that Jazz Haddock knows so much. He has to be involved somehow," Lei muttered. She'd printed up his driver's license picture and now tacked it onto the board above the date/time of her interview with him.

Haddock's seamed face frowned at her from the photo. He must have hated having to go to the DMV for that photo, that involvement with "the system." She drew a question mark above his head with the Sharpie and wrote knows too much, too quick to point out blame, too much research under his photo. Jenkins glanced up from his e-mail.

"Totally agree. That health food guy is suspect number one."

Lei went back to her seat, opened the binder again. Once again she compared the file contents on the missing Jenkins had pulled up with those Haddock had compiled. She found that Haddock had actually provided more thorough profiles, nicknames, and descriptions of several of the missing than just the missing persons data sheets Jenkins had printed up. "J-Boy, check this out."

She passed the items over to him and started a new timeline under the one beginning with Jay Bennett. That timeline began with the first "pair" of missing in 2005. She filled in the names and as much detail as she could find on each missing person on the timeline:

Kassie Feldman

Peter Krakouwer

Neil Powers

Grey Smith

John Samson

Tracy Enders

Brize Calloway

Susan Herzog

Hal Bloom

Jay Bennett

Lei did a quick count again: ten victims.

She circled the number.

She stood back, still holding the uncapped Sharpie. Suddenly the magnitude of what she was looking at overwhelmed her. Somehow it hadn't really sunk in before. She felt her throat closing, the telltale dizziness that signaled dissociation narrowing her vision with encroaching black. She dropped the Sharpie as she fell into her chair, digging her nails into her thighs in desperation. Fortunately Jenkins was absorbed in reading Haddock's binder.

The pain grounded her. The black receded.

She was here now; she was safe. She sucked breaths in through her nose, out through her mouth. In, out. In, out.

They were in over their heads. Deeply, totally in over their heads. She knew it down to her bones. She just hadn't let herself think about it yesterday. She needed to talk to someone, and there was only one person she knew she could trust—with her fears, with the case, with the politics of the station. When the symptoms abated she stood up, picked up her phone.

"I need to make a phone call."

"Uh-huh. I'm pulling up background on Haddock now." Jenkins's fingers flew over the keys, absorbed. The gelled spikes of his blond hair seemed to vibrate with excitement.

Lei headed down the shiny hall lined with corkboards papered in memos and alerts toward the front door of the station. She pressed down the button on her phone that had the number worn off from use—but hadn't been called in six months.

CHAPTER TEN

"STEVENS." His brusque answer in her ear felt instantly reassuring. Her breath blew out in a whoosh as the pneumatic doors of the station slid open.

"Michael. It's Lei." She strode over to sit on the break table under the plumeria tree at the side of the building.

"You're not the only one with caller ID. What do you want?" His tone was cold, a bracing slap. She gathered her thoughts.

"I'm sorry to call you, but I need to talk about a case. It's huge." Her voice trembled and she tried to firm it. "I need some advice."

"So I'm good for advice, huh? Glad I can be there for you when you need something." A long pause. She knew his cop curiosity would overcome the bitterness, and sure enough, after another long moment he said, "What's going on?"

"It's a serial. I've stumbled on a pattern of missing people going back at least five years. I told my captain about it on Friday, but he's not moving on it besides letting me work the recent missing guy… There have been so many victims, and it has gone on so long with no one doing anything. This is big."

"Tell me everything," he said. And she did.

A long silence followed. The wind tumbled her hair, and a plumeria spiraled down, a creamy pinwheel. The ocean gleamed in the distance, the horizon a blurred blue line as the phone crackled with static and all that couldn't be said.

"You need to go to your captain. He should bring in the FBI," Stevens said.

"No. This is my case. I know I need help though, maybe a task force..."

"Go and talk to the captain again. If there are as many as you've said, the FBI should get involved and, frankly, you want them involved. This is too big for little old Kaua`i; it involves vics from all over, and when it breaks it's going to be huge."

"I know."

She took the black stone out of her pocket, rubbed its silky surface. "Thanks for listening. I know J-Boy and I are in too deep with this thing, but I don't want to let it go. We've had such crap since we got here, and this is finally something real, something big."

"Too big. Sometimes being a good cop is knowing when to say when."

"I guess. It's good to hear your voice." Like a low, vibrating chord that struck deep within her, just listening to him made her feel safe.

"Likewise. Keep me posted. I might volunteer for that task force if you don't go FBI."

"I can handle this. I just needed...a second opinion."

"You need more than that for a case this size. But useful— that's me. Bye now."

He hung up abruptly, and she closed her phone. The dragging, bruised sensation in her chest—she didn't want to identify it even as tears prickled the backs of her eyes. A broken heart actually did ache. Damn, she missed him.

Her feet felt like lead as she walked back into the station. She flopped into her chair, gave it a spin. "We need to get a plan. I'm not sure what we should do next."

Jenkins turned toward her. "The health food store guy has a record."

"I know; he told me. Pakalolo?"

"Yeah. Possession and intent to distribute eight years ago. He ended up with fines, community service, and probation. Only had a few ounces on him when he was pulled over."

"He hates Captain Fernandez."

"Well. Nothing since."

Lei flipped through her spiral notebook, and the small square of tapa cloth Lehua Wolcott had given her fluttered out to land on the desk. She picked it up thoughtfully.

"Let me make one more call. Lehua Wolcott gave me this lead —I'm not sure what it's about, but I can fish around. Then we should go out for one more round of canvassing, maybe end up at the papaya farm, see if we can find Jim Jones. We were supposed to go follow up on the complaint out there anyway. I'd also like to see if we can get a meeting with the captain to get more eyes on this thing. I'm starting to think it's a little big for the two of us."

"Glad to hear you say that. I mean, ten missing people. Shit."

"Exactly." Lei pulled the phone over, punched in Esther Ka'awai's number.

"Coffee break." Jenkins disappeared.

Lei looked down at the little square of tapa cloth. She wasn't even sure why she was calling.

"Hello?" An older woman's voice.

"Hello, this is Detective Texeira with the Kaua'i Police Department. How are you today?"

"I'm glad to hear from you. I was hoping you'd call."

"Really? I got your number from a woman named Lehua Wolcott. Did she tell you I'd call?"

"She's my daughter. And no. I just knew you needed to contact me. So I'm not surprised you did."

Lei took a couple of relaxation breaths as the silence stretched out. This was more than surprising. It was bizarre.

"Well, I don't know what I'm calling for or why Lehua wanted me to call you. Maybe you can help me with that."

"No. I don't know either." The other woman seemed perfectly calm.

Lei looked down at the tapa square for the woman's name again.

"Well, Mrs. Ka`awai, I guess I'd better go then. I thought you might be of some help with my investigation."

"Call me Esther," the woman said. "And I will call you Lei."

"I don't remember telling you my name. How did you know my name?"

"Sometimes I just know things."

"Really." Was the woman psychic? "Do you know anything about people disappearing on the North Shore?" The words popped out before she had time to think about them.

"I've heard something. Perhaps I can help."

"Well. I shouldn't have said anything. I'll have to get clearance to consult with you."

"I'm an expert on cultural practices, a spiritual leader in the Hawaiian community. In case that could be useful to your investigation."

"I don't know yet. But it may be."

"Well, I'm here to help you with what you're going through right now."

Lei pinched the bridge of her nose. This conversation felt like falling down a rabbit hole.

"Okay. As it happens, something big is going on." Lei let her breath out, looking down at Celebrations in May and October in her notes. "And I might be able to use a consultant in Hawaiian culture—I don't know. But I need to have total confidentiality. Can I get that from you?"

"Of course. I am a kahu, a minister of the Word."

"Well, I'd like to meet you face-to-face, and I need to clear this with my captain. When can we get together?"

They set a date and time, then the kahu said, "When you wonder what to do, trust your heart."

"I can't trust my heart. It's unreliable."

"How do you know? Maybe you're right to have done what you did. There is more for you to experience, more to help with your healing, before you settle down."

"Who are you referring to? I thought you didn't know what was going on with me." She looked down at her empty ring finger.

"I don't know, but you do. Your heart knows." She hung up.

"It does not," Lei said aloud to the dial tone. "My heart doesn't know shit."

She closed her eyes, seeing both Stevens and Alika side by side. Though it was too soon to say what it was that Alika elicited in her, she knew she loved Stevens as much as she ever had anyone, as much as she was capable of—and yet being with him terrified her.

No, her heart didn't have a clue what was going on.

Jenkins came back in with a Styrofoam cup of black break room brew. "Ready?"

"As I'll ever be." She scooped the photos of the missing into a file, then stuffed it, her notebook, and the Nikon into her backpack. "Let's hit the road."

They drove back out to windswept Polihale, and this time even the tents of the park dwellers were gone. Partway back to Kapa`a, at Lydgate Park, they approached a young couple sitting in beach chairs outside a faded tent.

"I've seen this guy." The man, tanned and wearing threadbare board shorts, tapped the artist's rendering they'd worked up on Jim Jones. "His people came through yesterday."

"His people? You say that like he's got followers or something." Lei kept her voice even.

"He does," Board Shorts agreed. "They're all part of that

TruthWay group. They invited Jennie and me to their thing up at the papaya farm, but we don't swing that way."

TruthWay…and the papaya farm, popping up again.

"I've heard of TruthWay." Lei decided to try a common interview tactic—acknowledge a witness's comment, repeat it back as a statement, and see if they elaborate. "So you aren't into that kind of swinging."

It worked.

"Yeah. You know, firewalking, swapping partners…not our thing. Right, Jennie?" Jennie peeked up through tangled hair, and the gleam in her eye said she might not be opposed to a little "swapping."

"Know where the group meets?"

"Not really." Board Shorts got shifty. "It's a papaya farm somewhere on the North Shore. They got their own place, do their celebrations there."

"Well, thanks so much." Lei handed him a twenty. "Sure you can't remember?"

"Maybe."

She gave him another twenty.

"It's outside Kilauea. They call it the Jones family farm."

Back at the Subaru, Lei pulled up a tax map and identified the Jones family papaya farm, matching it to the complaint they were supposed to investigate. She glanced at her cell phone.

"Now we really need to make a run out to that papaya farm, but it's four thirty and I still don't have a dress."

"Got a date?"

"Believe it or not, I do."

"Red letter day! Who's the victim?"

"Shut up. It's that developer guy I met at Paradise Realty. He's nice."

"Ah, so now we know what it takes to get a date with Sweets—own a pool and a mansion and you're golden."

"You're worse than a little brother." They were passing through Kapa`a, and Lei spotted a boutique. "Pull over."

The Subaru had barely drawn to the curb when Lei jumped out and ran in. Ten minutes later she came back out with a bulging pink bag. She paused at the sight of a blown-up photo of Jay Bennett's face labeled missing—marked with Kelly's contact information—stapled to a nearby telephone pole. She ripped it off and hopped into the Subaru.

"Kelly's doing her bit to find him."

Jenkins peered at the poster.

"Good. We need all the help we can get. I can see you put a lot of time and effort into your shopping."

"Hey, he said 'dress,' so I got one." Lei shoved the bag onto the floor. "Let's roll; we should have time to swing by the papaya farm before I have to go on my date."

CHAPTER ELEVEN

LEI DROVE DOWN THE ONE-LANE, unpaved road in her truck, Jenkins following in the Subaru. They'd stopped at the station so she could pick up her vehicle, and now Jay Bennett's wary blue eyes watched her, flapping a bit from the poster held on to the glove box with a magnet. Head-high buffalo grass brushed the sides of the truck as she bounced through red dirt ruts.

Kilauea was a beautiful area planted in macadamia nut trees, coffee, lychee, banana, and papaya, all farms that had replaced pineapple in the last twenty years. To the north, the ocean shimmered, and some miles away, the rugged, drip-castle mountains that marked Hanalei raked the sky.

Papaya trees stood tall, their slender trunks topped with clusters of palmate leaves in soldier-straight rows, marking the edge of the farm. Six-foot wire mesh fence topped with barbed wire encircled the area, choked with weeds and scrub guava. Lei drove to the gate, a metal barricade secured with a padlock on a heavy chain. Lei got out and yanked on the padlock.

"Crap. Feel like a little trespassing?"

"Sweets, c'mon. We're detectives on the job. No probable cause here." Jenkins had pulled up beside her.

"I hear a scream?"

"Down, girl. Get back in the truck. You don't want to endanger anything we can get on them later, do you? We'll have to call and tell them we're coming."

"Shit. I wanted to get eyeballs on the place now." Lei looked contemplatively at the gate, but in the distance she could hear the bellowing of a large dog. "Awful lot of security for a papaya farm."

"We'll have to try again when they can let us in."

"I guess." She got back in the truck and fired it up.

"Have fun on your date," Jenkins said with a grin as he pulled out. "I want all the details in the morning."

"Shit," she muttered. "Almost forgot."

She drove slowly along the edge of the farm, scanning, but the whole property was securely fenced. There was nothing to see but acres of papaya trees, and nothing to hear but the distant thunder of the barking dog.

LEI PULLED under the vast portico of the Princeville Hotel, the door of her Tacoma opened by the valet. As she handed him her keys, she saw his eye run down her toned leg to the new slingback on her foot. She'd needed shoes too, and fortunately the boutique had some in her size.

"Have a nice evening, miss," the valet said as he got into the truck.

"Thanks. I will." Lei tugged down the short skirt of the narrow, strapless black dress she'd grabbed so hastily off the rack—a dress that turned out to be shorter and tighter than she'd estimated.

Alika Wolcott reached for her hand as she looked up.

"Wow," he said. His golden eyes crinkled in a smile. He took a red rose from behind his ear and presented it with a flourish. "You look amazing."

"Thanks," she said, the dangling weight of her aunt's greenish purple Tahitian pearl earrings making her feel regal. She tucked the rose behind her ear and gave a nervous glance at his dazzling height in black trousers and jacket over an open-necked silk shirt. "You're not so bad yourself."

He shrugged. "Man outfits. All the same."

He escorted her with a light touch on her back through the huge doors into the lobby.

Lei stared through a seamless bank of windows that framed an immense view of mountains, ocean, and sky. A black marble reflecting pool began at the entrance and ran the length of the lobby, appearing to fall into space as it sheeted in a waterfall to the next level below. Guests traversed a staircase on either side to the dining area. Lei caught her breath at the expanse, her eyes feasting on the vista.

"Oh," she said, and just stood for a moment. "It was worth coming just to see this."

"There's more. A lot more." Lei felt Alika's eyes on her face, the butterfly touch of his finger on her bare collarbone. "You have a scar here. What happened?"

"A perp bit me."

"Bit you? On the collarbone? I'm sure there's a story there."

"Not one I want to tell."

"What a witty conversationalist. I'll have to get you liquored up." Lei laughed as he escorted her down the staircase. "You're going to love the bar."

Lei craned her neck as they descended, looking at clear blown crystal chandeliers hung at different lengths on long, almost invisible cords from the ceiling. Droplets of fractured light danced in the waterfall beside them.

He pointed to the right. "There's the ballroom where the gala is being held." His hand touched her back again as he guided her to the left. "The bar is down here."

They descended another flight of stairs, walking into gloom woven with wavering light. Lei looked up and realized they were underneath the pool where the waterfall splashed. A Plexiglas ceiling allowed the far-off light of the chandeliers to fall around them like golden coins. The black marble floor added to the feeling of being in an underwater cave.

She looked up into the light, and—giving into impulse—spun around.

"Oh," she said, and smoothed her dress, an embarrassed smile curling up one side of her mouth. The rose had fallen on the floor. "I'm sorry. I had to do that."

He reached down and handed her the rose.

"I don't mind. I've often wanted to do the same." He opened his arms wide and whirled around. For a moment he was limned in gold. "Now that we both have no dignity whatsoever, let's go add some alcohol to the mix."

"You must've read my mind."

"What'll you have?" The bartender leaned forward to take their order over a bar made of translucent Plexiglas embedded with little glowing lights.

"Chardonnay," Lei said. She sat on one of the clear molded stools and spun around to get a full sense of the place. "It's underwater magic."

"Sometimes they turn on a disco ball in the main lobby, lower it down over the reflecting pool," Alika said.

"Want me to turn it on?" the bartender asked. Lei nodded, and the man pushed a button on the wall. They backed away from the bar and tipped their heads back to watch as a large disco ball lowered out of the ceiling of the lobby far above them, separated by layers of air, water, and Plexiglas. Sparks of colored light spun all over the room, and all the guests murmured.

The music increased in volume. One of her parents' favorite songs: "The Way You Look Tonight."

Alika took her hand without speaking and led her into the light-splashed space. They danced a gentle two-step around the room, and Lei felt the music moving through her. She relaxed into Alika's hand in the center of her back, her cheek near his chest, her hand in his as they circled the room, other couples joining in. The song ended and Alika walked her back to the bar.

Her chardonnay was waiting, pale and icy, along with his Scotch on the rocks. Lei sipped it appreciatively.

"I have a thing about that song. My father used to sing it to my mom. Back when they were happy. I hardly remember that, but she would play it when she missed him." Lei took another sip.

"Funny how music can take you straight back to another time and place. I danced with Ruthie Kahakauwila in seventh grade to that song."

For the first time she let her eyes wander over his silk shirt, well-cut black trousers, the bold line of his jaw. When he was turned away from her, she could really look at him, and she gazed at the clean line of his profile in wonder. Genetics were an unfair mystery. She remembered Stevens's rugged features with a pang—never quite handsome, his power and presence made him unforgettable, while Alika had both looks and charisma.

"Don't tell me your heritage—I want to guess." He leaned toward her and in the dim light captured her chin, turning her face toward him. Spangles of moving colored light dappled them.

"These lips—made for kissing—look Hawaiian to me. These eyes—full of fight and danger—look a little Japanese. And this skin." He bent her face a little more into the light. "Your freckles—this skin—you've got Portuguese too. A true island princess."

Before she could stiffen or pull away, his mouth touched hers in a kiss, haunting in its gentleness. Her eyes drifted shut, her mouth turned up, and then she felt him leave—a cool breath of air fanning across her face as he moved away.

She turned and took a big swig of wine. He was the first man she'd kissed since Stevens, and she still wasn't sure she was ready for any of it. She was terrified of her response—the prickling of her breasts, the way her mouth tingled, hungering for more of his.

He finished his drink and set a bill on the counter.

"Shall we?"

"Why not? Get it over with." Lei's nervous defiance was a familiar default mode. They walked into the ballroom where the event was underway. She blinked as she looked around, eyes adjusting to the bright light.

"Champagne?" a waiter with a loaded tray asked.

"Definitely." She hooked a glass off the tray, her arm tucked into Alika's as she took it all in. A well-dressed crowd formed a line beside a lavish buffet while a Hawaiian-music quartet played onstage in front of an open dance area. Lei broke away to examine velvet-covered tables forming a bay filled with silent-auction treasures. She looked back—an attractive woman had already cornered Alika. She turned to study the artworks, jewelry, flower arrangements, and fruit baskets in front of her.

"I like this." A long finger pointed to the delicate rose-pink of a densely woven kahelelani shell necklace in front of her.

"Me too." Lei turned to the finger's owner, a tall man with a gleaming kukui-nut lei over the aloha-print shirt he wore. "Don't see shell necklaces like that too often. Looks like the real thing, from Ni`ihau."

"It is. I know the woman who makes these."

"Well, I'm sure it will bring in some good money for the cause."

"Why don't you bid on it?"

"Too rich for my blood."

Alika materialized at her elbow.

"Mac Williamson," he said, with the kind of bluff heartiness that, among men, hid dislike. "Hitting on my date, I see."

The man ignored Alika, looking down into Lei's eyes. His were dark, gleaming, and nearly hidden by spiky brows. He took her hand in a big calloused one, kissed it with a gesture both old-fashioned and courtly.

"I'm Mac," he said. "What's your name?"

"Leilani Texeira." She was possessed of something close to

mischief as she dimpled at the tall stranger. "Mac. Short for something?"

"Mackenzie Ikaika Lono Williamson, to give you something to chew on. You should bid on the necklace. It would look good on you."

"I think I will," Lei said, and turned her back on both of them to write her name on the top line, adding what was for her an extravagant bid of one hundred and fifty dollars.

She gave the necklace a longer look. The tiny pink shells, smaller than a rice grain, were valued more highly than their weight in gold in the islands. Each one was handpicked from the sand and hand pierced by a needle, strung in intricate patterns that were passed down through generations in a Hawaiian tradition that was in danger of being lost. She turned back, to find Alika waiting and Mac gone.

"I've never seen him show interest in someone before," Alika said. A frown stitched a furrow in his smooth forehead. "That was weird."

"Great. Anybody who likes me is weird," Lei said. "Where are your manners, Mr. Smooth Talker?"

"No, I mean it. Mac's a hermit, lives out in Ha`ena on a big family estate with nothing but a caretaker for company. Strange for him to come to one of these things, let alone introduce himself. I've known him all my life and thought he was asexual. Not even enough there to be gay."

Lei must have been imagining the bitterness in his voice. She snatched another glass of champagne off a passing tray.

"C'mon." Alika took her elbow. "I've got people for you to meet."

They circulated until Lei was a little dizzy from champagne and names. Alika finally sat her at a little table near the musicians and went to get food.

Mac materialized beside her.

"Oh, hello! Where'd you disappear to?"

"Don't like him," Williamson said bluntly. "I went to get you something."

He set a little velvet bag in front of her. She looked down at it in surprise, opening her mouth to refuse whatever was there, but when she looked up he was gone again. The man was a giant jack-in-the-box. She was working open the little cords when Alika arrived with two plates loaded with fancy buffet food.

"What's that?"

"Gift from a gentleman admirer," Lei said, upending the pouch. A glowing pink Ni`ihau shell necklace, secured with a clasp made of a sunrise shell, poured out onto the table.

"Oh crap. This is way too expensive." Lei looked up, searching for Williamson's tall head, but he was nowhere to be seen. She got up and went to the auction table. The necklace she'd bid on was still there.

She went back to her seat and picked up the one he'd given her. Even more magnificent, its shells were a rare hot pink alternating with blush pink in swirling bands. The sunrise shell clasp made it a one-of-a-kind piece of authentic Hawaiian jewelry.

She put it on. Alika was still sitting, his mouth ajar. Lei waved a hand in front of his face.

"How does it look?"

"Mac must be smitten."

"I don't know about that, but I have to find a way to return this," Lei said, stroking the tiny rosy shells at her throat. They were already warm to the touch.

MUCH LATER, Alika waited with her for the valet to bring the truck back around. He'd draped his jacket around her shoulders. She inhaled his slightly spicy scent in its folds. He took her hand, swinging it lightly.

"I know why you took your own car. Wanted to keep me from kissing you at your doorstep."

"I can keep you from kissing me just fine," she said, picturing her father looking out the window and seeing them.

"But why would you want to?"

He folded her in, his mouth finding hers. She stiffened, but he held her gently, firmly. She felt her lips melting under his, the subtle touch of his tongue. She slid her hands up, filling them with the hard muscles under his silky shirt, feeling him tremble.

"Ahem." A polite cough behind her. She broke away, ducking her head. The valet stood behind her, the door ajar. Alika stepped forward, passed the man a tip, and handed Lei up into the cab. He touched the necklace at her throat.

"You made a few conquests tonight."

"Jealous?"

"Should I be?"

"Way too cocky," she said, smiling. "But somehow I can't help liking you."

"Oh good. So you won't pine away until I call you again?"

"I admit you're not a bad kisser." She put the truck in gear. "But Williamson knows how to show he likes a woman."

The truck accelerated and she smiled to see him looking after her, his hands in his pockets, brow knit.

For the first time in days she looked at her ring finger and it didn't hurt.

CHAPTER TWELVE

Saturday, October 23

SATURDAY DAWNED OVERCAST AND RAINY. Lei woke up to the distinct smell of pancakes. She put her feet out of bed and found the worn wooden floor unexpectedly damp and cold. She went to the back of the bedroom door and wrapped up in her old kimono, slipped into a pair of socks, and went into the kitchen.

Her father was at the stove, flipping a large, perfectly browned pancake that gleamed with the yellow of banana slices. He pointed to the pancake.

"You loved these when you were a kid. Mrs. Abacan, your landlady, gave me the bananas and some local honey."

"She's sweetening you up," Lei said, pouring herself a mug of coffee. She sat at the little table, and Keiki came over and put a broad head on her knee. She absently played with the dog's ears as she watched him finish the cake and slide it onto one of her little Corelle plates, drizzling it generously with honey.

"Thanks, Dad."

"I like the sound of that." He poured a dollop of batter so it spread across the sizzling griddle. "Making myself useful. Have a good time last night?" He'd been asleep on the couch when she got in.

"Sure did." Her fingers found their way to the necklace at her throat; somehow she thought she'd dreamed it.

Her father's eyes narrowed. "What's that? I don't remember you wearing that on the way out."

"It was a gift from a man who seemed to…take a liking to me."

"Can I see it?"

She unhooked it and handed it to him, coiling the necklace in his hand where it glowed like a handful of crushed rose petals.

"This is a really quality piece."

"I think it's from Ni`ihau." Only shells that had actually been picked up and worked by the colony of Hawaiians who still lived on that remote, tiny isle could be called Ni`ihau—the rest were just kehelelani.

"So who was he?"

"Guy named Mac Williamson." She shrugged. "It rattled my date's cage, and that was kinda fun. But the necklace is way too expensive; I need to find Williamson and return it."

Her father handed it back. "Beautiful. You know how to make the guys in this town pay attention."

"That was never my style. Have you called Aunty Rosario? Does she know you're out of prison?"

He shook his head, turned away to flip the pancake, then slipped it onto his own plate. There had been tension between the siblings ever since Rosario had given Lei the cache of twenty years' worth of letters.

"I know I should call her. Okay. Go get me your phone." Lei went and got it while he sat down and tucked into his massive banana pancake.

A few minutes later Lei left them talking and went out on the back porch with Keiki. She looked down the strip of lawn past the bedraggled shower tree to the turgid brown river. Rain pattered on the tin roof, on the leaves of the hau bush. Branches, clots, and mounds of submerged debris swirled in the swollen river. As she watched, the patter became a thunderous roar that drowned out everything else. She went back inside with Keiki plastered against her side. The dog's ears flattened to her skull in apprehension, big body shivering.

"Settle, girl. It's just rain." The dog was not reassured.

Her father closed the phone just as it rang again. He handed it to Lei.

"J-Boy, whatcha calling me for on a Saturday morning?"

"Just thought you should know they're predicting flooding in Hanalei Valley," Jenkins said.

"Crap, really?" Lei walked over to the window and looked out again. The view was completely obliterated by a wall of falling water. Jenkins's voice was breaking up. "What?" she shouted.

"I said, if you can't get across the bridge tomorrow, you can go out to Ha`ena and canvass the park dwellers," Jenkins yelled over the roar of the rain. "They'll all be snug in their tents."

"Sounds about as fun as a root canal," Lei said. "Wow, this rain is coming down."

"Kaua`i does have one of the highest rainfall counts in the world," Jenkins said. "Guess we get to see it firsthand."

"I better go talk to my landlady about what they do when it floods. I know it happens every year, so they must have it figured out."

"Hope you make it in tomorrow."

"Me too. There's not much we can do now. Keep in touch." Lei closed the phone. She turned to her father, who was cleaning off the stove. "I better go talk to the Abacans about flood control."

"Good idea."

Lei went out the front door and found her rubber boots, banging them upside down to scare out any insects. Sure enough, a cockroach fluttered away. Roaches and centipedes tended to hide wherever it was dry in the islands. She stuck her sock-covered feet into the clammy boots and took a clear plastic rain poncho from a hook on the door. She threw it on over her robe and squelched across the saturated grass to the neighbors' house.

Lei knocked on the door, but the rain on the roof muffled the sound, so she pounded. Charles Abacan, Mrs. Abacan's son, opened the door. He was a tall man for a Filipino, with a basketball belly that strained his undershirt and chin whiskers like antennae. Lei averted her eyes.

"Where's Mrs. Abacan?"

"Come to talk about the flooding? Mama doesn't know anything more than I do, which is that it looks like it's going to flood."

Lei looked at him with dislike. He was in the midst of a divorce and had come home a few weeks ago, bringing children who clustered behind him, staring at her. Alcohol fumes wafted her way—and it was pretty early in the morning to be drinking.

"Well, what do you do to get ready?"

"Mostly the river floods below us. We're on a bank above where it flattens out and curves at the bridge. That's where it floods, spreads out over the taro fields and just flows through the valley till it hits the ocean. But every three or four years it comes up under the houses. You see the pylons your house is on?"

He pointed with a dirty forefinger. She looked back through the pouring rain.

"Well, that's the flood control. Comes right up under the house but won't wash you away."

"Great," Lei muttered.

He cupped his hand around his ear. "What's that?"

"Nothing. Think I'll move my truck though." They both looked at where it was parked in front of the house in a low area off the pavement. Mrs. Abacan appeared, wiping her hands on her apron.

"Why don't you come in, dry off?" she asked.

"No, thanks. I'm fine." Lei wasn't about to stand around in her robe in front of Charles. "Good to know the house is flood proof."

"I wouldn't call it flood proof, more like flood prepared," Charles said. "Come on over if you want company."

"Thanks, but we're fine." She retreated off the porch to move her truck, and parked it on the opposite side of the road against the elevated bank. She made her way back to the cottage. The rain continued to thunder down.

She sloshed through the yard and toward the river. The chocolate-brown water had risen several feet and lapped hungrily at her lawn.

"Everything okay?" her father called from the back porch.

"We're going to have a flood. Other than that, terrific." She climbed onto the porch and hung up the streaming poncho, and pried the wet boots off her feet.

Wayne handed her a towel and she rubbed her disordered curls into an even more riotous mess. She hung the towel up on the back of the chair, went into the bathroom, and squirted some Curl Tamer into her palm. She walked back out as she squished it into her unruly hair. Her father watched this with amusement.

"I should try some of that sometime," he said as she shaped her hair into something less like a bird's nest. Lei looked out the window. Keiki made no move to follow, keeping her nose on her paws, eyes nervously darting.

The water had come up another ten feet on the lawn. Lei watched a whole tree float by, rolling slowly in the current, branches clogged with debris but still rotating slowly as it spun. Below the cottage in the direction of the bridge, she could see the flood spreading to cover the road.

"It feels wrong to just sit here waiting."

"I know. I've been through a few floods myself when I was growing up on Oahu. Lotta times there's nothing to do until it's time to head for high ground."

Just then the lights flickered, and with a little buzz, the power went out.

"Dad, we need to dig out my emergency stuff. I never unpacked it."

She opened the broom closet and sneezed. With the heavy rainfall darkening the room, the closet was too gloomy to navigate. She pulled the boxes out and handed them to her father. They stacked them in the middle of the kitchen and broke them open. Her father held up an apron.

"What's this for? Doesn't seem like you."

"Ha-ha. Just be glad we have a gas stove, or I don't know how we'd cook anything." She pawed through the box and found a heavy police flashlight. Of course, the batteries were dead. She had a small emergency radio, but that was dead too. At least she had a radio on the truck if they needed to call for help.

Eventually they located the candles and matches and then used the time to unpack and put away the contents of the boxes. She felt a prickle of something like happiness even in threat of the oncoming flood, to see her father so carefully unwrapping her cheap glasses from the newspaper she'd packed them in.

Lei looked out the window. The line between rain and river had blurred even further.

Her phone shrilled on the counter.

"Texeira."

"Ginger 4, this is Dispatch."

"Warning me about the flood?"

"Negative. Witness walking on the beach has called in a Code 17–9."

"What am I supposed to do about it?"

"Patrol units are stuck on the other side of the bridge. Don't want whatever it is to get moved by the flood. Captain wants you to go bag 'n' tag if you can get to the beach. It's by the pier."

"I have four-wheel drive. I guess I can try to get there, but the road looks washed out from here."

"Ten-four, Ginger. Just give it a try. Dispatch out."

Lei shut the phone, took a deep breath.

"Crap," she said. "Someone's called in a body or body parts washed up on the beach. I gotta try to get down to the pier."

"It looks totally washed out," Wayne said from the window. A swath of brown water had crossed the road a hundred yards down from the house.

"No one else can get there or they'd have sent someone. They're afraid it's going to wash away if I don't collect it."

"Collect it! What the hell!"

"Don't think it's a whole body," Lei said. In her bedroom, she changed into light nylon running pants, strapped on her holster, and loaded the Glock, clipped on her badge. "I'm just going to try to get down there, but if I can't, I'll come back."

"No way," Wayne said. He'd been changing too, into jeans and a parka. He tied his shoes on. "I'm not letting you go out alone."

Lei looked at him thoughtfully, hands on her hips. It could be useful to have his help if they got stuck or otherwise in trouble. On the other hand, taking a convicted felon along to recover reported evidence could create a host of problems later.

"What about Keiki?" Wayne asked. Keiki had crawled under the bed in the bedroom, but the dog stuck her head out at the sound of her name, brown eyes worried.

"We'll have to leave her with the Abacans. They'll know what to do if they have to evacuate."

They left the shivering Rottweiler with the family. The kids were overjoyed—Keiki less so. Lei and her father sloshed out to the truck.

Lei's heart thudded as she hopped up into the cab and turned the key. She looked over at her dad and saw his knuckles showing as he gripped the armrest. She smiled.

"Hang loose," she said, local slang for "relax." He looked over and winked.

She took out the radio and called in.

"Dispatch, this is Ginger 4 heading out for the 17–9 at Hanalei Pier. I have civilian Wayne Texeira on board for emergency help."

Hopefully the extreme situation would mitigate any legal problems related with using a felon for backup.

"Copy that, Ginger. We're monitoring."

She put the truck in four-wheel drive and rolled forward. The road was still clear below the house, though slick with rain. She eased into the water as it rushed across the road. It steadily rose as they rolled forward, the truck rock steady in four-wheel drive. She slowed to a crawl, trying to remember the geography of the road, which had become impossible to see. Wayne pointed.

"Follow the markers."

She reoriented, looking at the roadside steel markers that vibrated with the pressure pushing against them. They felt the power of the water as the truck shuddered. Wayne opened his door a little to check the water level.

"I think we should reverse as soon as it touches the undercarriage," he said. "We're about an inch away."

"I know," Lei said tensely. She braked and the truck obeyed sluggishly as a log barreled by in front of them. She rolled forward again. The road ascended to meet the bridge off to the right, but Lei kept going, bearing left, back down into the flood and toward the beach.

Without speaking, they inched forward into the flat of the valley, the vehicle shuddering and pulling to the right. She fought it, keeping it on the road with both hands and following the steel markers, and they gradually moved into shallower water until they were able to pick up speed.

"I think we made it!" Lei exclaimed. Wayne leaned back and took a long, trembling breath.

"Got a few new gray hairs here," he said, grabbing his forelock.

Lei laughed, a release of tension, and they turned right toward the pier. Just past the last of the houses in Hanalei town, the flood began again. Lei halted the truck, mid-axle.

"Dispatch, this is Ginger 4. Where is location of 17–9? Pier area under water."

"Roger that. Witness says Pavilion Park."

Lei shook her head in disgust, put the truck in reverse, and splashed backward to the Pavilion parking lot, which was slightly elevated and only a few inches underwater. She turned off the truck. The overworked engine ticked in the silence, punctuated by the patter of the rain on the roof. Her father zipped up his parka and put the hood over his head.

Lei put the clear plastic hood of her rain poncho up as well and reached in the back for a handful of evidence bags. She opened the glove box and took out a pair of latex gloves.

"Put some on," she told her father. "I might need your help." He followed suit, and they stepped out of the cab into a wet, gray world.

They squelched past the cinder-block bathrooms and down the long slope of open lawn dotted with built-in barbeques toward the beach. Chocolate-brown, angry waves churned against the sand, and great clumps of flotsam pushed up in waist-high mounds along the beach. Lei looked for the civilian who had phoned in the discovery.

She spotted a man with a German shepherd under a rain-battered kamani tree. They walked toward each other, and Lei held up her badge.

"Detective Texeira," she said.

"Tom Owens," the older man said. He was in full rain gear, bristly beard pearly with moisture. "I'm a retired firefighter, and Chelsea and I like to keep an eye on the community in weather like this. We came out to check what was happening with the beach and she got all excited and led me to this."

He gestured for them to follow him. Lei and Wayne picked their way across the debris, their progress impeded by slippery mounds of vegetation washed down from the banks of the river.

The shepherd barked when they got to one of the mounds. Lei suppressed apprehension and followed to where Tom was pointing.

Tangled in the pile of wet debris was a hand. Mottled, mahogany-brown fingers curled as if in supplication, palm upward. Without the dog, it would have escaped notice, blending perfectly with the branches where it rested.

Lei's heart picked up speed. A hand was good—the prints might be viable.

"I looked all around," Tom said. "I had Chelsea search, but this was all we found."

Lei reached inside her poncho and brought out her little digital Nikon, photographing the hand in situ.

A wave broke nearby, and brown foam rolled up around their feet.

"This is why I called it in as an emergency," Tom said. "I think this pile is going back out to sea."

"Looks like it." Lei walked behind the mound, leaning over to photograph it from above. The flesh was ragged and bloodless, and she could see abrasions on the protruding bone.

"I don't think this is a recent piece of remains," Tom ventured, turning to Wayne. Neither Lei nor Wayne said anything, so he went on. "I was thinking maybe someone was buried and the flood washed the body out, and this hand got broken off or something."

Tom had addressed all his remarks to Wayne, who remained expressionless and silent. He certainly looked like a cop, radiating a natural authority. Lei smiled a little at the irony.

"Can you collect Tom's contact info while I bag the evidence?" She handed her father a notebook and pen from her backpack.

"Name and address?" Wayne asked.

While they were occupied, Lei took one of the plastic evidence bags out of her back pocket, lifted the leathery hand out of the tangle, and slid it into the bag. Another wave surged up around the pile of wood, underscoring the urgency of retrieval. She put the bag into her backpack.

She turned back to Tom. "Your theory about a burial floating up is pretty good. Can you and Chelsea walk with us down the beach and see if we can find anything more? Her nose will come in handy since this body part isn't exactly fresh and the color makes it hard to spot."

"Sure." Tom's beady eyes gleamed with enthusiasm. He snapped his fingers, loosened Chelsea's leash, and the dog put her nose down and set off. Lei and Wayne followed a little more slowly.

The beach was hazardous between the mounds of debris and heaving brown surf. They traversed the length of it slowly, ending at the creek on the other side of the bay. The usually gentle stream was impassable, a violent brown flood a hundred yards wide. Nothing further was discovered but a drowned pig.

Back at the car, Lei peeled off her latex gloves and shook Tom's hand. "Thanks so much. Call if you find anything else."

"Will do." Man and dog disappeared into the drizzling rain. Lei stowed the backpack in the rear of the cab as they got in the truck.

"Didn't look fresh," her father commented, handing her the notebook.

"I know. I guess I was kind of hoping it was some evidence of the guy I'm looking for, but on the other hand, I'm relieved it's not him—there's still a chance he's alive."

It was awkward not being able to discuss the investigation with her father—she wished she could talk about the hand like she might have with Jenkins. She turned the key and listened with relief to the roar of the engine—it hadn't succumbed to the wet.

They made their way slowly back—the river hadn't risen any further, and having done it once, both of them were a little more relaxed. Lei parked the truck up against the raised embankment on the opposite side of the road from her cottage.

"I'll get Keiki; you can deal with the evidence," Wayne said. Lei nodded and radioed in the collection of the hand and their safe return, then sloshed her way into the house.

She took the hand out of her backpack in the kitchen, giving it a quick visual survey before Wayne came in. It was the dark brown of earth, and desiccated as a piece of leather. The soaking had caused the tissue to plump back up, but even so it had a mummified look to it.

And in the light, saw marks on the bone were clearly evident.

Wayne and Keiki came back in, and Lei held up the plastic evidence bag with its grisly contents.

"Observe me put this into a paper bag," she said, slipping the ziplocked bag with the hand into a plain brown bag. "I'm sealing this." She taped the brown bag shut with packaging tape and wrote the date/time on it in Sharpie, signed it with her initials.

"Not that I'll be such a good witness if you have to testify about this chain of evidence," Wayne said. "Convicted felons related to the investigator might not make for much credibility."

Lei pushed her Hot Pockets and frozen vegetables aside and put the brown paper bag in the back of her freezer. With the power out, it was the best she could do.

"Won't come to that. Besides being an emergency situation, more than likely this is just a burial missing its body."

Though who would saw a hand off a body that was buried in a grave? And why? The lab might be able to find out more, and in the meantime, hers was a true cop freezer, with body parts among the frozen peas.

The river decided to give them a break and stopped rising five feet short of the back porch. Without electricity, Lei and her father sat on the steps overlooking the river and drank decaf coffee into the misty night.

It was time to tell him.

She took a breath, blew it out. "I need to tell you something that involves someone from your past. Do you remember a guy named Charlie Kwon?"

"No."

"Small-time dealer. Worked for the Changs in Hilo. Back when you were in the game."

"Okay, yeah. We had words a few times."

"Well, he moved in on Mom after you got popped—he got her into the hard stuff, hooked. He did it on purpose."

Her father's face had gone stark. Eyes dark pits. Fingers curled so hard around his knees they were white. Lei looked away to say the rest.

"In prison he bragged he got a twofer with me and Mom—because he molested and raped me." She blew out a breath, looking out into the moonlit river, anywhere but at her father. "Not just once, for months. Mom overdosed when he left her, and that's why I ended up with Aunty Rosario—child welfare sent me to her."

"Rosario never told me anything about Kwon. Oh. My. God." He whispered it like prayer. His hands curled into fists. "Where is he?"

"Lompoc. Finally busted for molesting kids."

"I'm so sorry, baby. So damn sorry." He stood up, paced back and forth on the creaking porch behind her. "A pedophile. My God. Oh my God."

Lei stayed silent. Everything she thought of sounded like a platitude, and she'd never been that good with words. It wasn't her job to make this okay for him. It still wasn't okay for her. She reached into the loose pocket of the sweatpants to rub the black stone she always carried.

He sat back down. His piercing eyes fixed on Lei.

"'Do not take revenge...I will repay,' says the Lord," he quoted.

"That might be good enough for you, Dad, but I need my moment alone with Kwon. And don't you get in any trouble; I've got plans for him when he gets out. Unfortunately, not for a couple years."

"I'm just sick about this. Like it wasn't enough I lost you both to the game..." His voice trailed off. He sank his head into his hands, and she heard him mumbling a prayer.

Lei felt the shadow cast by Kwon dissolving somehow. Telling that awful secret, telling it to someone she'd blamed for leaving her vulnerable, seeing her father's pain... It felt like light and air moving across a wound left too long covered up. And maybe his prayers helped too. That loser pedophile didn't deserve the energy it took to stay pissed. In the meantime, Wayne shared the burden, just as he should—she wasn't carrying it alone any longer.

"I'm so sorry, baby," Wayne said again, and in the soft darkness, it was enough. For now.

Lei climbed into bed later that night and snuggled into her silky cotton sheets. She was safe. Her father was here, her dog was here, and, hanging where she could reach it on the headboard, her gun was here. Her eyes drifted shut, and she realized she was still wearing the Ni`ihau shell necklace. Her fingers touched it as she fell asleep.

CHAPTER THIRTEEN

Sunday, October 24

THE TIMEKEEPER PULLED on his rubber boots and slicker. The worst of the rain had passed, but this had been a serious flood and early in the season. He clumped out to the barn and saddled up the quarter horse. Her steady, even temperament would be needed in these weather conditions.

The mare labored uphill through the wet grass and sucking mud. He patted her sweating neck with affection and she snorted in reply. The trail got steeper, and a little rill of water poured down around her hooves. They kept going, splashing through fattened streams until he turned off on the side trail to the cave.

The stream had been in flood during the height of the storm; he spotted tufts of leaves and detritus high in the bushes and nearly to the opening of the cave, but it hadn't gone into the narrow, slitlike mouth.

He left the mare ground-tied outside and went in with a flashlight and another gallon jug of water. The interior was mostly dry, and he swung the flashlight beam to the Chosen, deep inside the sleeping bag he'd dropped off. He nudged the man with his foot.

Matted blond curls emerged as the Chosen poked his head out. The man's eyes were red-rimmed as he glared up into the flashlight beam. He'd peeled the duct tape off his mouth and chewed through it on his wrists. Livid red scratch marks circled his neck where he'd tried to loosen the collar.

"You're going to kill me, aren't you." The Chosen said it as a statement. "What I can't figure out is why, and why you haven't done it already." He coughed, and it didn't sound good.

The Timekeeper took the bucket of slops out and dumped it into the stream, went back in and set it near the man.

"My name is Jay. Jay Bennett. There will be people looking for me."

The Timekeeper looked over at the duct tape, handily placed on some rocks out of reach, and decided not to bother. He hadn't brought food either; the Chosen wouldn't need it to stay alive for the Time he had left.

He walked out of the cave with its dark and stench and mounted the mare, continuing up the trail to a wide mesa. The island spread out below like a hula dancer's skirt: yellow sandy beaches, turquoise ocean stained brown around the shore from the flood, green jungle. A rainbow draped a colored scarf off to the north.

He breathed a sigh of contentment to be here, so close to his Source. The Voices were getting bad, and he couldn't wait for the Day.

Samhain. The day he gave them what they wanted.

He rode the mare across the rocky mesa. At one end, a crag raked the sky. He dismounted at the base and ground-tied the mare, then parted the concealing shrubbery to disclose the stairs carved into living stone and earth.

He climbed up carefully. The stairs were slick, and even though the rain had stopped, it was a long way to the bottom and it didn't pay to hurry. He grabbed on to roots and the tough growth of waiwi, strawberry guava, and finally came to the place where the Source was strongest.

The heiau altar was intact, a great flat-topped, fire-blackened boulder that had been used for worship by early Hawaiians. All around the spire were special spots where he left his offerings after dedicating them. He checked and they were intact, tucked deep under stones marked with petroglyphs by those who came before him.

He wondered how his other site, the one in Hanalei Valley, had fared. He'd had to go there some years ago when the Voices demanded their due at that forgotten heiau. He hadn't been able to burn the offering because of the possibility of being spotted. He didn't like it because it was near the river, which meant human traffic. But the Voices would not be disobeyed.

He sat down in front of the altar stone and looked out across the breathtaking view. Skeins of rain swirled across the ocean in the far distance. The brown slurry of floodwater soiled the turquoise water over the reef—and the sun peeked out, brightening the rainbow.

He tipped his head back, felt the brush of the rain on his skin, a touch like a wind-borne kiss. The Chosen would never feel this again, and he let the man's name rest in his mind a moment before the Voices squeezed it out again.

LEI BLEW out of Hanalei toward work, the power of the truck putting speed to her urgency. The beach was too washed out for running and the hand seemed to burn a hole in the backpack holding it on the seat beside her. She'd radioed in to speak to the captain and got on his schedule as first appointment of the day. As she hung up the radio, her cell rang.

"Hello?"

"Still dry?" That deep, warm, teasing voice. Alika. The man

should be running a 900 number.

"Barely," she said. "The flood came pretty close."

"I was thinking about you. Hoped you were okay."

"I'm always okay."

A long pause. "So. You aren't pining for me?"

She laughed. "Naughty."

"You called me that already. Gotta come up with something new."

"Arrogant ass?"

"Hmm. Overused."

"Okay. Egotistical bastard."

"Ouch, that one hurt," he said. And he did sound hurt. He went on, turning brisk. "I wondered if you had any time today."

"What, I hit a nerve with that last one?"

"As it happens, I am a bastard. But I asked for it, so I can't hold it against you."

"I'm sorry." She whipped around a slow-moving commuter. "You know I was only teasing. There a story there?"

"Not one I want to tell." He waited a beat as she remembered saying the same to him. "I wanted to see if you'd like to come over for dinner."

"I've got a full day ahead, not sure when I'm going to be done." She found herself speeding, her heart beating a little faster than it should, and she took her foot off the gas, slowed her breathing. She wasn't going to let this guy get to her.

"It's fine. I was just thinking to have you over to the house. I'm in a cooking mood."

"Well, okay. As long as I can just call you later if it's not working out."

"Such enthusiasm. Good thing I'm egotistical and can take it. So do I get to call you a name?"

"Sure. Lay it on me."

"Ginger. Spicy Ginger, who haunts my dreams."

The dial tone buzzed in her ear and she closed the phone. He must have heard her call sign, and she wondered how.

At the station she and Jenkins barricaded themselves in the conference room, setting up the board she'd begun and preparing to review it with the captain. Lei showed Jenkins the sealed bag containing the hand. She'd put it in a small plastic cooler with a couple of bags of frozen peas, all she'd had in the freezer that morning.

"This could be the evidence of foul play we've been looking for!" Jenkins's cheeks were pink from shaving and enthusiasm. "I found out more about the stones, what they mean. All three are used in witchcraft ceremonies to enhance the power of the ritual. I think they could point toward some kind of religious sacrifice and have something to do with Samhain, on October 31."

He'd put the stones in a little plastic tackle box. He pointed to the green one. "This one, chalcedony, is the most powerful. It's supposed to invoke and channel the creative power of the universe. The jasper is for blood—when blood is given in sacrifice jasper cleanses it. And opal is for magic. It's supposed to amplify the power of the sacrifice."

"So there's literature out there on human sacrifice?"

"Oh yeah. So these stones are significant, and I think when we do more canvassing we should be asking if anyone found stones on a shoe like those that were at Bennett's disappearance site."

Lei finished attaching the pictures of the missing in chronological order. She pointed to the total number of victims, looked over at Jenkins.

"I called Stevens for advice when I saw this. He thinks the FBI should be called in."

"Crap," Jenkins said, running his hands through his hair and turning it into haphazard misdirected spikes. "We won't be able to do shit if that happens, and we found this case."

"I found this case," Lei said. "You listened to me. Get that straight."

"Okay, yeah. Well, the FBI would totally take over."

"I know. I plan to just lay it out in front of the captain, see if he'll let us do a task force and work it that way."

Just then Annette, the cap's secretary, stuck her head in. "He's on his way."

Lei smoothed down her blazer, seriously wrinkled from the damp. She ran the wand of lip gloss over her mouth and patted her hair—it hadn't yet had time to misbehave.

"Relax," Jenkins said. "He's too old for you."

She opened her mouth to retort when the conference room door opened and the captain walked in, dapper as ever.

Michael Stevens followed him.

Laser-blue eyes under slashing brows found hers instantly. Her heart jumped as she drank in the sight of him. Rugged height, shadows under his eyes, rumpled dark hair falling over a high forehead, and that invisible something that made him larger than other men—oh yeah. She still felt something, and it exploded in her chest and expanded south.

"Stevens!" she exclaimed. "What're you doing here?"

"I'm bringing him in on your case," Captain Fernandez said. "My old friend Lieutenant Ohale called me last night, seemed to think things were even more serious than you'd led me to believe, and said Stevens had volunteered to help out with the task force he was sure we were putting together. Ohale thinks we're going to need someone with his level of experience."

A wave of betrayal washed over Lei. He'd used a moment of weakness to snake her out of her case! She shoved off from the table, fists clenched.

"What the hell!" She started toward him, realized Jenkins was restraining her. Stevens never looked away, but she saw tension in the corners of his eyes.

"Settle down, Detective," the captain said. "Did you hear me tell you I want him to help out?"

"Did he tell you we were engaged, and I dumped him? This isn't about the case; this is personal."

"If you can't make it work, I'll have to give it to him exclusively," Fernandez said. "It's too much for our station to handle, and I need more than rookie detectives working it. As I said, I'm putting together a task force."

Lei shook her arm loose from Jenkins's grip. She smoothed her jacket down, took a couple of deep breaths. She wasn't going to give up so easily.

"This is my case. And I took some serious risks to get this." She reached into the cooler beside her, carefully broke the seal on the paper bag, and took out the plastic ziplock evidence bag.

The severed hand looked forlorn and hideous, slipping back and forth in pinkish fluid, a parody of a wave. She pointed to the protruding bone.

"Tool marks. I think this might be related to the investigation."

Lei set the bag containing the hand down on the conference table. Stevens still hadn't spoken, but now he came forward and picked it up, held it against the light. A thin fluid, probably water from the rain, had collected in the bottom of the bag as the hand thawed from her freezer to the station.

"Blood's long gone—but the tissue looks rehydrated, like it was drained and dried and then plumped up again in the flood. The brown color could be from soil, or just a byproduct of the mummification this underwent. One thing I agree with—this was no ordinary burial that just washed up during the flood. Someone sawed this off the body. I can't tell if the hand was recently cut off, or was removed premortem." He turned to Captain Fernandez. "Do you have a lab here?"

"We can do basic stuff, blood type, fingerprints. But that kind of analysis? No. Gotta send it to Oahu."

"Recommend you do that, sir," Stevens said. Lei snatched the bag out of his hand.

"We can at least do the fingerprints here, see if there's a match to any of our missing. I'll take this down to the lab. J-boy, can you orient them on where we're at? The murder board's over there."

Lei pushed through the door and hurried down the hall. She hated to leave the conference room for even a moment, but Stevens so casually taking over was more than she could handle. At the same time, she couldn't deny the tiny relief she felt at seeing him, the kick of attraction.

She wished she could have stopped herself from panicking on the whole marriage thing. She did a few relaxation breaths as she arrived at the lab, then gave a quick knock before pressing down the steel door handle.

Becky Banks, lab tech, sitting kitty-corner to the door, looked up. Round blue eyes and a white grin that showcased expensive orthodontia gave a falsely cuddly impression. Becky was the closest thing to a female friend Lei had at the station. She'd explained her position relative to the door was good feng shui, and she always knew who was trying to sneak up on her.

"Lei! Whatcha got for me?"

"Prints on this if you can," Lei said, holding up the bag, swishing the hand.

"Eww, gross." Becky squinched up her nose. "Well, as you can see, I'm a little backed up." She gestured to the stack of slides and samples next to her microscope.

"C'mon, how often do you get to potentially ID a hand? Can you bump it up? Captain's orders." Lei was exaggerating, but was pretty sure he'd have wanted a rush on it.

"Okay, I'll see what I can do."

"Thanks. You're the best." Lei stashed the hand in the refrigerator.

"You know it," Becky said, addressing her microscope.

By the time Lei got back to the conference room, she had her emotions under control and was ready to play nice. This resolve lasted until she opened the door and saw nobody there but Stevens, sorting through the pictures of the missing. He looked up.

"J-Boy? Since when did he earn a handle?"

"It's a Kaua'i thing. You can't distract me with that crap.

Where'd he go? Where's the cap?"

"They're setting up a 'war room' in Conference Room B. I guess they use this one for interviews and such."

"So what the hell are you doing here? Seriously," Lei said, hands on her hips. Her eyes actually felt hot with rage.

"I knew you'd be mad, and you know what? Screw that. I don't have to pussyfoot around your emotions anymore, make everything okay for you. We aren't together, in case you haven't noticed, and I don't give a shit if you're pissed."

"Damn you, Stevens. You always have to be the savior."

They glared at each other a long moment; then Stevens shook his head.

"Get a grip so we can work." He opened the file, spreading the photos of the missing people in a swath across the table. "I came over because this case needs someone experienced on it, and I don't trust your captain to reach out for help the way he needs to. He's had five years to investigate this and he hasn't, so no, I wasn't going to sit by and wait to be invited to join some mythical task force. This isn't about you or me. It's about missing people who deserve some justice!" He was yelling by then, face flushed.

Lei felt black closing in around her vision, old trauma triggered by a raised voice. He's not going to hurt me, she told herself. You know he never will. She put her hands behind her back and pinched the web of flesh between her thumb and forefinger and the black receded.

"Okay." She sat down and looked to make sure the door was shut, then said, "That doesn't mean I have to like it. Anyway, one of the suspects, Jazz Haddock, thinks the captain either has been paid off or has turned a blind eye all these years. It is weird that no one picked up on a pattern this regular, going on this long."

"This is Kaua'i," Stevens said. "That's what they'll tell you; that's what everyone said when I asked around. Kaua'i is like...the outback or something, the last bastion of the Wild West. All kinds of shit goes on here no one talks about."

"I know. It's a funny place to me. Station politics. Cults and strange people, insiders and outsiders." Lei looked down, and her gaze fell on her empty ring finger. She pulled her eyes away, found his. They were shadowed by his lowered brows and dark with emotion.

"I'm glad to see you again. Just to see you. But not over this." He gestured to the photos.

"I know." Lei swallowed. "It's overwhelming."

Jenkins stuck his head around the door. "We're set up, if you guys are done making up. I'd feel better if I saw some kissing."

"Shut up, J-Boy." Lei glared at him.

"C'mon, Sweets, just joking," Jenkins said, withdrawing his head. Stevens scooped the pictures back into the folder.

"Don't tell me that's your handle."

"No, that idiot J-boy is the only one who calls me that." Lei led him out of the conference room and down the hall. "I'm going by Ginger around here."

"Now, that suits you," Stevens said, and she heard the smile in his voice. A fist of sorrow squeezed around her heart. She didn't want to see that smile. She pushed open the door of Conference Room B unnecessarily hard, and ran straight into Fury.

Furukawa's arms were crossed over his chest. His teeth were bared in what for him passed for a smile. "You been holding out on me, Ginger."

"Don't owe you shit," Lei said, stepping up and giving back some attitude. "This is my case and it's way beyond the office politics. What are you doing in here?"

Flea waved from across the room, where he was looking at the stones in the tackle box.

"Captain called us in to help. Task force."

Captain Fernandez was flipping through Jazz Haddock's binder in evident fascination.

"Wish I'd listened to that hippie pothead," he said. "He's sure done his homework."

"I think that's why he needs to be considered suspect number one," Lei said. She belatedly remembered her manners. "Guys, this is Michael Stevens from the Big Island. He's been there three years, from Los Angeles before that, where he saw more hard-core crime in a month than we'll see in a lifetime."

Captain Fernandez looked up. "I expect you all to give Detective Sergeant Stevens the respect he deserves. He's on loan from Hilo with my blessing. Thanks for coming, Detective—you're highly recommended by Captain Ohale."

Stevens inclined his head. "Thanks. Looking forward to working with you."

"Now, Lei broke open this case with Jenkins helping, but I think even they'll agree we need to go with someone more experienced taking the lead. I'd like to have Fury, with the local knowledge, and Stevens, with the big-city detective background, co-lead the investigation."

Lei had known this was coming, but disappointment squeezed her into silence. Fury and Stevens took each other's measure, a long stare down and squaring off as they both folded muscular arms. Fury fired the opening round.

"Captain, I don't think that's going to work. Stevens, 'scuse me for saying, isn't from around here. How's he going to know how to call the plays?"

Stevens shot back, "How many serials you hunted? This is looking like a bad one, and I've worked a few. How long you been letting some whack-job disappear people in your community without the slightest notice from law enforcement?"

Fury stepped up, bristling. "It's easy to miss what's happening with the hippies. They come, they go, always mooching off the people who live here..."

"What, these people don't matter because they live in your parks? You might be local, but it still smells like redneck to me."

Captain Fernandez raised his hands. "Settle down. You both make good points. I can see someone needs to call the shots, and I think we need to be open to other perspectives. It's looking to me like attitudes within the department might have contributed to missing this pattern, so with that in mind, I'm going to make Stevens primary for now, with Fury as partner and second."

Fury's wide nostrils flared as he breathed loudly, his hand drifting past his weapon and landing on his belt. Jenkins tried to lighten the atmosphere.

"Well, at least it seems like everyone agrees Lei and I are the real crime spotters around here."

No one bothered to answer, but somehow it shifted things.

"Stevens," the captain said. "You told me some thoughts earlier. Care to tell the group?"

Stevens gestured to the table. "We might as well sit."

Everyone did. He pointed over to the board Lei had made, now mounted on the wall. "We've begun collecting what we know. It looks like there is either a perp or perps who are taking homeless people in May and October. First noted disappearance: 2005."

He recapped the salient points of the case, demonstrating a remarkable memory for facts and dates, and giving Lei full credit for following up with Jay Bennett's disappearance and uncovering the trend.

"Lei found Bennett's wallet with all his money and other possessions, something no homeless person would just throw away unless he was taken, or committing suicide. She then looked into his possessions for clues to his state of mind and searched for a clue to follow up on, leading to the connection at the Health Guardian. Another investigator might have written him off as a probable suicide. It's the homeless and transient status of the victims that has allowed this trend to go on so long."

Captain Fernandez shook his head. "I don't like the way the hippies live in our parks, but that doesn't mean I want some serial killer picking 'em off on my island. Let's get a plan going and get rolling on this thing. Oh, and I expect you to keep a lid on it. The last thing we need is the media getting wind of this."

The meeting moved forward then, with Stevens and Fury taking the lead on cataloging the binder and following up on Jazz Haddock and his connection to the case. Flea was to work up background on the missing to develop a profile and consult an expert on the stones and rituals angle. Lei was to follow up with the cult connection—Jim Jones and the papaya farm—and Lei and Jenkins together would continue canvassing the parks to see what they could pick up from the current crop of park dwellers.

"I think it might be a good idea to explore a Hawaiian cultural angle," Lei said. "I have a contact from a well-connected Hawaiian family, and I want to see about bringing this person on to consult with us if aspects of the case relate to Hawaiian cultural and religious matters. If there's some sort of pagan worship going on, I think this referral could be a helpful resource."

"Who is this 'well-connected Hawaiian family'?" Fury asked. "I know all the North Shore people."

"Her name's Esther Ka`awai. Lehua Wolcott gave me her name as a possible resource. I called her, and I think she might be helpful."

She slid the little square of tapa cloth over to Fury.

"Esther Ka`awai." He looked up. "She only works with a referral from someone she knows. You said you called her already?"

"Yeah. She took my call and was willing to consult. She said she could guarantee confidentiality."

The captain stroked his tidy goatee, looking at Fury. "Who these people stay?" he asked in pidgin.

"I know the Wolcotts—one big mixed missionary and Hawaiian family. They get plenty land on the North and West Side," Fury said. "And Esther, she famous. They say she's psychic, but she's studied and practiced Hawaiian culture all her life. We call her kahu kupuna, which is a spiritual leader and counselor in the Hawaiian community."

Stevens's eyes had been on Lei the whole time. "How do you

have a connection like this? You've been on the island only a few months. And what did you tell them about our investigation to have them give you this kind of insider intel?"

Lei felt a hot blush hit her hairline. Dammit. She was going to have to explain further.

"I met the Wolcott family during the Island Cleaning investigation. They were the real estate agency that reported the burglaries on the beachfront mansions, remember?" She looked at Fury. "Anyway, she said she had a feeling Esther could be helpful. I don't know why; I haven't told anyone what we are working on. As far as she knows, it's the burglary case."

"Seems pretty random," Stevens said, his tone skeptical.

Fury looked down at the little tapa cloth square, fingers holding it gently. "I think we should bring her on. There's probably no one on Kaua`i with a stronger knowledge base of Hawaiian culture, and if she says she can keep a confidentiality agreement, you can take her word for it."

"You'll forgive me if I insist on getting that in writing," Stevens said. "Call me a cynical Mainlander, but I'm finding this all a little woo-woo. Still, I think running the sacrifice/history angle by a local expert is not a bad idea."

All eyes turned to the captain, who had taken the little tapa square.

"All right, Texeira. But have her sign a boilerplate confidentiality agreement, the kind we use for outside experts."

Back at the cubicle, Lei took a coin out of her desk.

"I need some air, J-boy. Let's go out after those hippies again. I think we should go to all the parks between Lydgate and Ke`e Beach today. What car do you want to take?" She flipped the coin, reversing it on her wrist.

"I call tails," Jenkins said.

She looked. "Heads it is. Next stop, Lydgate Park."

CHAPTER FOURTEEN

LEI PULLED up at her cottage. Jenkins, beside her, had his seat reclined, taking a little nap. They still needed to go back out to the station to check in with the rest of the task force, but they were both tired and hungry from working their way through all the county and state parks. They still hadn't tackled the North Shore ones, where more contacts were likely to be—and it was already two p.m.

"I went shopping," Lei said to Jenkins. "There's food in the house, even if it's health food."

"I'll eat anything," Jenkins said, getting out.

Keiki came bounding up to the gate, and Lei signaled her back. Keiki already knew Jenkins from other times he'd come over, so she just sniffed him and let him pet her broad head.

Wayne came to the door. "Hey, you're home early."

"Pit stop," Lei said. "We're still working, but need some lunch."

"You're in luck," Wayne said. "I've been working on a chili with those beans you had and the stuff you brought home." As they entered, a wonderful smell wrapped around them.

"I could get to like this. Thanks, Dad."

"Who's this?" Her father looked hard at Jenkins. She laughed, threw an arm around Jenkins's bulky shoulders.

"Dad, meet my partner on the force, Jack Jenkins. He goes by J-Boy. J-Boy, this is my dad, Wayne Texeira."

They shook hands as Lei went into the kitchen.

"Oh man, that smells so good." She took the lid off the chili and inhaled.

"It'll be better tonight, but I'll let you have a preview." He dished the chili up for them. They ate ravenously and drank glasses of fresh-squeezed lemonade he'd made from local lemons Mrs. Abacan had brought over.

Jenkins sat back and hid a little burp behind his hand. "Best meal I've ever had at Lei's house, sir. She's good with a can opener and a gun but not much in the kitchen."

"Shut up. I have other interests, is all."

"And we're glad you do. Keeping the community safe is a pretty good hobby." Wayne gave Lei's shoulder a squeeze as he went back to the stove.

Just then her cell phone buzzed. She checked the caller ID—an off-island number.

"Hello?"

"Aloha! This is Aaron Spellman from Corrections Aftercare Solutions. I'm your father's reintegration specialist. I'm calling to let you know your father's place at the restoration center is ready."

"Oh." Lei walked out of the room. Just when she was getting used to having her father around and enjoying some home-cooked meals. Her gut clenched around the chili—maybe she wasn't ready for him to go yet. "Didn't you guys used to be called probation officers?"

"It's a whole new system now. Private contract. We've been tasked with lowering your state's recidivism rate, and so far our program's showing very positive results. We're looking forward to having your father as our guest."

Guest? Mandatory guest by any other name.

122

"Are you sure you have space for him?"

"Sure as shootin'. I pulled some strings to get him out of your hair ASAP."

Lei found her hand sliding into her pocket to rub the worry stone.

"How soon does he need to go?"

"Well, as soon as possible as he's scheduled for some classes and a job profile workup tomorrow. Any chance you can get him here tonight?"

"It's going to be tough," Lei said. "I have some work commitments here, but I guess so."

"Thanks. The duration of the restoration program is three months. By the end of that time we hope to have our clients established in a job and their own living situation. But he will still need your support and our monitoring for some time to come after that."

"Of course," Lei said. Well, at least her father would still be on the island, and maybe she could help him find something not too far away when his "restoration" was complete. "Okay. I'll take him in and call you when he's been dropped off." The specialist gave her the address in Lihue and she shut the phone. She walked back into the kitchen.

"Dad, that was your probation officer with Aftercare Solutions. The halfway house is ready and they want you tonight, as you're scheduled for some kind of job profile testing tomorrow." She firmed the tremble in her voice. "Can you pack up while Jenkins and I make a quick run out through the parks?"

Her father poured her a refill of lemonade from a plastic milk jug he'd used to mix it up. His hand wobbled, but his voice was steady.

"Sure. I'll be ready to go when you get back."

"It's three months, they say. They try to get you a job and set up with a place to stay by the end. It's not like we won't get to see each other," Lei said.

"Yeah, I know." He went back to the stove and stirred the chili.

Jenkins cleared his throat and stood, placing his dishes in the old-fashioned ironstone sink.

"Thanks for the lunch, Mr. Texeira. It was delicious."

"Welcome." Wayne's back was still turned.

Jenkins led her back out to the truck and they got in.

"Bummer," Jenkins said. "The man's a good cook."

Lei laughed, a little bubble of tight mirth. They drove in silence to the first of a series of parks. There was a fairly big cluster of tents at Anini Beach, but none of them fit the profile of the campers they'd encountered at Polihale nor recognized photos of the missing.

Under the ironwoods next to the river, at the great swath of deserted beach called Lumahai, they found a family who'd met Tiger and his followers—but they didn't know where they "hung out" when they weren't at Ha`ena Beach Park or Polihale.

Back at the truck, Lei's cell phone rang—Esther Ka`awai.

"Thought we were supposed to meet a half hour ago," Esther said.

"Oh no! I'm so sorry," Lei said, jumping into the truck and firing it up. "I got caught up in some canvassing and forgot. You said you're in Wainiha? We're only ten minutes away, and I got the go-ahead to have you work with us on this case."

"Come alone," Esther said, and hung up. Lei looked over at Jenkins.

"She said to come alone. This lady isn't the kind you cross. How about you drop me off and go finish a quick run-through on the remaining parks? By the time you get back, I'm sure I'll be done. I don't expect you to find many people out there with the weather the way it's been."

In no time they were pulling off precipitous Wainiha Road into a muddy driveway. Three large brindled dogs encircled the truck, barking. Lei waited until the figure of a woman appeared on the deck on the second story of the elevated pole house.

"Come," she said, and the dogs instantly withdrew. The woman made an imperious gesture and went back inside. Lei turned to Jenkins.

"Okay, be back in an hour."

"Gotcha."

Lei got out and climbed the stairs on the outside of the house to a deck with a panoramic view of rain-pummeled Wainiha Valley. She watched the truck pull out with a little pang of apprehension, then turned to face sliding-glass doors.

They opened and Esther stood there, a smaller woman than she'd appeared from below. Long silver hair wrapped around her head in a coronet, and a colorful muumuu brushed the floor. Sharp brown eyes assessed her from a broad, impassive face.

"Come in," she said.

Lei slipped off her shoes, as was done in Hawaii, and entered the great room. Lauhala matting covered the floors, and graceful old pieces of koa furniture formed a seating arrangement around a coffee table made of an aquarium filled with Japanese glass ball fishing floats. An oval of beveled glass formed the top.

"My grandson made it for me," Esther said, seeing Lei's eyes on the unusual table. "He makes his own furniture designs."

"I like it. He's talented."

"Thought you might. Have a seat."

Lei sat. She'd brought her backpack with the confidentiality agreement she'd printed out beforehand.

"I got the go-ahead to have you consult on the case. Before I can tell you anything about it, I have to have you sign this confi-dentiality agreement. Standard stuff for any outside expert we bring in."

"Fine," Esther said, taking a pen from a mug by the old-fash-ioned dial phone. The older woman signed, and sat back in her aloha-print chair.

"Don't you want to read it first?"

"Not particularly." There was a stillness about Esther, a calm but vibrant energy Lei could feel. The kahu's dark eyes gleamed with intelligence in the dim light. "What do you need to talk to me about?"

"The case? Well…" Lei took a breath, not sure where to begin.

"No. What do you need to talk to me about, personally?"

"I don't know. I thought you were consulting on the case."

"I consult on a lot of things and I am here for you, not the case. So what do you need to know?"

Lei took a breath, let it out. What the hell.

"I'm confused. There are two guys. I don't know which one I'm supposed to be with, or if it's neither of them."

"What does your heart say?"

"No idea," Lei said. "You said that before, and I don't know what you mean by it. There's no clear answer. One of them I love. We were engaged, and yet when it came time for the wedding, I panicked and ended up here because this is where my transfer came through. Then I met this other guy…" Her mouth turned up in an involuntary smile. "Hot guy—a player, not my type at all. But he seems to like me, and there's something there. Something that could be pretty fun. I'm tempted to find out. Then Stevens reappears and I feel guilty…" Her voice trailed off as she remembered the amazing shell necklace she was still wearing. Her fingers came up to touch it.

"And there's a third person," Esther prompted.

"No." Lei shook her head. "There's this weird but nice guy. He gave me this necklace and I need to return it. But that's not anything."

"It's something." Esther put her hand out. It was weathered, as if she spent time gardening or working, but her palm was softly pink. "Let me see that."

Lei took the Ni`ihau shell necklace off and put it in Esther's hand. Esther covered that hand with her other one, closed her eyes. Opened them, gave the necklace back.

"This necklace carries a lot of mana," she said. "Power. It's good protection for you. You should not give it back."

Lei laughed. "Not like I want to, but my aunty raised me not to accept expensive gifts from strangers. I don't know; I'll have to see if I can find Mac first."

"Mac Williamson?" The older woman's eyes sharpened. "I know him. He's one of my students, a haumana studying the culture."

"Huh. Well, what do you think about these guys and me?" Lei said. "It's embarrassing, but I need advice."

"Make no sudden moves," Esther said. "You are someone who makes snap decisions, and now is a time to proceed slowly and with caution."

"Thanks. I'll do that. It's a start. So what do you know about the disappearances on the North Shore? You said you might know something about it."

"I hear things. Nothing solid, just rumors. That there is a cult that uses people in their rituals."

"Oh my God, you heard that? Why didn't you go to the police?"

"With a rumor? Just gossip about the homeless disappearing. I have nothing helpful." She made a flicking gesture. "Is this the case you want me to consult on? What is the tie to the Hawaiian community?"

"We don't know yet. We just got our first confirmation that there may actually be foul play involved." Lei explained what they had so far with the May/October pattern and the discovery of the hand. "I thought you might know something about the slipper and the stones left at the latest disappearance site."

"We sometimes use stones as an offering. We wrap a ti leaf around a stone and leave it out of respect at sacred places. What kind of stones were these?"

"Not native." Lei described them.

"Sounds more like a haole witchcraft thing," Esther said disapprovingly. "I follow Christ, and so do my students. We don't use anything but our native materials."

"So you're a Christian."

"Does that surprise you? I've already been praying for you."

Lei threw her hands up. "It just all seems kind of weird. I'm still thinking you use a crystal ball or something."

"Now you are just being disrespectful." Esther folded her lips into a disapproving line. Lei felt those dark eyes measuring her and finding her wanting. "There are mysteries, but God's word is always truth."

"I know that, Aunty. I'm sorry." In Hawaii one respected elders, especially kupuna such as Esther, even when they were confusing, elliptical, and maybe even a little psychic. Lei's Mainland upbringing had made her a little rusty.

Esther appeared mollified by Lei's apology. "I need to see those stones. Feel them. They may tell me something." She stood. "Call me when you can bring them to me."

"Thank you." Somehow Lei wasn't surprised to hear the rumble of her truck pulling up, the barking of the dogs as Jenkins arrived. "I'll call you soon."

CHAPTER FIFTEEN

LEI TURNED into the parking lot of the restoration center, a two-story, false-front building in Lihue's old downtown area. Dusk had fallen, and the truck's headlights reflected off the mirrored glass doors. Attempts had been made to fix up the place by the shiny paint, and a new lighted sign hung above the entrance.

"Ready?" she asked her father as she turned the truck's lights off.

"As I'll ever be." He reached back and took his duffel from the backseat, and they got out. Wayne pulled the front door open and they stepped into a well-lit reception area. A young woman behind a half-moon corner desk stood up to greet them.

"You must be Wayne. I've been looking forward to meeting you." She came around, her hand extended. They shook. "I'm Shellie Samson, Aftercare Coordinator. I'm the social worker here."

"Good to meet you," Wayne said. "I'm Wayne Texeira, and this is my daughter, Lei."

Lei stepped forward. "Sorry we're so late. I got the call about two p.m. and still had a lot of work to do."

"Not a problem. I actually sleep here at the center when I'm on shift. Why don't you follow me, Wayne, and I'll show you your room and orient you on the building and our schedule for tomorrow."

"Well, so far this is an improvement over the past when we just kicked our ex-cons out to the curb and told them to check in with a PO," Lei said with forced heartiness. "What do you think, Dad?"

"It's fine." His weather-beaten face looked strained. She blinked hard as she hugged him, squeezing his tall, wiry frame. He didn't let go of her either.

"Bye, Dad. Call me anytime, and I'll stop by to visit when I'm in the area."

"I'll miss you," he said in her ear. She nodded and turned away abruptly.

"Bye. It was nice meeting you, Shellie."

Lei pushed out through the glass doors to the truck, refusing to cry. He'd been gone from her life for so long, and it felt too soon for him to be gone again. After their long separation, she was surprised at the ease they'd found with each other.

He's a resilient man, and he's going to do fine here, she told herself firmly.

She pulled out and got on the road for Hanalei, a ninety-minute drive when conditions were optimal and there was no traffic, and let her mind wander back over the rest of the afternoon after Jenkins had picked her up from Esther's house.

Jenkins hadn't found any further witnesses, nor anyone who knew about the disappearances. His drive through the wet North Shore of the island had got his clothes muddy and her truck filthy. Later, Fury had called to have Lei and Jenkins watch tomorrow's scheduled interview with Jazz Haddock.

Apparently Mr. Haddock was not too happy about coming in, though he couldn't know how seriously they were taking him as a suspect. What a long day, and tomorrow looked equally so. She stomped down on the gas for a little speeding to shorten the drive.

Her cell rang.

"Texeira."

"Are you going to be able to make it for dinner?" Alika. She'd completely forgotten he'd invited her.

"Of course. I'm on my way." She actually was very close to his turnoff. "Can I get a swim first?" Memory of his pool made her itchy with longing.

"Sure."

Ten minutes later she rang the bell at the spectacular model home. He opened the door wearing his board shorts and a smile.

"Hi."

"Hi." They just grinned at each other for a long minute; then he trailed his hand down to take hers. "Come on in. I've got things cooking."

"Can we swim? I'm dying to get in that pool." She held up her suit and the cotton robe he'd loaned her last time.

"Sure. Why don't you go out to the pool and I'll check the oven. White or red wine?"

"White."

He padded away and she went to the bathroom, changed, then walked to the open sliding doors. The underwater lights were on in the pool, the Portuguese tiles shimmering cobalt under the clear water. Spotlights played up the fan palms and red torch ginger of the landscaping. Lei dove in.

Alika came to the door, a glass of wine in each hand, backlit by the kitchen light. He set them on a side table.

"How about a race?"

"Can your ego take losing?" He dove in, came up beside her.

"We'll have to see about that." Lei grasped the side of the pool and braced her legs against the wall. "On your mark. Go!"

She blasted off the side explosively, unleashing all the pent-up energy and frustration she'd felt throughout the day. Her arms churned and legs kicked, and she did an underwater reverse at the end, blasting across the pool until she hit the ledge on the far side.

Alika was already there, his muscular arms spread in a parody of relaxation across the pool edge.

"Ready for dinner?" He didn't even seem winded.

"Bastard." He turned his face away, and she said, "I'm sorry. I forgot."

"Gonna need more than that." She swam over to him, looked into his eyes—they'd gone dark. She brushed her lips tenderly over his, a reminder of their first kiss in the underwater bar, a kiss all about promises.

"You gonna tell me why that word gets to you?"

"Usual reason. My mother wasn't married when she had me—and my father wouldn't acknowledge me."

"Shit. I put my foot in it."

"Yeah, you did, but I know you didn't mean it. How about you kiss me and make it better?"

"Tell me more first."

"It was the usual story. They met in college. He was a white guy, well connected. She didn't know he was married. She came home, dropped out of school to have me. She married Shawn Wolcott, and he adopted me. He's been all the dad I could want."

"I'm sorry. Again. I've got some scars from the past too."

"Tell me about them."

"Maybe another time. I'm hungry."

"You came to the right place." He turned and heaved himself out of the pool in one fluid movement, wrapping himself in a towel. She hoisted herself out a little less gracefully, and he held out a towel. She dried off quickly, then wrapped herself in the robe, scooping up the wine and following him into a kitchen redolent with tasty smells.

He reached into the oven, pulling out a roast in a deep pan, surrounded by small whole red potatoes and garnished with rosemary sprigs. He used a pair of forks to transfer it to a cutting board and brought a carving knife to bear on one browned end. Lei's mouth watered.

"Oh my God, I've died and gone to heaven." She inhaled a waft of rosemary and spices. He smiled and filled their plates with potatoes, green beans, and slices of pink, perfectly done beef. He carried the plates to the dining room table, a great slab of mango wood set with two places.

Lei took a bite of the roast, closing her eyes in ecstasy.

"Oh, that's good."

"Glad you like it." They ate in silence until Lei's rumbling stomach began to settle down.

"So." Alika sat back and swirled the red wine in his glass. "How are you liking our third date?"

"Third?"

"First—poolside frolics. Second—the lighthouse benefit. Third —dinner at my house. I'm working on a fourth, something I think you'll like."

"Hmm." Lei frowned. She took a sip of the crisp wine. "I would rather we just kept it casual. Maybe I'll ask you out next time."

"Sounds good. What's the plan?"

"You don't let up, do you? How about a morning run? You must do something besides swim to keep in shape."

"I do. I paddle canoe with the Kilauea team, so I'd have to skip practice for our run. I also surf whenever I get the chance—in case you thought I was a slacker, just sitting around raking in money."

"Okay, then. Meet me Wednesday morning at the pier at six thirty a.m. Keiki deserves a good run."

"All right." They clinked glasses.

"So, I noticed something." Lei pointed to the living room, where an aquarium stood in front of the leather couches, filled with antique Japanese glass balls and topped by a round of beveled glass. "I've seen one of those before. Where'd you get it?"

"Designed it myself. I do some furniture designs as well as house plans."

"So…you know Esther Ka`awai."

"Yes—she's my grandmother. Why?"

Lei shook her head. "This is too weird; but now that I think of it, your mother was the one to give me her name."

"What's this about?"

"Esther's consulting on my case. Lehua gave me her card, but never mentioned she was a relative. Looks like keeping secrets around here gets tricky."

"Not for my grandmother. She's a steel trap—she has more dirt on people on this island than anyone, but she never gossips."

"She said she was a kahu of the word, but I don't know what that means."

"She was referring to her church. It's a small group, but they all have assigned roles... Hers is the guardian of our oral traditions, in the old way. You're lucky to have her on your case."

"I get that feeling. I also get the feeling she took me on for her own reasons. She has quite the reputation."

"You're lucky," Alika repeated, and drained his wine. The discussion seemed to be making him uneasy. He tossed his napkin on the table. "Care for another swim?"

"No, I'm too tired. It's been a long day. I should be getting on the road."

She was a little rattled by the interconnectedness of the people she was getting to know on the island... Maybe these kinds of coincidences were part of spiritual forces rumored to be woven into Kaua`i's very fabric—and maybe it was "just a small island."

"If you must." Alika got up and they cleared the table. She collected her discarded clothes.

"Thanks for a wonderful meal."

"You're welcome. You look like you needed it."

He set his hands on her waist, pulled her in. She turned her face up, her eyes drifting shut as his lips settled on hers, confident and exploring, boldly taking. His hands moved down, reaching to open the robe, wandering over her smooth stomach and circling around to stroke the muscles of her back.

Stevens. He'd kissed her so differently in the beginning. So gently. Slowly. Letting her get used to him. Letting her know she was safe.

He was here, somewhere on the island.

She broke away, pulled the robe back into place. "Thanks again."

"Hey. Everything okay?"

"Sure. Just—not quite ready for this. I'm…getting over someone. We were engaged."

"Really? You never said."

"I don't like to talk about it." Lei found herself blinking again, for the second time that day—and Alika was the last person she should tell about the riot of emotions seeing Stevens had brought on.

"Good to know. I like a woman who doesn't want to talk about the exes. Sorry if I was a little enthusiastic, but hell. You can't blame me for trying." He made a gesture that encompassed her, bare feet to damp head. "You're the total package, and I'm a little bit hooked."

She couldn't help smiling, rising on her toes to kiss his sculpted mouth.

"I think I might be, too. See you soon."

CHAPTER SIXTEEN

Monday, October 25

THE NEXT MORNING Lei took a seat behind the Formica counter that fronted the one-way mirror into the interview room where Stevens already sat, selkie-dark head bent over a file. Her eyes traced the long line of his bent back, one big hand folded to prop up his cheek, laser-blue eyes shadowed.

Wherever he was staying, he wasn't sleeping well.

Jenkins sat down beside her, a full cup of Starbucks at his elbow. Captain Fernandez and Flea took the remaining chairs in what they called the "peanut gallery."

They watched as Fury preceded Jazz Haddock into the interview room, Fury's outthrust chest reminding Lei of a bantam rooster spoiling for a fight. Stevens gestured to the chairs around the steel table.

"Have a seat."

"Thanks," Jazz said. "Like everything about this, do I have a choice?"

Lei noticed the aging hippie's grayish pallor, gaunt face pearly with sweat. Probably scared the shit out of him to be in there. It was never fun being in the interview hot seat.

"We appreciate all the research and work you've put into this," Stevens said, tapping the binder. "It seems like you've been trying to bring some attention to these disappearances for a while. Do you mind if we tape this interview?"

"Go ahead. Not like I have a choice," Jazz said again, appearing a little mollified by Stevens's compliment. "If I coulda got that redneck Captain Fernandez to look into this, it might have saved some lives."

Lei didn't need to look over to see the captain's rigid response to this comment. Stevens went on.

"So how long have you been collecting this information?" An easy question, since the dates in the binder made it obvious.

"I noticed a regular pattern of people disappearing in the last five years, and what I've collected is in the binder. My family and I have been on the island seven years."

"What we find particularly interesting is the note here." Stevens pointed to a handwritten note in the margin of one of the clippings of a missing person. "Samhain and Beltane?"

"Yeah. After the second year I was collecting information, I realized people were disappearing in May and October. I wondered what the significance might be. The dates put me onto it first; then I kept hearing things…that made me wonder."

"What kind of things?"

"Rumors. Of witchcraft, maybe a cult connection. Some of the campers would tell about animal disappearances. Then there were the stones."

"Stones?"

Everyone in the peanut gallery sat forward.

"Yeah, the stones that were left behind. Campers found three stones several times at the site where someone disappeared. I think the stones have significance."

"We have to find some forensic evidence showing foul play.

These disappearances are certainly weird, a pattern, and something we are seriously investigating, but we can't say for sure these people are victims yet." Stevens was still fishing, waiting to see what Haddock would reveal on his own. The addition of other stones was already more than the store owner had told Lei.

"You can't, but I can." Jazz threw his shoulders back proudly. "I'm the Guardian of the community, and I know when it's in trouble. I know people are being taken and killed. I even think I know something about who's doing it."

"Please." Stevens made a sweeping gesture. "Let us in on it!"

"Why should I give away the only leverage I've got? Not without something in exchange."

"Exchange for what?" Fury spoke for the first time. He'd taken the "bad cop" role, standing against the wall with arms folded and a scowl on his face. "I wasn't aware there was anything we could help you with."

"Exchange for an apology from Captain Fernandez—for not taking this seriously when it was happening right under his nose."

Stevens looked up at the mirrored window. The captain bent forward to the microphone embedded in the Formica.

"I'll talk to you." His voice had a tinny echo in the audio system of the interview room.

"Now." Jazz folded his arms.

The captain leaned forward. "Turn off the tape."

Fury hit the switch on the wall that turned off the video camera.

The captain stood up, straightened his jacket, shot his cuffs, and put his gold-braided hat on. He left the booth and went around to the interview room door, went in. Walked over to the table and reached out his hand.

"Jazz Haddock. Long time no see. Thanks for coming in." Jazz took his hand and they shook. The captain took his hat off, tucked it under his arm.

"I should have taken your complaint seriously. I apologize for any misunderstanding we may have had over the years and if my department treated you with anything less than fairness."

"Accepted."

"I want to keep my island safe, and everyone on it. That means everyone. Please give these men your full cooperation so we can move ahead with this investigation."

The captain clapped his hat back on, spun on his heel, and left the room. A few minutes later he took his seat beside Lei again. His jaw was bunched with tension, but his apology had worked, because Jazz got a paper out of his back pocket and smoothed it on the table.

"These are the facts about the perpetrator I've been able to develop—one: He lives here. Probably somewhere remote, where he takes the victims. Two: He drives a truck. There were truck tire marks at some of the sites when I asked fellow campers about it, and a truck would be a great way to easily transport someone.

"Three. He may have help. I think someone assists, what have you, because a lot of the missing were young and in good physical condition."

Lei's mind flew to Jim Jones. He seemed the perfect candidate, as either the murderer or the helper, and his suspicious behavior and disappearance had only made Lei more eager to bring him in. The papaya farm cult would make the perfect hunting ground and hideout—who knew how many bodies might be buried there as fertilizer. Lei rubbed the stone in her pocket and fought the urge to get up and pace.

"Four. He's got some means. I think he has a cover life, but this kind of activity requires a flexible schedule. Five. He's physically fit. The victims have been a variety of sizes and body types; he seems to be able to handle them all."

"We were hoping for a name," Fury said.

"I don't have that for you."

"Not bad for speculation." Stevens took the list. "Now, how about you? Where were you Tuesday, October twenty-third?"

Jazz gave a short laugh. "Oh, it's that way, is it? Well—I hate to disappoint you—I was opening my store with my wife, Penny, like I do every morning. I wouldn't have the chance to drive all the way out to the North Shore and grab a strong young man and kidnap him." He lifted one skinny arm, flexed it. "I hire young people like Jay Bennett to help me do the heavy lifting these days."

"We'll be verifying that. I think that's all for now, and again, we really appreciate your cooperation." They escorted Jazz out.

The captain flung his hat down on the Formica counter. "I thought he had a name for us!"

"It was gracious of you to talk to him, Captain," Lei said. The other men left her alone with him. The captain picked the hat back up, turned it in his hands.

"He was gloating."

"No one thinks less of you for apologizing to him. They'll respect you for it. You said you want to protect everyone on this island—and that's what the guys will remember."

A long pause, then Fernandez stood up.

"You're all right, Texeira," he said gruffly, and clapped his hat back on as he left.

LEI STUCK her head into Becky's cubicle. The young woman was hunched over her microscope, busy with a slide. Lei knocked on the doorjamb.

"Hey. Any luck with our mummy hand?"

"Yeah. I matched the prints and sent it to Oahu." Becky looked up, stretched, hopped off her stool, and moved over to the computer, gesturing to a wheeled stool.

Lei rolled it over to the computer.

"Prints matched a missing person, John Samson." Becky turned the screen toward Lei, showing a photo of a mid-thirties white man with long hair and a beard. "Missing since 2003. Kind of amazing the hand's intact."

Lei's pulse jumped—this was the first solid evidence that one of the missing was a homicide, just as they'd hoped.

"Can you log this and e-mail it to the captain? I'll make sure the rest of the team knows."

"Well, you'll like this too." Becky scrolled to a blow-up photo of the hand. "See this?" She pointed to a ragged edge of bone. "Serrated marks. This didn't come off as a result of decay or the flood—it was sawed off."

"Premortem or postmortem?"

"That I can't say. It's on its way to Oahu for a full tox screen and DNA analysis. Hopefully they can tell."

"What've you got?" The brusque inquiry made them both jump. Stevens stood in the doorway, brows a dark slash over intense blue eyes.

"Come see this." Lei gestured. "This is the hand I picked up from the Hanalei flood. Becky did prints on it—and it matches one of our missing."

"I don't believe we've met." Becky hopped off her stool, ripped off her latex glove and, smiling, shook Stevens's hand. "I'd have remembered if we had."

Lei hadn't noticed Becky's petite, curvy figure until now, how attractive her tousled blond hair and bright blue eyes were. Becky made a show of straightening a miniskirt so short it disappeared beneath her lab coat.

"Great to meet you." Stevens flashed the smile Lei remembered, one she hadn't seen in months. "This is very good news."

"I aim to please." Becky did a little curtsy.

"Well, I'm out of here." Lei slid off her stool. "I'll let you get caught up on the details."

"Just a minute." Stevens's hand clamped around her upper arm. "Let's go together. I have to brief you on something. Private conversation."

Lei gave a little wave to Becky as Stevens pointed at the doors.

His large hand encircled her biceps as if she might run. She yanked her arm away and strode ahead. They swished through the sliders and into the parking lot. Lei headed for the little shade tree growing against the side of the building. They sat on the picnic table beneath it, facing the ocean's blue smudge visible in the distance.

Stevens cleared his throat. "This is more awkward than I thought."

"What did you think it would be like? We broke up; now we have to work together."

Lei's voice trembled and she stilled it, thrusting her hands into her jeans pockets. She rubbed the black stone.

"Well, I didn't realize you'd be seeing someone so soon. Who sent the roses?"

"What roses?"

"Your cubicle. Who is he?"

"None of your business." Lei felt a hot blush blooming up her neck. She'd obviously missed something.

"I think it is."

"We broke up. I moved here. Life goes on."

"I guess I thought you were just having another panic attack, that you needed some space. I just don't understand you." He looked away.

"I don't either." Lei looked down at the stone in her hand.

"Well, I wanted to tell you I miss you, and I'd like to…spend some time together."

"I don't know. We're in the middle of an investigation. Don't you think we should try to focus on that?"

"Sounds familiar."

She remembered him saying what she'd just said, how hard it had been keeping their hands off each other during last year's investigation. Stevens's phone shrilled, and he picked up, walking away from her back toward the station. She followed slowly, studying the breadth of his shoulders, the curling brown hair that he'd let grow to touch his collar.

She missed him. She missed snuggling against his big hard strength and listening to the measured thud of his heart; she missed how safe she felt with him.

Somehow that hadn't been enough to get past her fear.

Lei headed straight to her cubicle, hands sweating. Her eyes widened at the huge bouquet of blush-colored roses she'd been too distracted to notice on the way to the interview room. A tiny cream-colored card was set in a plastic holder protruding from among the glossy foliage.

She took the little card off, flipped it over.

Remembering last night. Alika.

"Oh my God," she said out loud. "Crap."

Stevens had probably looked at the card, but even if he hadn't, the roses took up most of her cubicle. She stared at them numbly.

Jenkins came in. "Woo-hoo! Nice roses! Stevens trying to get you back?"

"No." Lei pushed the roses off into a corner where they didn't take up so much room. They hit her in the head when she sat down in her chair.

"Just 'no'? What, got a secret admirer?" Jenkins wheedled. Lei stuck the little card in the pocket of her jeans.

"What Jazz Haddock was saying really makes me like Jim Jones for this, and we never did get an interview with the folks out there at the papaya farm."

"Hey now, no distracting me. What about those roses? Who sent them to you?"

"None of your business."

"You're my partner. Everything's my business"

"It's Alika Wolcott, the developer dude, okay? We've got a case to work on. Let's focus on that." Lei flipped the black stone back and forth between her fingers. "I wonder if there's some way to really see what's going on out there—maybe by getting in undercover."

"Stevens isn't going to like it." Jenkins's statement seemed to encompass both the roses and her idea.

"No, this could work." Lei did a few spins in her office chair, her head tipped back. The pent-up tension of the morning, the frustration and edginess of talking to Stevens, had begun to transmute into an idea she could take action on. "Jazz could bring me in and I could be a hippie chick 'seeker.'"

"What makes you think he'd take you in?"

"I don't know. I might need to show him I'm serious, that I can do it." She grabbed one of the Bics, jotted a little cartoon on the pad of scratch paper by her desk, held it away to look at it.

"You need to run all this by Stevens and Fury," Jenkins said. He'd begun to chew the corner of his index fingernail. "Let's go talk to them."

"No. I don't think so." Lei reached for her backpack and cotton blazer. "I'll be back in a few hours."

"It's on your head." Jenkins raised his voice to call after her, rare irritation twisting his mouth. "You gonna ditch me, go off on a tangent, it's on your head."

"That's right," Lei said, over her shoulder. "I'll let you know how it goes."

CHAPTER SEVENTEEN

Lᴇɪ ᴘᴜꜱʜᴇᴅ through the screen door into the barbershop in the shabby old-town area of Kapa`a. A dusty striped pole spun slowly outside, and the chair was occupied by an elderly Filipino gentleman who looked at her disapprovingly over half-glasses and his paper. The barber ignored her as she sat on one of the plastic seats, reading an ancient National Geographic.

Finished, the barber dusted the chair off, the latest hair offerings joining drifts on the linoleum floor.

"What you like?"

Lei got into the chair.

"Take it all off." She rubbed the black stone to still her hands, knotted in her lap.

"Crazy, you," the barber tsked. "Whatevahs." He turned on his clippers.

Fifteen minutes later, Lei walked out rubbing her head, shorn like a lamb to within an inch of her scalp. She couldn't bear to look in a mirror. Next stop—tattoo shop.

She came out an hour later with henna tattoos and several imitations that looked like the real thing: a henna sun sent rays out from her navel, an ankh decorated one wrist and an "om" sign the other; and a colorful lotus blossom bloomed on her lower back.

She drove on to Lihue and made her way to the costume shop, a little place near the community theater. She'd shopped there several times doing detective work, and Shevonne, the owner, looked up in surprise as she came in.

"Oh my God, is that you, Lei?" she exclaimed.

"Going for a new look."

After the costume shop, she hit the local hemp clothing store, where she came out with yet more packages. She drove back to Kapa`a, and at the park, went into the women's washroom and put on her disguise. Eventually satisfied, she got in her truck and drove to her destination.

THE TIMEKEEPER FINISHED the last of his Tae Kwon Do workout and dove into the ocean. The water was cool, and he stayed submerged as long as he could, swimming beneath the surface, sleek as a seal.

"Lazy good-for-nothing. You and your brother and sister, nothing but pains in my ass." Her voice rang in his ear as loud as the day she'd spoken those words. He broke the surface, gasping, looking around.

Nothing but beauty as far as his eyes could see—the sculptured face of Bali Hai mountain, horseshoe of yellow beach, and ocean gone cobalt with early morning.

"Get your ass back to work or I'll take it out on her," she said. His sister, too frail to withstand her. His sister, whom he'd failed.

"Okay, Mom, I'm going," he said aloud, and swam hard for the shore.

CHAPTER EIGHTEEN

JAZZ HADDOCK GLANCED up from his last customer and Lei pushed the organic lamb chops and other groceries toward him at the register. He took the items without comment and rang them up. "That'll be twenty-seven ninety-nine."

She handed him the cash, and as their eyes met, his widened in recognition. She put her finger over her lips and pointed to the beaded curtain. He gave a tiny nod and handed her back her change. The next customer engaged him in conversation, and Lei sidled casually through the curtain, trying to keep the beads from rattling. She parked herself on the couch, the string bag bulging with food at her feet.

Jazz's "office" was dimly lit, the evening light slanting through the window and falling on the coffee table, where a bamboo tray held a variety of round semi-precious chunks of stone and a loupe.

She picked up the loupe and looked at the stones. They were roughly the same size as the ones they'd recovered from Jay's shoe. A nasty suspicion came to her as she held one of the walnut-sized rocks, an opal, up to catch the light. Jazz pushed through the beaded curtain and shut the office door, putting his hands on his hips.

"I said all I needed to, down at the station. What's with the disguise?"

Lei set the stone back into the tray. "What are you doing with these rocks?"

"Collecting. You never answered my question."

"Yeah. Collecting. I think these were 'collected' from the other disappearance sites. You've been holding out on us." She folded her legs Indian-style under the hemp skirt and placed her hands on her knees, thumb to forefinger in the classic meditation pose, her "tattooed" wrist symbols clearly visible.

"You guys never asked if I had them. I answered everything I was asked truthfully."

"I think you know a lot more than you told us," she said, as if he hadn't spoken.

He clamped his lips shut, sat in the lounger. A few long minutes passed, and Lei closed her eyes, breathed in through her nose and out through her mouth.

The pose really was relaxing.

"How do I look?" she finally asked.

"Like a hippie. What the hell are you doing?"

"I need to get into the cult you told me about, the Truth-Way. I've been all over the North Shore with my partner, showing pictures and canvassing; we can't find Jim Jones and that group of campers, or anyone who seems to know anything about the disappearances. We do know they meet and hide out at a papaya farm owned by a Jones family. I want to get onto the papaya farm, and you said you know people there."

Jazz looked at her for a long time. She could see him assessing her outfit: the natural-fiber fringed dress, the strings of tulsi beads decorated with a bronze peace sign, the tattoos, and finally the waist-length black wig, which did more to change her looks than she'd hoped.

"Lose the beads. Too much."

"Okay." She took the strands off and handed them to him. "Will you help me?"

"You aren't talking to the other cops about this, are you?"

"Nope. I don't think I'd get the green light. I plan to tell them after I'm in."

Jazz sat back, playing with the tulsi beads. "These are used for prayer, you know. You use them like a rosary, and say the Hare Krishna on each one."

"Good to know. You're going to have to tell me everything you can, and coach me on the details. Like, I don't know what the Hare Krishna is."

"You should know that TruthWay can be dangerous. I know. I was a part of it."

"I knew there was a lot you weren't telling us. I thought you said you wanted to help, you wanted the investigation."

"I don't think TruthWay has anything to do with it."

"That's not for you to decide. Sometimes when you're too close, you can't see what's in front of you." Lei gestured to the stones. "I need to take those in too."

Another long moment, then he nodded. He got up and took a plastic ziplock bag off the desk, emptied the tray of stones into it.

"Okay. I do want the investigation—wherever it leads. I'll get you in."

LEI GOT into her truck outside the health food store. The adrenaline buzz that had carried her this far had worn off, and now, as she glanced in the mirror, her wide brown eyes looked apprehensive under the wig's black bangs. She was all but unrecognizable, even to herself, and walking into the station in her current getup was going to cause quite a shitstorm.

At least she had the bag of stones, Haddock's cooperation, and a good chance of getting inside that papaya-farm stronghold.

As she drove, Lei remembered the name of the man whose hand she'd recovered. John Samson. She hadn't had time to investigate him at all, but she knew someone with the same last name. Maybe they'd be able to find another lead.

She called the restoration center and got Shellie Samson, the social worker.

"Shellie, do you by chance know anyone named John Samson?"

"I do," Shellie said cautiously. "He's my husband. Why?"

The adrenaline was back. Lei focused on the road and controlled her voice.

"Do you know where he is?"

"Why are you asking?"

"You first."

"I was married to John Samson. He left me. Just up and left, no word, nothing. So eventually I divorced him."

"Tell me about how he left."

"We came to Kauai on vacation. One morning he just... Well. He told me he wanted some alone time, was going to take a hike on the Na Pali Coast. We'd been having some problems, and he said he wanted to think things over. He never came back."

"You filed a missing persons?"

"I did... I know you're Wayne's daughter. Why are you asking me these questions?"

"I'm a detective with Kauai Police Department. We've found some evidence regarding your husband." The sadly gruesome hand burst into Lei's mind's eye.

Shellie gasped—and Lei hurried on. "Can you come into the station and answer a few questions for us? I promise I'll fill you in on what this is about."

"Of course." They set an appointment for later that day. Lei closed her phone.

This investigation just kept unfolding in front of her, coincidence wrapped in happenstance pointing to the next lead. Now there was no choice. She had to make the call.

She pushed the worn button on her phone and held it down.

"Stevens."

"Hi, it's Lei."

"I know. Where'd you go? We had a strategy meeting and Jenkins said you had an errand." Bless her loyal partner.

"I'm on my way." She filled him in on the Samson situation as she turned into the station parking lot, where her courage failed at the sight of the automatic doors. "Can you meet me outside at my truck? Got some confidential information."

"Okay."

She put on sparkly lip gloss and fluffed up her long black wig. She knew it was silly, but she couldn't help it. Stevens opened the passenger door of the truck. His eyes raked her from head to foot.

"What the hell are you up to?" He held the door open and then reached over to tweak her wig off. It was held in place with a bit of adhesive, and she yelped as it pulled her skin. She smacked her hand to her forehead, eyes watering at the sting.

"Wow." His eyes wandered over her head, the long black wig streaming from his hand. Lei trembled as she touched her shorn scalp, and that made her angry. She yanked the wig out of his hand and slammed it back on her head.

"You're an ass." She blinked rapidly and got her voice under control. "I'm going undercover."

"Oh really? Last I checked, I was primary on the case." He got into the truck beside her, slammed the door.

"Nothing was breaking. I had an idea and I went with it. I've got a way into the cult through Jazz Haddock."

"I knew that guy was holding out on us, but I didn't expect it from you. Take that wig back off. I want to look at you."

"No. I like it on."

"You didn't even look at your head, did you?"

"Who cares about my head! What's important is that Haddock

is going to put me to work in the Health Guardian to gather intel. When I've established my cover, he's going to bring me out to the TruthWay cult's Sunday 'love feast.'"

"I don't even know where to begin with this. You sure there's a connection?"

"No, but I suspect that Tiger–Jim Jones character. He would be in a great position to disappear people, and Jenkins and I narrowed his location down to this Jones papaya farm cult group. I really want to get eyes on the place, the people, look for something."

"You've been busy. Busy, and not telling anybody else what you were thinking." His voice was flat.

"Yeah." She picked up the bag of stones, set them on his lap. "But I am getting somewhere. Haddock had these from the other disappearance sites. Also, I found John Samson's wife. She's coming into the station this afternoon. Claims not to know where he went, said he just went hiking and she thought he left her."

"Son of a bitch. So our missing man has a wife right here in town! I put Fury on running down the victims' identities, and Samson's last listed address was California."

"Yeah. Apparently they came on vacation. Shellie just stayed."

A long pause as he absorbed this, looking at her changed appearance. He finally spoke. "So it's a done deal."

"It's too good an opportunity for you to make me pass it up. But I definitely need backup. Haddock says the cult is scary, and after doing all that canvassing in the parks, I'm concerned about being made."

"You should be. This whole thing is sketchy." He glanced over at her again. "Please take the wig off—or are you too scared?"

"You can't get me with that old 'I dare you' thing."

Still, she found herself putting the wig carefully on the armrest and tilting the rearview mirror to look. Full lips and tilted almond eyes looked enormous without the riot of curls to balance her face. She shut her eyes, feeling exposed, and felt his hand on her shoulder.

"I can't believe how beautiful you are." His breath was warm in her ear. "You shouldn't be—it's dangerous."

She found herself turning, her eyes still closed, her arms reaching for him blindly as he pulled her in. His touch filled her senses, an instant kindling she'd kept tamped down. She wound around him as far as she could reach, with the steering wheel and armrest in the way, and he stroked her body, squeezing her hard as he kissed her, as if to impress her shape on his hands. A combustible clash of need, desire, and anger left her knees shaking and her lips burning when he finally lifted his head.

His eyes were bluer than she ever remembered.

"Don't play with me. I can't take it."

"I'm not playing. I just can't marry you. That's all I know." She moved farther away, trying to get her breath back.

"I hate it when you go off half-cocked, like this hippie disguise thing." She saw the longing and fear in his eyes. "Someday it's going to cost you."

"It's already cost me. I told you a long time ago I am who I am. I didn't want to tell you anything because you'd just shut me down."

"Impulsive is what you are. Reckless. But—you've got good instincts, I'll give you that."

Lei had parked the truck alongside the building where they were out of view. Stevens seemed to be getting his composure back, turning to look out the front windshield.

"I've got a couple of loose ends I need to run by you," Lei said.

"Uh-oh."

"Nothing too big. Esther Ka`awai wants to 'feel' the stones; she thinks she can tell something about them by doing that. And I don't think I can go in the station looking like this. I want to go right over and get started at the Health Guardian."

"I'm going to have to bring Haddock in for more interviews," he said. "I'll have Jenkins bring you the stones from Bennett's disappearance site and you can take them out to the Ka`awai woman."

"Yeah, I figured you'd have to talk to him, but since I'm going undercover...can you dial it back? It needs to look like he's not cooperating with us. He says it's dangerous, that people who try to leave disappear."

"The guy was hardly cooperating. But okay, we'll take it slow, meet him somewhere neutral. I want to talk to Haddock, make sure this plan with you is on the up-and-up, and I need to brief the captain on all this. Why don't we meet at the district safe house in Kilauea?" The county-owned residence was used for various purposes by the police department and could provide much-needed privacy.

"I'll call Jenkins and Haddock and let them know to meet us out there."

"You just don't want to have to walk into the station and deal with Fury getting a load of your outfit."

Lei snorted a laugh. "You're right about that."

He went serious again. "You should have talked to me about this first. Or your partner, at least."

Lei suppressed a stab of guilt. "The investigation is the most important thing, and I just knew...no one would like the idea. It was time to think outside the box."

"You just aren't supposed to decide that on your own. Jumping the gun again, Sweets."

"Figures that J-boy's nickname for me is the one that sticks. If it's an apology you need, okay. I'm sorry. I'll be a team player from now on." She mentally crossed her fingers.

He seemed mollified. "So when is Shellie Samson coming in? I'll have to be back in time to interview her."

"Three p.m.," she told him, putting the wig back on and tweaking it in the mirror. He gave it a long look.

"I think I like you better bald."

"I'm not bald. Just almost. Okay, gotta get on the road."

He didn't take his blue, blue eyes off her. Electricity between them made the hairs rise along her arms and her heart thunder in her ears. He reached out, fingers tracing a line up her throat, along her jaw, and circling around behind her head to pull her over for another kiss, a tender invasion that left Lei's body flushed and tingling.

"We have to stop this."

"I wish we didn't have to."

"But we do. And I need to come up with a cover story. I'll see you at the safe house."

She smoothed down the already-crumpled hemp dress. The pull toward him was strong, and he rubbed his hands on his jeans as if to keep them from reaching for her, opening his door and stepping out. Her phone rang.

"I have to take this." He nodded and shut the door, striding away. Her eyes followed his graceful loping stride as she flipped open the phone. "Texeira."

"Lei, it's your dad."

"Hi, Dad. I called earlier—how're you doing?"

"Fine. It's going good. When can we get together?"

"I don't know. I was in Lihue today and could've swung by; but I'm not sure what the coming week's going to be like."

They set a tentative time to get together as she got on the road. Lei made the call to Jazz Haddock and Jenkins, then put her foot down for Kilauea.

CHAPTER NINETEEN

LEI AND JENKINS sat at the battered police-station discard table that furnished the safe house kitchen. She had a ball cap on, but Jenkins had pried it off first thing, and she'd endured his questions and castigations. Stevens joined them, pulling out one of the kitchen chairs and straddling it.

"What did the captain say?" Lei tried not to sound anxious, but her voice wobbled.

"Wasn't happy but said the plan has potential. Proceed with caution and keep him informed. Also no more 'cowboy antics' or he'll bust you down to patrol. And I quote."

Lei blew out a breath. "Guess I deserve that."

"Yeah, and I think he wants to give that message to you personally next time you're in the station."

"Better be out here undercover awhile and bring home da kine," Lei muttered, the pidgin expression for "the goods." Jenkins got up and hunted around in the fridge, returning to the table with a loaf of whole wheat bread. He dumped a pile of slices onto a plate.

"Dude. Really?" Lei said, as he picked up a slice and took a bite. "Who knows how long that's been there."

"No breakfast. We Ohio boys need fuel for the day."

"Haddock better get here soon. I'm still deciding whether or not to charge him with obstruction for holding back those stones. I called a geology professor we consult with at University of Hawaii on Oahu. We e-mailed him photos of the rocks for identification, and he's going to research their uses in witchcraft and other religious rituals. I think we're going to find there's something significant about them. I mean, how many people have the time and money to collect exotic stones out here?" Stevens took one of the bread slices, bit into it.

"That might have been true at one time," Jenkins said, "but with the Internet, anyone could be collecting anything from the privacy of their home."

"I think the best approach is to let me keep working the infiltration plan. I need to start living my cover story as Lani the hippie-chick seeker. I think the cult is suspicious, and they've survived this long by keeping an eye on everything that's going on, probably with a lot of help from Jazz Haddock. Speak of the devil." Lei turned her head toward the door.

The rattle of the VW van's motor sounded like a sewing machine as it pulled in next to the other cars. Lei went to the coded gate and let him in. She followed the health-food store owner into the house. Stevens and Jenkins stared Jazz down as he came in.

"Believe you've met Detective Sergeant Stevens," Lei said. "And this is my partner, Detective Jenkins."

Jazz was a touch defiant as he took one of the cheap aluminum chairs. "I'm here. What do you want from me?"

"How would you like up to five years for obstruction of justice for withholding information and evidence in a homicide investigation?" Stevens asked.

"Bring it," Jazz flashed. "I've had reason to make sure you were going to take this seriously before I disclosed anything more."

"All right, 'nuff already," Lei said. "You're on board now and that's what's important. So let's put that behind us and move forward. Why don't you tell us everything you know about TruthWay and its leadership."

Jazz looked at his gnarled hands. Jenkins took out a yellow pad and pen; Stevens put a tape recorder in front of the older man and pressed Record. But Jazz didn't start speaking until Lei gave his arm an encouraging pat.

"It started out as a way to connect with people," he said. Jenkins and Stevens exchanged an ironic glance, but Lei shook her head at them as the aging hippie took a deep breath and looked around the modest little kitchen. "Do you have anything to drink? Some water?"

Jenkins filled a glass at the sink and brought it to him. The older man took a long drink, the three detectives watching him. He sighed, wiped his mouth with the back of his hand.

"The TruthWay began in 1971 in the hippie encampment on the North Shore. The founders just wanted to celebrate life, each other, and this island. They wanted something different than the canned bureaucratic religions our parents had." He took another fortifying sip.

"The group borrowed ideas and practices they liked from various different religions. Dance as a form of worship from the Native Americans. The use of hallucinogens and marijuana from Sufism and native practices. Meditation from Buddhism, and the idea of oneness and nirvana—only we believed we could achieve that state here on earth, through the pursuit of spiritual pleasure, and that there is no afterlife, only a connected Now."

"Spiritual pleasure?" Lei wasn't familiar with the term.

"It's a concept the cult has. Hedonism with a twist." His seamed mouth turned down. "As time went on I saw that, instead of becoming more enlightened and loving through our practices, we were becoming driven by addictions, jealousy, apathy." His voice trailed off. "My brother, Cal, and I have been involved for seven years—since we got here. I tried to leave, but by then Tiger was in place as our leader, and he has a no-departure policy."

"What does that mean?"

"It's clear that once in, you stay in. I don't ask questions." He folded his lips shut on secrets he wasn't ready to share.

"What has your role been in the cult?"

"I helped organize our celebrations. I don't have a role now, not that there are many. That's part of the Canon—we don't formalize positions."

"Sacrifice anything as a part of your celebrations?" Stevens asked.

"No. Not a part of the cult's practices, as far as I know. However, Tiger's adding to the Canon all the time, and I wouldn't put much past him."

"The Canon?" Jenkins interjected. "You said that before."

"The cult's book of beliefs and practices. It's kept by a cult member elected Lore Keeper. Right now that's Peggy Jones, one of the owners of the papaya farm headquarters."

"Is that where the cult meets for…worship?" Lei wasn't sure what to call it.

"Yes."

"I bet that's where Tiger, aka Jim Jones, is holed up," Lei said. "How soon can I come join the festivities?"

"Soon. I want to get you established as one of my employees on a spiritual quest."

"I'll be at the store later today." Lei held her foot up and jiggled it. She'd put on a chiming anklet of tiny metal clappers. "With bells on."

"So that's the cover story?" Stevens asked.

"Yes, I'm Lani. Single name. Looking to find myself through fun and spiritual frolics."

They spent another hour working out details for communication. Lei would check in with Jenkins twice a day by phone and would keep away from the station, just going from home to the Health Guardian unless she could unobtrusively work something in for her cases.

"They're watching me," Jazz said. "They know I'm talking to the police."

"Then we'll just have to leave you alone so the attention dies down."

The older man nodded. "I'm not sure how far they'd go to protect the cult, and I don't want to find out."

CHAPTER TWENTY

LEI HIT THE GAS, her cop light flashing in the back window of her truck. Jenkins and Stevens followed. At the end of the older man's tale, all their cell phones had gone off, one after the next. They'd pushed Jazz out of the house and locked it up, Lei tossing the belled anklet into her truck.

A body had been discovered in a gulch in Kapa`a.

It wasn't long before she pulled up behind the medical examiner's van and the patrol vehicles on the side of the road in a rural area outside of town and got out, stepping into long grass. Yellow crime scene tape already marked the area.

She waited for Jenkins and Stevens and then pushed through the underbrush, picking her way down a slope covered with scrub guava trees and lantana. A knot of officers marked the discovery at the bottom of the gulch; she slipped between them.

The medical examiner, Dr. Hasegawa, crouched over a small, curled white hand and pale arm protruding from the red clay soil. Becky, standing behind him with her arms loaded with tools and sample bags, gave Lei a quick smile and Stevens a longer one.

"Hey. What's the situation?" Lei asked.

"Some kids out exploring with their dog found the body," Becky said. "They saw the hand sticking out of the dirt. That big rain we had washed a lot of the soil off her—she wasn't buried very deep."

"Trowel," Dr. Hasegawa snapped.

Becky handed him the implement.

He carefully uncovered more of the body, using a wide-bristled brush to flick the dirt off and the trowel to dislodge the soil.

"Can we help?" Lei asked. Stevens crouched behind Dr. Hasegawa, his eyes scanning the ground.

"Get these uniforms out of here and any other nonessential personnel," the ME said. "Senior detectives only."

Impatient to a fault, he was known as a hard-driving perfectionist. The doctor wore rubber boots and a coverall, properly dressed for his work, and his eyes behind their wire-rimmed glasses never left the body.

Lei turned to the patrol officers, who'd heard and were already shuffling off, grumbling. The detectives leaned in to get a better look as the woman's face emerged, a waxy gray-blue tinge to the skin, swollen and mapped by enlarged black veins. Black hair, tangled with soil, formed a muddy halo around her face. In spite of the decomposition, Asian features were apparent, and the only mark on her was a dirt-filled bullet hole in the center of her forehead.

Lei found her hands had balled into fists, nails digging into her palms. The pain anchored her. She sucked a few relaxation breaths, but the sweetish smell of decomp ruined the effect.

They watched as Dr. Hasegawa got Becky working as well, and soon the two of them had the remains clear of the shallow grave. The dead woman wore shorts and a T-shirt with the Island Cleaning logo on it. Her feet were bare and clean of anything but remnants of clinging soil.

"I think I know who this might be. Lisa Nakamoto from Island

Cleaning." Lei wished she'd remembered to put Vicks under her nose, an old trick against the smell.

"Who?" Stevens asked.

"She's been missing. She was involved with the meth lab operating out of the Island Cleaning building and probably involved with the vacation rental burglaries. Fury and the narco guys have been looking for her and the other workers ever since the lab got busted."

"Don't see any blood trace around or in the soil," Dr. Hasegawa said. "And she didn't walk here. So you'll need to find the original scene."

"Looks like it might have been a nine millimeter." Stevens leaned close to the bullet hole.

"We can't determine that without the bullet or casing," Dr. Hasegawa said, bagging the woman's hands for trace. Becky's camera clicked as she took photos of the body. The rest of the crime scene team arrived, and the detectives backed off to let them do their business.

"I know what a nine mil bullet hole looks like," Stevens said stubbornly as they walked toward the cliff. "I've seen a lot of head shots—looked like an execution."

"Well, I vote we go get some lunch, let the techies do their thing," Jenkins said. "We're probably not going to get this case anyway."

"You never know." Lei pulled on guava saplings to climb back up the vegetation-covered slope. "And the mansion burglary case is ours. Lisa is connected to that."

"Thought you were doing the serial one hundred percent." Stevens flipped the brim of her ball cap as they reached the top. "Thought you were going to immerse yourself in the undercover role."

"Damn," Lei muttered. "I did say that, didn't I? I'm going to the Health Guardian after this. Okay. The usual for lunch?" She raised an eyebrow to Jenkins.

"Yeah. Let Anuhea get an eyeful of the fresh meat in town." Jenkins whacked Stevens's back. "Follow us."

Lei followed Jazz into the verdant dim interior of the Health Guardian. She took the sacking apron Jazz handed her and tied it on over her hemp dress, filling a pocket with the honey-flavored organic candy he wanted her to give out. She'd styled the black wig in a simple braid, and plain reading glasses sat uneasily on her nose.

Lei couldn't rid herself of a creeping sense of urgency even though she wasn't on the new murder case. Fury had joined them at lunch after visiting the dump site and all the talk had been about possible reasons for Lisa Nakamoto's murder (though identity hadn't yet been confirmed) and the whereabouts of Darrell Hines, her dealer boyfriend. Lei detached herself reluctantly, donning a role that had begun to feel like a silly long shot. She'd stopped at the drugstore, throwing the glasses on at the last minute.

"Pretty simple setup," Jazz said. "I'm going to use you for busing, stocking, cleaning. The customers order at the bar over there and take their food to the tables outside. You just bus the tables and keep things neat, and do whatever needs doing." He led her over to the juice bar, where a bemuscled and ponytailed young man worked the blender.

"This is Dan. Dan, Lani. Show her the ropes." He vanished through the clashing curtain of bamboo beads into the back.

"Hi." Lei extended her hand to shake. She felt unexpectedly shy, blinking myopically through the reading glasses. In fact, they were keeping her from seeing, so she took them off and stuck them in a pocket of her apron.

"Hey, Lani," Dan said with easy friendliness. "Come back here and I'll show you where things are." She slipped behind the bar for the rest of her orientation.

Many hours later she signed out with a wave to the helpful Dan. Her wig itched unbearably; the tattoos on her wrists were peeling from dishwater and her feet ached. She hopped into her stuffy truck with a sigh of relief just to be sitting, and turned on the engine and the AC. Her eyes wandered to the poster of Jay Bennett taped to the glove box, and she reached to rip it down—tired of his accusing eyes on her—when her cell rang. She picked up instead.

"Hello?"

"Yo, Sweets."

"J-Boy. Calling to see how I survived the Health Guardian?"

"Yeah. Stevens wanted me to check in. Said I'm your 'liaison' with the task force from now on."

"That's right. Well, nothing much interesting. No new intel and my feet hurt. I dropped a lot of comments about being on a personal journey, searching for spiritual meaning, blah-blah. No takers. On the plus side, I learned how to make a spirulina smoothie with a protein booster."

"I've gotta drop by and see you in action. Spirulina? What the hell is that?"

"Blue-green algae. Highly beneficial to the nervous system. Anyway, I did get invited to a drum circle at the nudie beach. I think Dan the juice bar guy is hoping I'll take it all off and boogie."

"You gonna go? Want a chaperone?" Lei had to laugh at Jenkins's hopeful tone.

"Nah. I can handle Dan. Seriously doubt he's even heard of the cult."

"What did Jazz have to contribute?"

"He just lay low in the back. I hardly saw him. But all in all, it was okay as a first day. What's happening with the Lisa Nakamoto case?"

"Not much. Fury is working it with Flea Arizumi. He's looking to interview any of her connections."

Alika was a friend of Lisa's, and he'd been concerned about

her disappearance. Good thing Lei was going running with him tomorrow morning or she might have had to turn him over to Fury as a lead.

Instead, she could talk to him herself and see what he knew.

CHAPTER TWENTY-ONE

Tuesday, October 26

LEI STOOD next to her truck, stretching in the early morning. Light filled the air like gold dust, gilding the river mouth and illuminating the mountains across Hanalei Bay in a sharp demarcation. The beach was mostly clear, the debris from the flood having washed out to sea with a recent swell, and Lei couldn't wait to get going. Keiki tugged at her leash impatiently, sniffing the air.

Alika's black Tacoma pulled up next to hers, one of the only vehicles in the sandy parking lot. A two-man canoe was strapped to the sturdy pipe racks framing the truck bed.

"Hey," Lei said.

Alika jumped out of the cab and beeped the door locked.

"Good morning." He walked toward her, his golden-brown eyes alight. Before she could react, he pulled her in for a kiss. He knocked her ball cap off—and he tasted fresh, like minty toothpaste. Her hands moved up, learning the muscled contours of his body. She eased away, and met his eyes.

"Good morning to you, too."

Alika took his time taking in her changed appearance. "What happened to your hair?"

"Going undercover. The hair had to go—I have to wear a wig."

"You'll do anything for your job. I respect that."

A charged look passed between them. He stepped in close, bringing his hands up along her shoulders, stroking her neck, traveling slowly up to rub and caress her shorn head. It felt indescribably good.

One hand cupped her skull gently as an egg while the other wrapped her in close against him. She sank into his kiss as naturally as diving into the ocean. Lei felt a warm languor filling her veins with honey, a blissful mindlessness taking over. She couldn't help contrasting the clash of her encounter with Stevens with the entrancement of Alika's arms.

It seemed she craved them equally—salt and sweet.

Keiki butted her head against Lei's thigh, breaking the spell.

"So. Let's do this." She scooped up the cap and put it back on.

"I had another idea. I'm missing practice with the club, so I borrowed a canoe for us to take out."

"I've never paddled before."

"What? Local girl like you? They didn't raise you right over on the Big Island," Alika teased as he whipped off the straps securing the canoe.

It took both their effort to lift the fiberglass shell, sleek and cigar-shaped, off the racks and carry it to the water. Alika went back and brought out the iako, or outrigger, a stabilizing contraption made of carbon-fiber plastic with an attached ama, or float. He clipped it into brackets on the hull. The sleek canoe was completely sealed, all of a piece, with adjustable molded seats flush with the top of the hull and recesses for their feet in a molded plastic interior.

Keiki whimpered anxiously. Lei shared her feeling as she looked at the tippy little craft.

"Oh no. Keiki counts on her run for exercise."

"No one's around. Why don't you let her off the leash and we'll paddle along the shore? She can run and keep up."

Lei unclipped the leash, giving the dog the signal to sit. They launched the canoe, pushing it into the water and jumping in. It tipped precariously and Alika stabilized them with his paddle.

"Keep your weight distributed across both sides of the hull with your hands," he instructed until she was settled in her plastic seat. He showed her how to dig deep on the downstroke and switch sides, and after some initial wobbling, Lei picked it up. She glanced back and saw Keiki sitting where she'd been told, looking mournful.

"Keiki, come!" She called, and burst out laughing as, instead of running along the beach, the dog leapt into the water and swam after them.

"She'll get her exercise, all right," Alika said.

They paddled along the shore just outside the wave line, the big dog's head bobbing in their wake as she tried to keep up. Every twelve strokes on one side Alika would call, "Hut—ho!" and on the hut Lei was warned to change, and on ho she was supposed to switch sides. She sprayed Alika and herself with water and smacked the paddle into the side of the canoe, but she soon found a rhythm that made her shoulders burn with satisfying effort. Keiki finally figured out she couldn't keep up and swam in, trotting along the shoreline with eyes on her mistress.

They paddled the length of the bay and drifted a bit at the end, getting their breath. Lei watched the light play through the clear water in dancing streaks, bouncing off the smooth, pale sand of the bottom.

"Whew, that's a workout." She plucked the sweat-soaked tank top away from her body.

"Jump in and cool off." Alika stowed his paddle under an elastic strap and stripped his shirt off over his head. He lifted an iron bar that had been tucked up into a compartment in the hull and tossed it overboard. A length of nylon rope spun out behind it. The water wasn't deep, only fifteen feet or so, and Lei could see the bar hit the sand on the bottom. "We don't need to worry too much because the wind's not up yet, but never get out of a canoe without an anchor."

"Aye, aye, captain." Lei gave a mock salute and stowed her paddle as he stood up, rocking slightly, and dove into the crystalline water. She didn't have a suit on but decided her running clothes were fine. She stood up, and the canoe promptly pitched her into the water.

She came up spluttering, and Keiki barked in alarm from the shore, jumping in and making for Lei like a big black missile. Alika laughed, and they both dove down to find pebbles for Keiki to fetch.

Alika finally grabbed the gunwale of the canoe on the side with the outrigger and hauled himself up. Lei enjoyed the sight of his tanned back flexing as he lifted himself up and into the canoe. He sat in his seat and stabilized the rocking little craft with his paddle.

"Now you."

Lei was able to eventually haul herself aboard, hooking a leg over the side and sprawling in her seat. She saw laughter in a flash of his gold-flecked eyes.

"Don't say anything," she warned.

"I know better. You're actually doing great for a beginner."

They paddled back to the pier and hauled the canoe up, boosting it onto the sturdy racks. Alika lashed it down.

"I've got something to tell you." Lei bent and stretched her knotted shoulders. "Lisa Nakamoto's been found."

"She all right?" He leaned over, stretching beside her, muscled arms surprisingly limber.

"No. She's been murdered."

He stood up. A darkness passed over his face, twisted his mouth. He covered his face for a second with his hands, blew out a breath.

"I can't believe it. What happened?"

"We found her body yesterday. The rain had uncovered it. Got a call late yesterday—a positive ID on her."

"Oh my God. Shit like this just doesn't happen on Kauai."

"You'd be surprised at what happens on Kauai, sheltered boy. Lisa was into something major with that meth lab. It's priority one to find Darrell Hines, the guy who you told me got her into it. The detectives on her case are interviewing all her friends and family, so I was wondering if you had any more information we could follow up on."

"I may have a lead for you. Are you working her case?"

"No. I'm on another one that's taking a lot of my time. But I'll be able to get any intel you give straight to the team who's on it. We're also concerned about the rest of the cleaning crew. They must be in hiding."

"I had a bad feeling about Lisa." Alika turned and they headed toward the showers, Lei clipping the leash on to Keiki's collar. "I knew she was into something over her head. I wonder if she tried to turn them in and they killed her."

"Maybe." Lei put Keiki under the shower. She rinsed the dog down while Alika showered under the other rusty metal spout. She handed him the leash as she got under the cold stream of water.

Done rinsing, she hung her head down and shook it, stood back up. Her cropped hair was almost dry.

"There—good to go. I think I'm getting to like having a buzz. So what was that lead you had for me?" She took Keiki's leash and headed for her truck.

"I think my grandmother knows Darrell Hines's mother," he said, following. "I met the lady at my grandma's. She might know where he is."

"Pretty good tip. I'll call that in right away."

"Wish I could do more. Lisa—I can't believe she's gone. She didn't deserve that."

"Nobody does." Lei lowered the tailgate for Keiki to jump in and grabbed a towel out of the back. "I'll call Esther right away and check this out. I have something else for her to look into anyway."

Alika reached over to rub her head. "I'm getting used to this. Okay, I'll call you later."

Lei could tell he wanted to kiss her again, but she turned away, hopping into her truck and turning the key. She headed back to the house, thumbing open her cell phone and calling Esther, who said she could fit her in later that morning. She then called Fury to tell him she was following up on a lead related to Darrell Hines.

She was relieved when he didn't pick up—he couldn't scoop the lead away from her to follow it up himself. Lei squelched a niggle of guilt. Yeah, Lisa Nakamoto wasn't her case, but he'd shut her and Jenkins out so thoroughly they didn't have any further leads on the robberies. So fair was fair.

She would also take the three stones out for Esther to "feel." Who knew what the psychic kahu would be able to tell her by handling them.

CHAPTER TWENTY-TWO

"COME SEE MY TEACHING ROOM." Esther gestured for Lei to follow her. They went through the living room and down a set of interior stairs to a small chamber. High louvered windows let light in. The floor was lined with lauhala matting, and the walls covered in tapa cloth decorated with traditional patterns. One wall was covered entirely by Hawaiian musical instruments: several ukulele (miniature guitars) in various sizes, ipu (gourds) used for percussion, slotted bamboo pu'ili sticks, poi balls, various sizes and shapes of drums, and feathered uli'uli` rattles.

Esther went to a round fat cushion at the end of the room and sat cross-legged, her muumuu settling in graceful folds around her. She seemed in no hurry, gazing at Lei with impassive eyes. Lei could see the breadth of her calm forehead and boldly marked brows in Alika's features. Once again Esther's hair was braided into a crown around her head; this time a rose folded out of palm frond decorated the coronet.

Lei took out the ziplock bag with the three stones Jenkins had brought her from Jay Bennett's remaining possessions.

"These are from the most recent disappearance site." She poured the stones into the older woman's seamed brown hand.

Esther set her hands palm over palm, the stones between them, in her lap. Lei sat back on her heels as the older woman's eyes fluttered shut.

"We don't use stones like these in our ceremonies." Esther's voice rang like a cello. "These stones are not from here."

"I know that much. We think they're from all over the world, being used to enhance some quality of a ceremony." Belatedly she realized Esther wasn't listening—her ear was tuned to something different.

"This is a dark place." Esther's eyes were still closed. "There are four torches."

Lei bit down on her lip to keep from asking the questions that bubbled up.

"It's a bad place. Blood all around. Death." Esther dropped the stones out of her hand onto the lauhala mat as if she didn't want to touch them another moment. Lei leaned forward and scooped them back into the bag.

"What did you see?"

"It's not a seeing; it's a knowing. I know those stones are soaked in blood."

"There wasn't any trace on them. I checked early on."

"Metaphorically. Perhaps."

"Okay." Lei frowned. Esther was being enigmatic again, and now she felt the telltale buzzing in her ears that signaled an episode of her own. Blood. Death. The words vibrated in that dark place in her mind.

"A cave, maybe?" Lei struggled to focus.

"Maybe. It's still, dark with just the torches, and the blood..." Esther's voice trailed off.

Lei reached over to pinch herself as her vision narrowed, the walls closing in as her dissociation symptoms returned full force. Her eyes fluttered shut as she sucked a relaxation breath in through her nose, out through her mouth, digging her nails into her arm in desperation to stay present.

It didn't work.

The next thing she knew she was lying on her back on the matting. She heard a low pule, or prayer, and her feet were being massaged. Wonderfully, marvelously, powerfully massaged. She lifted her head, looking down her body. Esther's face broke into a luminous smile. Her strong hands continued to rub and knead Lei's feet. The smell of coconut oil filled the room.

"You had me worried, girl."

"That hasn't happened to me in…ages." Lei sat up. "I get triggered sometimes and I—check out."

"Where do you go?"

"I don't know. I never remember."

"Do you want to remember?"

"I don't think so. I think the disappearing is to…escape something."

"Maybe your soul is wandering."

Lei felt the hairs rise on her arms. She pulled her foot out of the older woman's hands, tucked it beneath her, rubbed her arms briskly.

"I don't believe in that kind of thing. My shrink says it's dissociation related to trauma. I was molested when I was a little girl."

"Same thing," Esther said imperturbably. "Your soul leaves the body. It goes where it feels safe. It comes back when danger is over."

"Only—that might have made sense when I was a child being sexually abused. It doesn't work for me now. Here I am, in the middle of an investigation, in the middle of your teaching room—having one of these episodes."

"Nothing is an accident. Everything comes the way it wants to."

"What does that mean?"

"What does it mean to you?"

"I don't know." The irritation she used to struggle with last year during her therapy, angry rebuttals to Dr. Wilson, didn't seem

179

to happen with the mysterious Esther. Not that Esther was her therapist or anything.

"I can help you heal, though," Esther said, as if Lei had spoken aloud. "Maybe there is something different you can do with these 'episodes,' as you call them. Maybe they serve a purpose. If you stop fighting them, they might yield their message."

"Speaking of message." Lei stood up. "I have a lead to follow up on. Do you have any contact info for Darrell Hines's mother?"

"We'll discuss these episodes again; don't think I've forgotten. I'll be praying about them. And yes, I know Celia Hines. Why do you want to speak to her?"

"Another case, not the one we're working on." On impulse, Lei asked, "Do you know Lisa Nakamoto, by any chance?"

"I knew her mother much better, Ann Nakamoto," Esther said. She went to a corner of the room, where a screen shielded a little bamboo desk. She flipped through an old-fashioned Rolodex and jotted down Celia Hines's number on a blank card. "Why do you ask?"

"I'm sorry if you knew her, but—Lisa's been murdered."

"Oh no." Esther's hand dropped to her side, the card fluttering out of her fingers as her chocolate-brown eyes grew wide. "Lisa was a friend of Alika's when they were growing up and Ann was a friend of my daughter's—Lehua will be devastated. She was so upset when Ann died of cancer."

"I'll let you break the news, then." Lei cringed at telling kind, regal Lehua Wolcott something devastating. She wondered briefly about the muffled quality of Alika's response to the news of a childhood friend's murder—almost as if he'd been expecting it. Well, he had been worried about Lisa.

"I have to call Lehua." Esther headed for the old-fashioned dial phone on the desk. "You can let yourself out. And keep that necklace on."

Lei reached down and picked up the fallen card, touching the

Ni'ihau shell choker at her throat. She hadn't taken it off, even to sleep.

"I will. Thanks."

Esther was already dialing, and said over her shoulder, "Come back next week. Same day, same time. And call me if you need to."

Maybe she was going to therapy, Lei thought as she ascended the stairs. Except when did therapy involve psychic stone readings, prayer, and foot rubs?

Only on Kaua'i, where the usual rules didn't seem to apply.

LEI CALLED Stevens as she carried a glass of wine out to her back porch that evening. She needed the wine after passing on all the information she had on Darrell Hines to Fury—as usual he hadn't appreciated her initiative.

"Esther seems to be psychic. She held the stones, says there's a dark place with four torches and blood all around. Maybe a cave."

"I'm not that interested in psychic mumbo jumbo. Anything solid on the cultural angle?"

"She said the stones aren't used in any Hawaiian ceremony. So whatever he's doing is some other religious practice—or the stones mean something else entirely."

"Seems like a dead end for now. The UH guy basically confirmed what you're saying. The stones are nonnative to Hawaii, and not used in any cultural rituals he's ever heard of." Stevens blew out a breath. "I just got done interviewing Shellie Samson. She walked out yesterday, refused to believe me. So today we had to show her fingerprints and a picture of the hand."

"What fun." Lei pictured the social worker's shock on hearing her husband was a victim of foul play.

"Poor lady. She'd been angry at him so long, it took some convincing that he was murdered."

"That hand is the first body part we've found confirming any of the missing were murdered. I'd give anything to find the site where it was buried; I bet that would tell us a lot."

"You and me both. Speaking of, the captain is calling in the FBI now that we have confirmation of murder. He says the numbers are just too big for us to handle with our resources—since Flea and Fury are already pulled onto the Nakamoto case."

Lei's stomach dropped at the mention of the FBI. She took a big swig of wine to settle it, frowning at the peaceful river.

"I'm just getting started on my undercover thing! Dammit. I'm not surprised, but—what's that going to mean for our investigation?"

"Don't know. He's been making the calls today and more will be revealed. In the meantime, we know Samson's hand came from Hanalei Valley within the path of the flood. I've been working on a plan to take the guys and some cadaver dogs and do some major hiking."

"Better wear hip boots and serious mosquito gear." Lei looked out at the tangled masses of hau bush and tall grass growing along the river. "When's this going down?"

"Don't know yet. Having trouble getting the K-9 unit. They're doing a drug sweep with the dogs at the airport for the next few days."

"Talk to the captain. He'll get the dogs pulled for you."

"On the agenda for tomorrow. So how was your start at the health food store, Sweets?" His voice was lighter, teasing. Lei leaned her elbow on a knee, rubbing her short hair and enjoying its soft, springy texture.

"It's actually hard work. I'm busing tables and waiting on people in the café area. Nothing much interesting on my second day either." Lei traced the "om" symbol on her wrist with a finger, the phone caught between her shoulder and ear.

"It'll be interesting to see what the FBI think of the cult angle as a lead, what they make of your undercover operation. I'll probably use J-Boy on the cadaver hunt since you'll be busy waiting tables for the health food store."

"I'm happy to miss the hunt. I live right on the river, so I know firsthand how hard you're going to have to work. So how are you and Fury getting along?"

"It's professional. Once I showed him who's boss, we've been fine."

Lei laughed. "Good luck with that. I'm sure he's just waiting for you to trip up."

"Yeah, it's all right. So, keep me up to speed on anything you see or hear tomorrow."

"Of course." A long pause. Lei found herself reluctant to close the phone. Memories of being in his arms flashed through her mind, lighting nerve endings like tiny electric shocks. She listened to his breathing across the miles, a tangible connection.

Not so many miles that they couldn't be crossed.

"I miss you. Can I come over, bring some Chinese for dinner?" He was the first to say what they were both thinking.

"I don't think that's a such good idea," she said softly. "It can't lead to anything—and I can't trust myself alone with you."

Another long pause.

"I don't give a shit where it leads," Stevens said finally, his voice rough with emotion. "You're making me crazy."

She pictured dark brows lowered over laser-blue eyes, the hard set of his mouth. His rough-planed face was better than handsome. It was lived in, intelligent, charismatic. Sexy.

"I'm sorry. I never wanted you to come here. You're making me crazy too, because I can't be with you. I can't be what you want!" Lei cried.

He hung up, an abrupt severing.

"Dammit!"

She couldn't seem to stop hurting those who wanted to love her. She was messing with Alika's head now, too. God, how she hated herself—and it was all Charlie Kwon's fault. That pedophile was the one who'd made her Damaged Goods. He was the one who'd made sure she was too messed up to know how to love.

Or be loved.

She felt an overwhelming urge to cut herself, to feel that purging fire of pain that somehow released inner anguish and sometimes brought relief. Her mind pictured the knife drawing a shallow line of welling blood. Maybe she'd carve their names into her arms. Blood and darkness, that was all that was in her; that was all she was.

Self-loathing mounted, that she was even so tempted, that she could regress so far even in her own mind. She looked at the insides of her arms, laced with white threads of scar tissue from the past, rubbed them hard, a replacement she'd learned in therapy. Keiki, who'd been napping at her feet, leapt up to nose her, whining.

Lei went down into the darkened yard and threw herself into her Tae Kwon Do routine. In the dark, kicking, spinning, and leaping, her mind emptied of confusion. Chest heaving, legs trembling, she eventually exhausted herself until there was nothing to do but go to bed, hoping things were better tomorrow.

CHAPTER TWENTY-THREE

Wednesday, October 27

"HEY, your tip about Hines's mother paid off." Jenkins's voice was becoming her lifeline as she checked in during her midday break the next day at the Health Guardian. "Fury said to thank you for the intel you gave him yesterday. They've got a line on Hines—he took a plane off Kaua`i a few days ago to Oahu. We have an alert on him at the airports and the Oahu PD is looking for him."

"Anything confirming Hines was involved with the ice production?"

"Yeah. His name is on some orders for supplies used at the Island Cleaning factory. They also got one of the cleaning team people; she's talking about the whole operation as we speak. Anything new at your end?"

"No. I'm starting to think Jazz is just doing this to get me as a free slave." She'd tied the wig back, but she was overheated, as usual. Her phone chimed and she saw an incoming call from Alika. "Anything else?"

"No. Check in tomorrow, Sweets."

"Will do." She clicked the phone over to the new call. "Hello?"

"Hey, Ginger. Any news on Lisa?"

"Investigation's proceeding. Thanks for your intel; you'll probably be getting a call from the main investigator, Detective Furukawa."

"Sounds like you can't tell me anything. That's okay. I was just wondering if you wanted to come for a swim after work."

"God, that sounds perfect." Lei swiped her damp brow with a forearm. "But I'm a long way from being off."

"No worries. I didn't mean at my house anyway. Somewhere special, out on the North Shore."

"Oh yeah. Today's totally sweaty; I can't wait to jump into something cool and wet."

"Okay. I'll tell you how to get there." He gave directions.

The location was only another fifteen minutes past her house. Rejuvenated by the prospect of going swimming, she went back into the café just as Jazz led a tall man out of his office.

"Lani, meet my brother, Cal. Cal, this is Lani, my newest employee."

"Hi." Lei had the reading glasses on, blurring the edges of a craggy face, and she took them off and shook the calloused hand that met hers. "Didn't know you had a brother on island. Good to meet you."

"Hello." Cal had dark eyes, shared his brother's lean build, and his skin was leathery, as if he spent a lot of time in the sun. "Pleased to meet you too."

The distinctive scent of marijuana clung to him like musk.

"Cal works on an estate out on the North Shore."

"Oh, I love it out there. So spiritual," Lei burbled, in character.

"Don't know what you mean. It's just land, and a lot of work to keep nice." Cal shook his head.

"Oh. Well, I just think, the energies…" She was left staring after Cal as he turned and walked away. She glanced at Jazz.

"He's not much of a people person," Jazz said. "Looks like you've got some customers."

"Looks like I do," Lei said, and went to the juice bar.

She'd been getting used to people affirming her vague comments about "energies" and "mana" and "spiritual centers," and Cal's rebuff snapped her out of that. She'd even kind of begun to believe it. Maybe it was Esther's influence. Kaua`i seemed to bring out the paranormal in people.

"Detective Texeira." Lei looked up, eyes widening at the sight of Kelly Waterson, a stack of flyers pressed against her pillowy chest. "I thought it was you."

Lei's head swiveled as she checked for who might have over-heard. No one in earshot. She hustled out from around the juice bar, towed Kelly to a table in the corner, gave her a little shove into a rattan chair, and sat down next to the girl.

"Not so loud. I'm undercover."

"You haven't called me back."

"I'm sorry. I didn't have anything I could report."

"Are you here for Jay's investigation? Because he hung out here. I wanted to put these posters around on the tables."

"I can't talk about it, Kelly. Just know we are doing all we can and things are progressing. Good initiative on the posters."

"I have to go back home soon. I have to get to work." The girl's eyes filled. Lei took a paper napkin out of the dispenser, handed it to her. Kelly dabbed her eyes. "No one seems to know anything. Jay's dad is offering a reward."

"Well, if you get any leads, make sure they come to us at the police station. All I can tell you is that we have more manpower on the case and a full task force going. We are taking Jay's disappear-ance very seriously."

Kelly stood up. "Okay. Call me. Keep me informed." The green in her changeable eyes glittered. "I'm serious."

"Of course." Kelly handed her a few of the posters and walked out.

Lei let her breath out in a whoosh, looking around. No one was paying attention. She picked up the posters and tacked one onto the front of the bar, her stomach knotted.

Jay's eyes could accuse her from everywhere in the café now.

SEVERAL HOURS later she turned off the main road onto a rugged, rock-strewn dirt track leading uphill at a steep angle. She put the truck in four-wheel drive and bucked her way up to the cleared area at the top, parking next to Alika's black Tacoma.

Alika leaned against the hood of his truck, working his cell phone. He looked up and waved. She snagged her swimsuit off the seat, slipping out of her underwear and wriggling into the bottoms. She reached behind and unhooked her bra, slipping it off one arm and then reaching in with the other hand to pull the bra out of her sleeve without taking the dress off. She dropped the polka-dotted top over her head and reached backward under the dress to tie the strings, then whipped the dress off and gave her scalp one last rub, enjoying the springy softness of fledgling hair without the scratchy wig.

Alika whistled as she got out of the truck in nothing but the yellow bikini and her rubber slippers.

"That was amazing. I kept hoping to get a glimpse of something, but you have changing in the car down to a science."

"We local girls know a few tricks." She put her hands on her hips, swiveling to take in the view.

They were halfway up a precipitous mountain in a rough clearing. A boulder-strewn path led farther up the incline. She could look down the road and see the ocean, a wind-whipped blue tumult in the distance. Jungle stretched away in either direction.

"So where's the swimming? Don't tell me you lured me up here under false pretenses."

"Oh, there's swimming, all right." He shucked his shirt off over his head. "You're not the only one who got sweaty today. I had to spend the day filling in for one of my carpenters, who called in sick." He reached back into the cab of his truck for a couple of towels and tossed her one. "Follow me."

He turned and headed up the trail. Lei wrapped the towel, a huge bath sheet printed with palm trees, around her torso and hurried up the trail after him.

The path ended at the lip of a cavern. Lei caught her breath at the soaring depth of it, rough stony edges softened with hanging ferns. She glimpsed the black shimmer of water far below. "Oh my God. This is awesome."

A draft of cool air wafted out and poured over her. Alika was already picking his way down the steep path inside to the water. His upturned grin gleamed in the dim light.

"You said you like go swimming."

CHAPTER TWENTY-FOUR

"WHAT'S THIS CAVE CALLED?" She picked her way down the precipitous rocky trail. "You can't even tell it's here from below!"

"It's Waikapala`e Cave. This is an old lava tube, and the water comes through the stone from underground springs."

They reached the bottom of the cavern, where crystalline water lapped at the shore, and Lei stuck her foot in. She shrieked and jumped back. "It's freezing!"

"You wanted to cool off." Alika tossed his towel over a nearby rock. He climbed onto an outcrop on the side of the cave. Small, sparkling white stalactites dripped into the pool. Maidenhair fern clinging to rocks reached for light coming through the cave mouth far above, a lacy scrim trimming the jagged lava.

Alika dove in, then burst up out of the water with a Tarzan yell, shaking his head.

The icy splash sprinkled Lei and she gasped, goose bumps erupting. She followed him up onto the outcrop and jumped in, holding her nose. The cold hit her like a fist, driving the air out of her lungs in an explosive burst, and she surged up to the surface with a matching yell. They laughed spontaneously, the sound echoing around the chamber and making the fragile ferns shiver.

"Follow me." Alika struck out for the shadowy rear of the cave. A little hesitantly, Lei followed. He swam all the way to where the rock face touched the surface and pointed down into the deep, clear water. The reflection of distant light was captured in the lime-lined depths, and she could see the cave went on underneath.

"We need to dive under and swim through a short tunnel. We'll come up inside a chamber. It's something you have to see to believe. You game?"

"Of course." Lei's heart pounded so hard it hurt her ears.

"Okay. I know my way, so I'm going to hold your hand. Just keep your eyes open and swim after me. It's less than thirty seconds. Let's fill our lungs."

They both oxygenated their bodies with deep breaths; then Alika took her chilled hand in his and dove under. She sucked in one last big breath and followed him, kicking and swimming with her free hand as hard as she could. With her eyes open she could see the light reflecting off the bottom of the cave far below, but above her head was terrifying black. Imagining being held beneath the water with nowhere to escape to pumped adrenaline through her veins and used up oxygen faster than it should have—so when Alika swam upward, she flew up beside him into the underwater cave with a gasp.

They treaded water, assimilating their surroundings. The water glowed, lit from reflections beneath, filling the dark, enclosed chamber with an eerie blue light.

"They call this the Blue Room." Alika's voice echoed in the roughly spherical space. Lei looked up—blue reflections danced across the rough ceiling, bounced off the walls. Her limbs looked foreshortened in the water, azure and alien.

"Follow me." Alika struck out for the side of the chamber. Along one wall, nearly invisible, was a narrow shelf. He hauled himself out of the water, turning to sit. He reached down and grasped her wrist, and with one powerful heave pulled her high enough for her to clamber onto the ledge. She turned around and sat beside him, their feet dangling into crystalline blue.

"This is amazing. Magical." Even though she whispered the words, they sent ripples around the enclosed space.

"Being here with you is magic."

"Bet you say that to all the girls," she said, trying for banter.

"None of them ever had the nerve to come here." His words fell like stones in a pond, sinking into her.

When his hand touched her chin, turning her face toward him, she felt like the only woman in the world. His lips were the point of heat in that universe, and she sank hungrily into the kiss, welcoming his tongue into the cave of her mouth. Her arms came up and around him just as he reached for her, the coldness of their bodies clashing on the narrow ledge in a timeless embrace.

She couldn't get enough of him. Her hands flew over him, rubbing marble-cold skin into warm pulsing life. His hands were all over her too, friction between them bringing her to the edge of frantic desire. He pushed her top aside to touch her breasts, and her nipples became tactile points of intense sensation. When his hot mouth touched her there she cried out, and the sound of it bounced around the cave. She moved up and onto his lap, powerful legs encircling him, a haze blinding her—and that was when she felt something odd.

Something poking her in the knee. Something small, roundish, hard. Something that shouldn't be there. She raised her head from where she'd been biting his neck, stillness falling over her like a cloak.

"What's wrong?" His harsh whisper had a ragged edge of desperation to it. "I don't have a condom, but…"

"It's not that." She moved off his lap and he groaned, reaching for her. She pushed him away, patting the ledge beside them until she found the object. Held it carefully. Moved over to sit on the ledge and lean out over the water for whatever reflected light she could pick up.

It was a cylindrical shape a little bigger than a cigarette butt, flared at the ends, light and slightly porous to her fingertips. Even in the dimness she could tell it was bone.

She straightened her top back into place. Continued to pat the surface of the ledge carefully as Alika watched, brows drawn together.

"What are you doing? Are you okay?"

"I found something important." She kept feeling, then shoved him. "Get off. I need to check this whole ledge."

He dropped into the water. She continued her slow patting of the ledge, then moved up onto the wall. About two feet up near the middle she hit pay dirt—a hollow depression in the wall, with a cache of bones in it. She touched them lightly, enough to feel their contours, but she didn't want to disturb them in situ and it was too dark for her to see into the depression.

She needed to see if the bone was what she thought it was. Lei tucked it deep into her swimsuit top, tightened the strings so there was no possibility of losing it, and slipped back into the water.

"What's going on?"

"I think I found something major. I need to bring some backup in here. They'll have to bring scuba gear." She swam for the entrance to the cave, the enchantment of blue light lost on her.

"What? What is it?"

"I think it's human remains. Seems like someone's been using the ledge for some sort of shrine."

"Oh shit. Now, there's a mood killer."

"I have to get to my phone. C'mon." She swam to the wall, looked underneath it to the tunnel, and gulped a few quick breaths. Before Alika could catch up, she ducked and swam through the tunnel, coming up on the other side and breaking into a fast crawl across the pool. Alika was just getting out of the tunnel when she climbed out of the water and wrapped herself in the bath sheet, digging the bone out of her top and holding it up to the dim light.

"Finger. Maybe toe," she muttered. She pushed her feet into

rubber slippers and bounded up the precipitous trail. Alika finally caught up with her back at her truck, where she was placing a call to Becky.

"Becks—I have something for you to check out. A bone." She held it up so the setting sun could light the macabre little object. She was almost sure it was human.

"So bring it in tomorrow." Becky's voice sounded tired. "I'll take a look if I have time."

"No. It's more urgent than that. I think this might be part of the big investigation I'm working on with Stevens." She described the bone. "It's a little blackened, as if it might have been in a fire."

"What about it being old? I mean, this could be part of some Hawaiian burial site or something."

"Maybe, but I doubt it." Lei described the cache of bones in the hollow in the wall. "The Hawaiians did hide their high-ranking dead in the cliffs in caves—but not a wet cave like this. And the bones at this site are small, nowhere near enough to be a whole body. That's why I'm calling you first. I want you to check it out, see if it's worth calling out the full team for."

"I won't get paid overtime, but okay." Becky sighed. "Give me forty-five minutes or so. I have my kit in the car, fortunately."

"Do you have scuba gear?"

"What?"

"Scuba gear. I think it would be worthwhile to check out the bottom of the cave, and you have to have your swimsuit and some dive lights at least, since you have to swim in through an underwater tunnel."

"Oh my God." Becky's voice went to a high-pitched squeak.

"Okay, fine. I'll call Stevens. He can help you; he'll want to be notified anyway."

"I'll do it if you call Stevens. And yes, you're in luck. I'm certified for scuba and own my own equipment," she said. They wrapped up and Lei pushed the worn button on her phone to call Stevens.

His voice was colder than the ice water in the cave.

"I told you Jenkins was your liaison."

"I think you'll want to know about this." She filled him in on her discovery. "I need you to hold Becky's hand. Come out and see the site for yourself."

A long pause.

"On my way."

She closed her phone, heaved a sigh. The sun was dead ahead, almost touching the darkening sea. She looked around for Alika and spotted him sitting on a promontory of rock, sunset gilding his torso. Evening cast a chill that bit through her wet bathing suit and towel. She climbed up next to him, snuggling against his warmth.

"Help's on the way."

"Good." He wrapped an arm over her. "Now, where were we?" His lips found hers. She put up with it for a few seconds, then withdrew.

"Sorry. I'm distracted."

"Some other time. It's cool watching you in cop mode." He shook his head a little. "You're so focused. The bad guys don't stand a chance."

"I wish. Listen, you don't have to wait. They'll be here soon."

"I wouldn't miss this for the world."

They watched the sun disappear, staining the clouds crimson, peach, and gold. Lei shivered.

"Let's get you into the truck, turn on the heater. I've got some food in there too."

"Food! Oh God, I think I love you." She laughed.

"Whatever it takes." He tried to nuzzle her neck, but she'd jumped up and was heading for the vehicle.

They were sitting in his truck, the engine and heater on, eating beef jerky when Stevens's police Bronco bucked its way up the steep track. Becky's face was white as she clung to the dangling safety strap, and the flashing light bar testified to the speed Stevens had used to get to the remote spot.

They all got out. Lei tightened the towel, tucking the ends in.

"Hey, thanks for the fast response. Check this out." She held the bone out on her flattened palm. Becky snapped on her Maglite. She picked it up, examined it in the harsh light.

"Human. Looks like it's been in a fire. Can't tell how old."

Stevens was already going around to the back of the SUV and opening the tailgate, revealing a pair of oxygen tanks and a welter of scuba equipment.

"Hi." Alika stepped forward, hand extended. "I'm Alika Wolcott."

"Becky Banks." The lab tech shook his hand.

"Oh, sorry," Lei said. "Becky, Stevens, this is my friend Alika."

Stevens looked up, a regulator in his hands. Lei couldn't see his expression in the dim light.

"Hey." His voice was terse. "How did you guys find the bones, anyway?"

"I brought Lei out for a swim, wanted to show her something special." Alika draped his arm over her in a proprietary gesture. "Guess it was even more special than I had in mind."

"Yeah, a big surprise." Lei slipped out from under his arm. "Did you bring enough equipment for me?"

"Oh, sorry. No," Becky said. "I've only got two rigs. Are you certified?"

"No, but I figure, how hard can it be? Damn. Well, we can show you where it is, anyway."

"I don't think that's going to be necessary," Stevens said. "We can take it from here."

He'd wrapped a towel around his midsection and was pulling on swim trunks and a wetsuit vest. "Becky, come get into your gear. The sooner we check this out, the sooner we can get on home."

"Sure." Becky hurried to obey. Alika and Lei watched, and it wasn't long before Alika led them back up the trail. Stevens and

Becky had the only two flashlights, and Becky gave an involuntary gasp as the cavern opened up before them. The flashlights bounced around the dramatic interior as they looked it over.

"Wow." Becky shone her light on the trembling maidenhair ferns around the surface of the water. "I wouldn't mind coming here on a date."

"It wasn't a date." Lei stumbled as she picked her way down the trail.

"I thought it was," Alika said, his voice mock-injured.

"Stay focused on what we're here for," Stevens said, shutting down any further discussion until the group got to the bottom of the cave.

"This is gonna be cold," Alika warned, dropping his towel. Lei reluctantly surrendered hers as well, and Stevens and Becky waded forward into the vast inky pool, rinsing their masks and turning on each other's oxygen tanks. Lei stuffed down a stab of jealousy as Stevens tapped Becky's oxygen readout, adjusted her straps, and gave her a thumbs-up. Lei turned and pushed forward into the icy water, following Alika's sleek head as he swam for the far wall of the chamber.

The water, previously enchanting, was now frigid, and the darkness so complete that without the flashlights lancing through the water below them, Lei would not have been able to see her hand in front of her face. It was disorienting—like swimming in freezing space.

The bubbles from Becky's and Stevens's regulators glittered silver gems as they swam beneath Lei and Alika, finding the tunnel and swimming through it ahead of them. Alika took her hand silently, and they pumped their lungs full, then ducked under and swam after the trail of lighted bubbles.

They surfaced in the Blue Room, which, without the eerie daylight effect, was only a roundish cave filled with black water. Stevens and Becky surfaced, shining their flashlights around the room.

"Over here." Lei headed for the ledge. In seconds, the flashlights had the little hollow pinned in their white glare. Becky climbed up on the ledge with a boost from Stevens, balancing with difficulty on the edge. She shone her light into the hollow containing the bones. Without a word she got out her camera, and the flash burned the scene onto Lei's retinas over and over, a grisly tableau she'd never be able to forget.

Becky turned to them, the mask pushed onto her head, lips pale with cold.

"Looks like some sort of offering cache. There's a lining of ti leaves in here and several nonnative stones. I'm going to bring the whole thing in for analysis." She pulled a waterproof evidence bag out of her vest and carefully scooped the contents of the hollow into it.

Stevens and Lei exchanged a glance. The nonnative stones clinched it—this was definitely related to their case.

"I'm going to take a look around the bottom. See if anything ended up down here." Stevens put his mask down and the regulator back in his mouth and sank in a stream of mercury bubbles. Lei and Alika watched his flashlight sweeping back and forth across the cave floor.

Becky let herself fall backward into the water with a splash. She tucked the sealed evidence bag into the front of her vest.

"Let me shine the light for you guys; then I'm going to join Stevens and search the cavern floor, make sure we get everything."

There was nothing for Lei to do but follow Becky's flashlight through the water and across the darkness. She shone it all the way to the edge, and Lei and Alika climbed out and wrapped themselves in their damp towels, watching the eerie crisscross of submerged beams moving through the black gloom of the cavern.

"This sucks."

"Yeah. I don't even know what the hell is going on and I have to work tomorrow." Alika's voice had an edge to it. Lei joined him on his boulder, snuggling close.

"Wish we had our own flashlight. We could at least get back to the truck and get warm. I'm sorry about all this."

He looped his arm around her in what was becoming a familiar gesture. They watched the intermittent movement of the beams and flare of the underwater flash, eerie as a soundless war.

"Don't think Stevens likes me," Alika said.

"Don't think he likes me either. Seems like he likes Becky well enough, though."

"Jealous?"

"Of course not." A flashlight beam speared them out of the darkness. Lei resisted the urge to spring apart and held her hand up to block her eyes.

"We found a few things." Stevens's voice. The beam moved away. They stood up as he splashed to the edge of the water. "Check these out."

They looked at what he held in his rubber-gloved hands—long heavy femurs and tibias, bleached and glowing in the flashlight beam. Becky splashed up beside him. She held a skull.

"Nice," Alika said. "We were swimming in that."

"If it's any comfort, the bones have been here awhile," Becky said. Water drained out of the eyeholes, splashing on the stones. "The water's got high alkalinity, so decomp happened a long time ago. These bones are beginning to calcify."

"Was that all that's out there?" Lei asked.

"No. But we thought we'd bring in our first load. There's more." Stevens was already putting his mask on after piling the bones on a rock.

"Can we get a quick light back to the car? Alika has to get on the road, and I think I should call for backup."

"Guess so," Stevens said. "Call Fury. He can come out. Tell him to bring scuba gear if he can. And you can call it a night."

Lei tried not to let the dismissal sting. After all, there wasn't anything more she could do, and cold was racking her with nonstop shivers. She and Alika took Becky's flashlight and picked their way back to the vehicles. Alika beeped open his truck.

"Interesting day."

"I know. I'm sorry about how it ended."

"I told you—I wouldn't have missed it—and I meant that."

"You can't talk about it. It's an open investigation."

"I'm not an idiot." His tone was brusque. He got into his vehicle and turned the key. "I'll call you."

"You better." She leaned into his open window to kiss him goodbye. He turned his head, and she set her lips on his sculpted ones—firmly and with intent. The brief stamp she'd intended turned into more, and her arms wound around his shoulders and neck. He reached out to haul her closer and she found herself hanging halfway in, toes barely touching the ground as he returned her kiss with hunger of his own. Her mouth buzzed. Her face was hot and body tingling with what he'd woken in her in the cave.

She extracted herself slowly, holding on to the window frame as she released his shoulders and slid back down. Her knees felt too wobbly to hold her up, so she clung to the doorframe of the truck. "Thanks for all you did today."

"You're welcome." He kissed her once more. "Okay. Stay safe."

"Will do." She got in her truck and turned on the heater as he bumped back down the rugged track. She was able to get ahold of Captain Fernandez, and after promises that he was notifying Dr. Hasegawa and rangers from the Park Service, she drove home and fell into bed. Keiki lay next to her until she'd thawed out enough to fall asleep.

CHAPTER TWENTY-FIVE

Thursday, October 28

LEI TOOK Keiki out for a run on the beach the next morning before her shift at the Guardian. She ran hard on the sand near the water's edge. She needed to shake off the effects of adrenaline and over-stimulation from the day before, but she couldn't stop thinking about the implications of last night's find. Her phone toned against her side. She stopped, leaning over to catch her breath as she answered it, oblivious to the dawn-blushed waves lapping the silvery sand at her bare feet.

"Hey, J-Boy."

"Sweets, it's been a long night. Stevens, Fury, Becky, and Flea found what looks like three skeletons in the water, and the shrine held hand bones and some of those stones like those at the disappearance sites. They're still reconstructing what goes with what, but the bones had tool marks as if the bodies were cut up first, and many have scorch marks. Stevens and the captain want the whole team to pull in to the War Room for a confab."

"That's a lot of bodies." Lei pinched her arm to stop her over-active imagination. "Sounds like a plan. When?"

"Nine a.m. What up? Every time you turn around something pops on this case!"

"I know. Weird, huh? Speaking of weird, I better call Esther and see what she thinks of the shrine in the Blue Room. Maybe there's a cultural angle to that."

"Good idea. See you at nine. Oh, and by the way, they caught Darrell Hines in Honolulu. Fury's flying over to question him about Lisa Nakamoto's murder."

"Glad to hear it." Lei's eyes squinched shut to block out the memory of Lisa's still, bluish face with the bullet hole in her forehead. It didn't work.

She finished her run in record time, burning nervous energy, and back at her house packed up her hippie gear for her shift at the Guardian after the station conference. She called Esther on the way into Kapa`a Station.

"You found something important." The older woman's voice was matter-of-fact.

"We did. How did you know?"

Silence.

"Well, anyway," Lei continued. "We found a cache of human bones in the wall of the Blue Room at Waikapala`e Cave. They were arranged on top of ti leaves, with nonnative stones mixed in —like the ones I showed you. Any cultural angle there?"

"Ti leaves. They have spiritual significance. People often wrap them around stones as an offering at the foot of bridges, waterfalls, and other places for good luck or to show honor and respect, though that is recent and not a true Hawaiian tradition. Ti leaf is believed to have protection against evil, and that's why people plant it around their houses. This arrangement sounds like it's borrowing some elements of our culture, but it is not a part of anything I know. It's a corruption of our ways."

"There were also bones from up to three people in the cave pool. The bones were separated, as if the bodies were cut up, and they had scorch marks on them."

When Esther finally spoke, her voice vibrated. "This is evil at work. I have to pray." She hung up.

Lei shook her head. She wished praying made her feel better, but though she'd tried last night it had brought no comfort—ten people were still missing. She pushed the accelerator down hard, and the truck surged forward. For now she preferred to trust in what she could see and touch.

Even so, she whispered, "Lord, help me find Jay Bennett. Protect him, please."

There wasn't anything else she could do.

LEI STOPPED at the morgue on the way to the station. Every available surface was taken up with bones in the process of being reassembled. Becky looked up from where she was bent over a collection on a rolling table, camera in hand, eyes ringed with fatigue and blond hair in a bedraggled ponytail. Dr. Hasegawa was at work beside her, holding a magnifying glass.

"Pulled an all-nighter, I see. What's the verdict?" Lei asked.

"Got three skeletons here—we're still trying to figure out what goes with what. See these scorch marks?" Becky pointed. Lei leaned in to look. "Some deterioration has occurred. It's surprising they weren't more disintegrated by the fire—he must not have wanted them to burn up completely. See these tool marks?" Lei nodded, examining the notched surfaces around the joints.

"I'm not really trained in this kind of forensic work. I'm asking the captain for some outside help," Dr. Hasegawa said. "This case is too much for our limited resources."

"Any ideas about cause of death?" Lei asked.

"Not yet. But this one looks clear." Becky reached over and retrieved a skull. The forehead was caved in with a dent the size of a baseball. "Head trauma. Some sort of blunt instrument."

"Hm. Could be how he subdues the victims."

Stevens entered, looking as sleep-deprived as Becky, but darkness under his eyes just made them bluer, whisker-shadow on his
jaw adding a rakish edge. "Dr. Hasegawa, Becks—how's the
jigsaw puzzle coming?"

"Slow. I already told the captain I need help identifying what
kind of tool was used to cut up the bodies, and on this." Dr.
Hasegawa held the skull up with its concave dent. The bone was
bleached-looking, the depression on what would have been the
forehead webbed with fracture lines that looked like cracks in old
china.

"I'm trying to take some good pictures we can e-mail to Dr.
Hasegawa's contact in the lab on Oahu," Becky said. "We're going
to be working on this awhile."

"Well, the FBI will be joining us this morning at our conference at the station. They might be able to bring in some experts or
specialized equipment. We'll let you know. Keep at it. You're
doing good work." Stevens directed this comment to Becky, and
Lei remembered the grin she' saw on Stevens's night-shadowed
face—a combination of respect and male appreciation. She hadn't
seen that grin in a long time.

Lei pushed past him and went toward the door. "Thanks for the
update."

"Better get to the station," Stevens said, following her. "We'll
call as soon as we know anything."

She felt him behind her in the hall and sped up, only to feel his
hand touch her arm. She yanked it away. "What?"

"You were pretty cozy with that Alika guy yesterday."

"I could say the same of you and Becky."

"It's hardly the same. I haven't even asked her out yet, and
you've had roses and a 'thanks for last night.'"

Her stomach dropped. He'd read the card with the roses. She
couldn't blame him; she'd have done the same. Still, the best
defense was always a good offense—her dead junkie mother had
taught her that.

"Keep out of my things. Playing the psycho-jealous boyfriend doesn't suit you, and you might not like what you find."

"I already don't."

They swished out through the front doors of the hospital, and Lei practically ran toward the parking area, where their vehicles were parked side by side. She beeped the truck unlocked. He leaned against the cab as she opened the door and got in.

"Thought I'd tell you Captain Fernandez asked me to transfer here. He says he needs someone with my perspective on his team. I'm thinking about it."

Lei's heart hammered. She didn't know what it was—terror, anger, happiness. Maybe a little of all three.

"There isn't room here for us," she blurted.

"What do you mean—us?"

"Becky. You. Alika. Me."

"For someone who dumped me, you seem pretty concerned about who I'm even thinking of dating."

"You said you were going to ask her out."

"That's what I mean—always jumping to conclusions. Maybe I want to think about staying—to see if you'll change your mind about us. You and me. Not them."

"Oh God. I can't deal with this now." She reached for the door to slam it shut, but he put his arm out and held it. She tugged to no avail, then turned the key. The truck roared into life. "This isn't the time or place. We've got a meeting to get to."

"I'll take that as a maybe." He let go of the door. She yanked it shut and rolled down the window for one last word. Stevens stepped in, and as the glass slid down, he reached in with both hands to cup her face, pulling her toward him.

His mouth was hard and a little painful, but the instant combustion of it stole her breath and objections. Lei's eyes closed, her hands coming off the gearshift and steering wheel to wrap around the column of his neck, pulling him closer.

The kiss seemed to be telling a story: all that had been, was longed for, could be. She sank into it, lost in sensation, a mutual claiming. Her fingers moved up to tangle in his curling hair, and she wasn't even aware of climbing halfway out the window into his arms.

Stevens finally eased away, looking into her eyes. His were a bruised-looking dark blue, clouded with all he didn't say. She was stunned by the hold he still had on her, by the need he so instantly awoke—and by terror that she'd hurt him.

Maybe that was why she couldn't marry him. Not that any of it made sense. Some part of her knew that and mocked the repeat of a kissing scene she'd just played out with Alika—only this time she was the one sitting in the truck.

"I'll take that as a maybe," he repeated, softly this time. "God knows I can't seem to get over you."

She cleared her throat. Nothing came out when she tried to speak. Instead she pressed the automatic button and the window rolled up between them, a transparent barrier. He put his hand on it and she put the truck in reverse, pulling away.

The shape of his hand remained for a few seconds on the window, outlined in a mist of condensation.

CHAPTER TWENTY-SIX

"SPECIAL AGENTS MARCELLA Scott and Matt Rogers." Captain Fernandez gestured to two gray-suited agents who were studying the white board with its branching timeline as Lei and Stevens slid into empty chairs around the conference table along with Jenkins and Flea. Fury was still on Oahu in pursuit of Hines. "I called and apprised them last night when the bones were brought in, and they wasted no time getting on the plane from the Honolulu field office."

"Welcome to Kaua`i. We're glad you're here," Stevens said deliberately. Lei remembered he'd always advocated for getting them involved.

The captain continued with a recap of the case so far. He filled the agents in on Lei's discovery of Jay Bennett's disappearance, the pattern of May and October missing persons, the connection to the transient hippie community she and Jenkins had discovered in the parks, the contributions of Jazz Haddock that had led to her undercover job at the Health Guardian.

"I'm on a schedule for my undercover role. I don't want to cause comment being late on my third day," Lei said.

"So tell me again how you think this role will lead to a connection with the killer?" asked Agent Rogers. He turned away from the board with a movement that hinted at the coiled strength of a powerful build and aimed flinty blue eyes at her.

"I'm investigating the cult angle. We think the TruthWay cult may be involved because of its leader's behavior when we interviewed him, and Jazz Haddock's connected with them and he's our best lead. We think the killer may have help in his activities." Lei tried not to squirm and babble under the agents' unblinking gaze.

The female agent, a Jennifer Beals lookalike, turned on a high-wattage smile complete with dimple. "Special Agent Marcella Scott. Good to meet you." She extended a hand to Lei.

"Lei Texeira." Lei shook her hand. The woman had a grip like a weightlifter, contrasting with a curvy figure that strained the top buttons of a plain white shirt. Scott seemed to be trying to downplay her dramatic looks—long glossy curls were tightly scraped back into a ponytail and there was no makeup on her flawless face.

"Seems like you had a lot to do with breaking this case open."

"I guess." Lei sneaked a glance at the clock.

"The cult angle is pretty thin; we know that," Stevens said. "But if the bones from the cave are some of our missing, which seems highly possible, disposing of bodies that way is a lot of work and may take more than one person. Besides, it seemed like a good idea to follow wherever Jazz Haddock is going. The man knows too much."

Stevens was covering for her. Lei felt a squeeze of gratitude.

"Gotta go," she said, standing up.

"We're going to give you a little more surveillance support," Agent Scott said, with that disarming dimple. "Soon as our observation van gets here, we'll be hooking you up with some more equipment, maybe even working another agent in."

"Seems like you talked the situation over before getting here," Captain Fernandez said.

"We did. And we got clearance, based on the discovery of the bones last night, for the full support of ViCAP and the BAU."

"Acronyms?" Stevens asked with a smile. He was able to put on charm too.

"Sorry. Violent Criminal Apprehension Program. We come in to work with you, but when the arrests go down, it's all you making the busts. The BAU is the Behavioral Analysis Unit. We have agents trained in profiling; we use these resources for hunting serials. Like I said, we have enough to work with on your case to deploy more agents and our mobile evidence investigation unit. They're on their way" Rogers set fists on his lean hips, pushing the gray jacket back to reveal the ornate Federal Bureau of Investigation badge clipped to his belt. Lei tried not to ogle it, but, damn, it was a pretty badge. She'd dreamed of working for the Bureau in secret fantasies.

"Wonderful," said Captain Fernandez, and the rest of the team nodded like marionettes.

They were losing the case to the FBI.

"Really, I'm late." Lei fled.

ANOTHER HOT, sweaty day in the health food store and she'd gathered nothing useful. By the end of the day she'd begun to wonder if Jazz allowing her to work in the Guardian had little to do with the investigation and more to do with getting a free slave. For the hundredth time she wondered how the FBI was going to deal with the case, and by four p.m. she noticed a white utility van parked across the street that she'd bet was the FBI surveillance unit. They never called her to check in. That didn't feel good, and made her scalp prickle. Maybe it was the heat and the wig—but either way, she finished the day irritable.

After firming up Jazz's commitment to let her come to that week's TruthWay celebration, Lei got into the truck and rolled her neck, wondering if she should call Jenkins and deciding not to. She fired up the truck and headed in toward Lihue instead of heading for home—she'd made plans to meet her dad for dinner.

She pulled into the parking lot of the restoration center and took off the wig, smoothing its strands, and then tried to fluff what was left of her hair. There was no discernible effect. She scrubbed at a spot on her tie-dyed T-shirt, ran the wand of her lip gloss over her mouth, and gave up any further efforts.

She pushed through the front doors. Shellie Samson sat behind the reception desk and looked startled at the sight of her.

"What happened to your hair?" she exclaimed. Lei rubbed her still-itchy scalp, gave a big smile.

"Staying cool," she said. "My dad around?"

"It looks good on you. I'll buzz his room." She toggled the old-fashioned call board. "Wayne, your daughter, Lei, is here."

"Be right down." Wayne's tinny voice came through.

"I'm sorry about your husband," Lei said after a few minutes.

"Me too." Shellie shuffled some papers, her eyes down. "Our marriage was kinda rocky when he disappeared. I wasn't into his whole hippie thing. So when he just never came home, I thought he'd decided to hit the road and start over. I never dreamed he'd been murdered."

The word seemed to stick in her throat like a chicken bone, and Shellie coughed, tears springing to her eyes.

"I'm sorry." Lei pushed the box of Kleenex on the counter over to Shellie. She wished she had her stone to rub, but there were no pockets on the hemp dress. She rubbed her hands on her thighs instead and paced back and forth in front of the stairway.

"It's okay. It's actually better knowing. I just feel bad now. I was so angry at him for so long when, really, it wasn't his fault." The tears were flowing now, and Shellie grabbed tissues and pressed them against her eyes.

Wayne descended the stairs, dark eyes taking in the scene.

"Her husband," Lei said, wiggling her fingers to remind him of the hand they'd found in the flood. His eyes widened. She turned back to Shellie, who was blowing her nose. "Well, are you okay? I was going to take my dad out for dinner."

"Of course," Shellie said, visibly pulling herself together. "Wayne has been a great guest of ours and is an asset to our program."

"Great," Lei said. "Well, I'll return him before you know it."

"Just sign in, Wayne, when you get back." Shellie handed over a logbook. He filled it out and followed Lei through the doors. They got in the truck.

"How's it going?" Lei asked.

"Okay." He stared at her shorn head. "What happened?"

"I'm undercover. Wearing a wig," Lei said. "You've seen my hair. It was never going to lie down and take that."

Her father laughed. Lei realized how seldom she'd heard it. He sobered quickly.

"What's this about Shellie's husband? That was his hand we found?"

She filled him in as she drove them to a nearby Japanese restaurant. They settled into bamboo chairs. Wayne looked around at the lighted kirin beer signs, kokeshi dolls, and dangling paper umbrellas that decorated the place. He turned to her.

"I miss that dog of yours."

"Yeah, she's been a little grumpy too. I've had to leave her alone a lot, been busy with the investigation."

"Well." He cleared his throat. "What do you think about me getting a place in Hanalei? I could babysit her during the day while you work."

"I have to think about that. Keiki's a guard dog. I like to have her keeping an eye on the house while I'm gone."

"Okay, it was just a thought." He fiddled with his chopsticks.

"No, it's a good idea. At least you could visit her, take her out during the day. She'd love that."

"Yeah." He finally looked up. "Ever consider a roommate?"

Lei was the one to look away. She didn't want to hurt him, but it seemed way too soon.

"Well, Dad, I'd have to get a bigger place. The cottage only has one bedroom, and I like the location on the river. I'd have to think about it."

"I'm sorry I asked. It's too much. I just liked taking care of Keiki, cooking for you—it made me think we could get something back of what we lost."

Lei didn't answer until after they placed their orders. She'd ordered her favorite comfort food, a big bowl of noodles. She looked her dad in the eye.

"No one wants to get that lost time back more than I do. I'd be willing to consider it if I needed to move, and we found a place that was right for us, and… I knew I could count on you."

"You can count on me. But of course you don't know that." He blew out a breath. "I did stupid things when I was young. Harmful, devastating things that I can't take back. But in jail I gave my life to Christ, and I got a fresh start. I know I can live a new way, putting others first. I want a chance to prove that to you—but I don't blame you for needing me to."

Lei picked up the little cup of tea and smiled. "Dad, this is a fine start right here."

THE TIMEKEEPER LED the Chosen by the cable on his neck, stumbling out into the clearing outside the cave. Sunset splashed the nearby stream with golden-red beams, and the song of the water across the stones was barely interrupted by the whimper of the man as he saw the stream.

The Timekeeper felt a stab of something almost like sorrow or compassion as the man fell on his knees by the stream, splashing water into his mouth and over his abraded wrists. He stuck his head entirely under the water, and the Timekeeper cursed, reaching in to pull him up by the hair. The Chosen spluttered as the Time-keeper flung him backward onto the bank.

"Please," the man said. "Just a little longer. I haven't seen light in days."

"Just until the sun goes down," the Timekeeper said.

"You always indulge them." His mother's voice in his ear, a sibilant whisper. He hated that her Voice was loudest, louder than all the spirits of the aina (land) he served. He sat and endured as a different Voice challenged his mother, and they screamed back and forth in his head as he watched the sun drop behind the mountain and touch the dripping hair of the Chosen with a gold almost like kindness.

When the shine was gone from his hair, the Timekeeper led the man back toward the cave and wasn't surprised when he made a run for it. The collar yanked him back, and a kick to the back of the knee brought him down. But it was the Timekeeper's fillet knife nicking off the lobe of his ear and pressed against his carotid artery with terrifying, surgical knowledge that compelled the Chosen to walk back into the cave with him, meek and bleeding.

"My name is Jay," the man whispered in the dark as the Time-keeper put the cable back on.

The Timekeeper didn't care. The Chosen had a purpose, and his name had nothing to do with it.

CHAPTER TWENTY-SEVEN

LEI'S PHONE buzzed as she was turning off the bridge toward the cottage, her headlights slicing through the thick warm night.

"Texeira."

"Never gets old, hearing you say that."

"Alika. What's up?"

"You're asking me that? What's up with the bones?"

"Can't really talk about it."

She didn't have to try to make her voice regretful; she felt terrible cutting him out of the loop after all he'd done the night before.

"I can tell this is going to be a tough part of our relationship."

"So." She put a smile into her voice. She had to work harder on getting over Stevens, and Alika was the perfect way to do that. "We're having a relationship, are we?"

"Of a sort. I liked where things were going until you found the finger bone." He laughed. "You're never boring, I'll give you that."

"You're not bad yourself. Thanks for all you did yesterday. So helpful. I'm counting the days until they pull me off the case, now that the Feds are involved."

"Feds?"

"FBI."

She pulled onto the grass verge at her cottage, parked the truck. Keiki ran back and forth in front of the fence, barking a happy greeting.

"Wow. Serious."

"More than you know. Listen, let's get together. Take it to the next level." It was past time she got over Stevens once and for all. She bit her lip as she walked up onto the porch and fumbled her key into the lock.

"What do you mean?"

"You know what I mean." Lei reached down to rub the Rottweiler between the ears. "Continue what we started in the cave."

A short silence.

"Way to cut to the chase," Alika said.

"I think of it as decisive."

"Well, much as some parts of my anatomy want to just drive over and get busy, I seem to remember telling you I was planning something more romantic."

"Okay, if you must. And apparently you must." Lei went into the kitchen, turning on lights as she went. "What do you have in mind?"

"Let me surprise you. Just be ready for me to pick you up Saturday morning."

"I like to drive. I'll meet you there."

"You have to trust me. I'll pick you up at eleven a.m. Wear something nice."

"Oh God. I'm so not this kind of girl. C'mon. You've seen my one dress. Now I'll have to get another one."

"I'll take you however I can get you."

"I'm in a hippie phase. I'm prone to hemp these days."

"It's what's underneath that counts. I'll see you Saturday." He hung up.

Lei folded the phone shut and set it on the counter, gazing out the window thoughtfully. On impulse she turned off the light over the sink, and dark fell over the kitchen. She walked out onto the little porch at the rear of the cottage. Keiki followed and sat beside her, leaning her warm bulk against Lei's side as she looked at the river.

The moon was up and the water glimmered. A tiny breeze blew across, rippling the long grass in dark silken waves. Lei watched a limb traced in silver light float by. Kaua'i was like the river, calm and beautiful on the surface, but filled with its own power—and sometimes a raging destruction.

The FBI coming in was going to change things dramatically. Their lab resources alone would be invaluable. Still, they would take over the case, leaving little—if any—role for her and the Kaua'i task force. There was no question KPD's meager resources weren't up to an investigation of this magnitude and they needed the help, but the contemptuous look in Rogers's eyes and the suspicious one in Scott's didn't bode well for her own role in things.

The phone rang and Lei sighed, saying goodbye to the river as she went in. She brushed through the barred screen door and opened the phone, turning back to close and lock the door when Keiki was back inside.

"Texeira."

"Sweets, it's J-Boy. Your task force liaison, for however long it lasts."

"Yeah, my thoughts exactly. What's the latest?"

"They're bringing over more agents. Flying some of their Behavioral Analysis Unit out from Virginia."

"Oh my God." Even though she'd been preparing for this, confirmation was a sucker punch. She went to the freezer for the emergency vodka, poured a shot into one of her jelly glasses, and sat down. Keiki put her head on Lei's thigh, ears swiveling anxiously.

"How long do we have?"

"Another conference early tomorrow and we'll see. I think a day max."

Lei threw the vodka back in one burning gulp. It rendered her unable to speak.

"You okay?" Jenkins sounded alarmed. "I should've come over to talk to you, but I thought you saw which way the wind was blowing this morning."

Lei coughed and pounded her chest. The alcohol hit her stomach, a bomb of warmth.

"I'm okay. Emergency shot," she wheezed. "Okay, yeah, I saw it coming, but that doesn't make it any easier to take."

"Yeah, the captain even copped to having some idea that there were more disappearances than there should have been, but that he didn't quote, 'have the resources' unquote, to investigate."

"I hope that doesn't bite him on the ass."

"Me too." They sat a moment in morose silence. "So, Sweets, how was health food patrol today?"

"Nothing popping. I'm having to work way too damn hard for nothing right now. I'm just waiting for this Saturday's antics out at the papaya farm."

"So Haddock's letting you attend the cult festivities?"

"Yeah. Says I needed this week to establish myself as his 'protégée' and now he can bring me out there. I'm counting on you for backup."

"No way I'd miss it. Well, with the Feds on board at least Becky's going to get some help with the bones. They're bringing out a forensic bone specialist with a portable lab. Costs a fortune, but they can even extract DNA from bone and may be able to identify the vics. Agent Scott said they're going to enter everything into that ViCAP database and see what they can find."

"I don't know what the ViCap is."

"It's a whole division with different aspects, and one of the main assets is the national database of missing persons and unidentified human remains."

"Thanks for filling me in on this. The captain did the right thing bringing them on at this stage. I just hope they let us do something. This feels like my case, like it keeps unfolding for me for some reason. I'd like to keep that going." Lei mixed up Keiki's dog food as she spoke.

"I know. That ViCAP program is awesome." Lei hadn't heard Jenkins sound so enthusiastic in a while. "They're scanning in photos of the bones, tool marks, the hand you found, and the MO, as far as we know it, and sending it all to the Behavioral Analysis Unit. Like I said, a couple of BAU agents are coming to help Scott and Rogers, and they'll be looking over everything in Haddock's binder, everything we've gathered."

"Should be interesting." Lei took a breath. "Marcella Scott. She seemed like a hardass."

"In more ways than one."

"Great, sexism from my partner. How's Stevens taking it?"

"Like a man." Jenkins chuckled. "Don't forget he was the one pushing for us to bring them in earlier. He and Becky are cooperating better than Fury and the rest."

"He and Becky seem to be getting pretty cozy." Lei wished she could take the words back the minute they were out of her mouth. She didn't want to sound like the jealous ex, but there it was. Again.

"Yeah, they seem to be hitting it off. You got a problem with that? Seems like you have some action of your own going."

"'Course not. Just kinda wish...he was still on the Big Island."

"Don't blame you. You guys are both moving on, I guess." He paused, a long beat. "Well, Anu asked me out. We're going to the movies."

"Great, J-Boy. You deserve a little fun." Lei injected enthusiasm she didn't feel into her voice. "Okay, see you at tomorrow's briefing."

Lei turned off the phone. She didn't have the capacity for any more interaction today. She went to the refrigerator and opened it.

She hadn't been to the store since Monday, and the few veggies left in the drawer were limp. She ended up making an omelet and writing herself a big note: buy food.

It was probably going to be hippie food, but she was beginning to be okay with that.

CHAPTER TWENTY-EIGHT

Friday, October 29

Lᴇɪ sᴀᴛ at the long conference table in the war room the next morning. A cooling coffee carafe, a stack of Styrofoam cups, and warm malasadas, delicious doughnut rounds drowned in sugar from the Kapa`a Bakery, beckoned from an open pink box. It was a typical debriefing except for the suits ranged around the wall in power positions.

She let her wig stream in a rebellious waterfall down the back of her chair. She'd aired and spot cleaned the hemp dress and was in that again, but there was no help for the peeling tattoos on her wrists. She picked at them as Special Agent in Charge Newsome, newly arrived from Quantico's Behavioral Analysis Unit, stepped forward to address the group.

"Kaua`i Police Department has done a great job with a huge investigation. But sometimes the best part of being great is knowing when to reach out for help. Captain Fernandez has chosen, wisely, to access the expertise and resources of FBI's ViCAP program. We're formally taking over the case. Detective Stevens, thank you." Newsome stepped forward and shook

Stevens's hand. "Agents Rogers and Scott will liaise with you for the next few days, but we'll be taking it from here."

Stevens's face was stony. He said nothing.

"Detective Texeira." Agent Scott spoke, and Lei snapped to attention. "You have a unique angle going with the undercover thing. We aren't convinced the TruthWay cult has anything to do with this killer, but from where you're positioned you can keep eyes on Jazz Haddock, who's our best suspect at this point."

"It's true that Jazz knows way too much about the missing and didn't surrender the stones he'd collected. Part of what I've been trying to investigate is his role in all this, but it's been hard to establish." Lei firmed up her voice and kept her hands in her lap, where she rubbed the black stone, anchoring herself. The FBI wouldn't intimidate her if she could help it.

"Yes, we agree he's a viable suspect." Rogers spoke this time. Along with SAC Newsome, two other new agents sat at the table. No one had introduced them. "We're digging deep into his records, forensic evidence, everything we can find in that binder. He's got some connection with this killer, and he trusts you. At least to a degree. We want to keep that going."

"And just when I'd decided he was exploiting me as a restaurant slave," Lei said. No one laughed.

"For now we'd like to keep you in place at the Health Guardian and going to the cult celebration this Saturday. Obviously, don't let Haddock know we're in the picture," Scott said.

"Obviously." Lei inclined her head. "Well, I've got a shift to keep. Got anybody who wants to join me in this undercover venture? We can catch up out at the safe house in Kilauea. I'm not sure how much the cult is watching me, and I want to keep trips to the station minimal."

"I'm coming in with you. We won't want you to go to the cult alone." Scott stepped away from the wall as she spoke. "I'm going to become your new best friend, and I want you to introduce me to Haddock." Her dimpled smile had a lot of teeth. "For today just do your usual; I'll meet you at the safe house this evening to strategize going undercover with you. We're also going to be recording you and keeping Haddock under surveillance from now on." She handed Lei a tiny earpiece and button mike.

"Sounds fun." Lei gave back some toothiness as she took the equipment. "I can't wait."

She stood and walked out, putting some swing in her step. Her mind flashed to the phrase "can be oppositional with authority" that Lieutenant Ohale on the Big Island had written in her last performance appraisal. She needed to get herself in hand, but situations like this just didn't seem to bring out the best in her.

"You going to be okay with all this?" Stevens had followed her out.

"I should ask you the same thing." Lei walked on. The double doors whisked open with a pneumatic sigh.

"I'm not thrilled about it—I wanted us to be able to break this case open. But with so many bones and so little resources, it was past time to bring them in."

"I know." Lei unlocked her truck. "It's weird, everything changing so fast, all these new people. At least I get to continue on the case for now."

"I'm still organizing the cadaver hunt. They're counting on our manpower; even with five agents here, the canvass of Hanalei Valley is going to take a lot of resources."

"Okay. Well, going now." The earlier kiss hung between them, haunting and magnetic. Stevens nodded and walked away.

LEI STOOD by the chain-link gate of the police safe house in Kilauea. Marcella Scott had called Lei to rendezvous there several hours into her workday. It had been a long morning at the Health Guardian with little to show for it, and now heightened tension thrummed through her.

A battered green Camaro pulled up, and Special Agent Marcella Scott got out of the driver's side. Sleek brown hair hung in braids with curling ends, and she wore frayed denim shorts, flip flops on her feet, and a tank top emblazoned with Bob Marley over a long-sleeved tee. Lei wouldn't have recognized her from the buttoned-down woman she'd met at the briefing.

"Ready to come work at the Guardian, I see," Lei said. "What I don't know how to do is sell you to Jazz."

"Let me worry about that. You remember Matt Rogers from the briefing." Marcella gestured to the brawny man who'd got out of the passenger side. The agent had mussed up his short hair and put on jeans and a T-shirt, but there was no disguising the military set of his shoulders as he swung a briefcase out from behind the bucket seat.

"Sure. Come on in." Lei led the two agents into the little house and locked the door behind them as they did a quick assessment of the modest living space. She led them to the Formica kitchen table.

"Kaua`i Police Department uses this house for witnesses, retreats, whenever someone's undercover. It's not much, but it works. They keep the fridge stocked with some basics. Something to drink?"

"Water's fine," Marcella said. Rogers booted up a laptop from the case. Lei got a water bottle out of the fridge, handed it to the agent, and opened a Diet Coke for herself.

"Here's the cover story. I'm your friend Marcella from the Big Island. Nothing to do with the investigation, but I need a job. I'm thinking I'll offer to take your coffee shop job in the Guardian, and you can focus on developing your relationship with Jazz. Offer to be his personal assistant. Get in closer. Poke around his office. Meanwhile, Rogers is going to be our backup, keeping an eye from outside in the surveillance van."

"Seems like you've got it covered." Lei took a sip of her Diet Coke, leaning back against the counter. "What's the rest of the task force doing?"

"Reassigned. They're back to regular KPD cases. We've been getting up to speed at the station all day and working on different scenarios. With four field agents and two lab techs here, we should make some rapid progress." Marcella cocked her head. "There was some interesting chatter on your comm today."

"Not that I noticed," Lei said. "Just Dan the smoothie guy talking story."

"We thought his interest in you might be more than usual. He was asking a lot of questions."

"He's just friendly." Lei made a flicking gesture. "Might want to get a little more than friendly, but I don't think he's got a lot upstairs. Speaking of which, what do you think of that guy Tiger? He's got potential as a suspect."

"We've been trying to find him in the system, but so far, no go. This Sunday I think Lani needs to bring her friend Marcella to the cult festivities. While we're there, I'll get samples and photos to help us ID him."

"I don't know if Jazz will go for that. He's going to be suspicious about just bringing you into the store."

"Let me handle it." Marcella smiled. "I think he'll be interested in what I can add to the celebration. I'm a trained belly dancer."

"Belly dancer!" Rogers exclaimed. Marcella's dimple deepened.

"Never know what you'll need to do in the service of our government. I also speak four languages. Did some time overseas. Belly dancing came in handy more often than I want to think about."

Marcella Scott was a woman with brains and a body who knew how to use both to solve her cases. Lei was just beginning to realize the potential of this.

"Maybe you can show me some moves." Lei eyed the agent over her Diet Coke.

"This I gotta see." Rogers winked at his partner.

"All you get is your surveillance scope." Marcella went on to outline the plan the FBI had put together for Saturday night.

Lei felt the frisson of apprehensive excitement that made the job addicting tighten her sternum. She could hardly wait.

Lᴇɪ ᴘᴜsʜᴇᴅ the clattering wooden beads that screened Jazz's door aside and stuck her head in.

"Hello?"

Jazz pushed back from the computer. A smile lit his face. "My favorite undercover cop. Just need a few more like you and we'd be really raking in the dough."

"About that." Lei came in and gave Marcella's hand a tug, closing the inner door behind them as the shapely agent followed her into the dim office. "This is my friend Marcella. She needs a job."

Jazz took a minute to roll his eye over the Marley shirt and beads the agent had on, and Marcella brought out the dimple and white teeth. "I'm a hard worker. I just want a chance to show you what I can do." She cocked a hip in short shorts.

Lei wondered if the agent was laying it on a little thick.

"She a cop?" He narrowed his eyes.

"Does she look like a cop? She's my friend from the Big Island."

"You didn't answer my question."

Marcella broke character, digging into her tight pocket and producing a creds wallet. "Special Agent Marcella Scott, FBI," she said.

Jazz recoiled away from them in his rolling chair. "Oh no. No. This isn't what I signed on for."

"We've done a little background workup on you, Mr. Haddock. Tax evasion is just the beginning of what we found. This store looks like an ideal front for drug dealing. Cooperate with our

228

investigation, or spend some time in Halawa Prison," Marcella said, the dimple still in place and the smile a little unnerving now.

"You don't understand. The cult trusts me. I can't bring more cops in. I'd be finished in this town."

"Look at us," Marcella said. "Do we look like cops? Yeah, we'll have a surveillance team on us, but you'll never know they're there and neither will anyone else. The only thing we want is the murderer who's disappearing people you claim to care about."

Jazz leaned forward, bringing a shaking hand up to rub his eyes. Lei saw Marcella taking in the dimly lit office, the rich scent of incense, the straining wail of sitar music in the background.

"All right."

"All right," Lei echoed. "And since Marcella's coming on, how about I help you organize back here? She can take the front. I'll take the back."

"I don't need office help."

Lei gestured to the teetering pile of invoices held down with a chunk of amethyst.

"You do too. It's not like we're investigating you or anything." She wished she could cross her fingers behind her back.

He shook his head. Marcella switched the charm back on.

"We appreciate your cooperation, Mr. Haddock. You're going to be a hero when we catch this guy."

"Okay, okay," Jazz muttered, and turned away. "Have Dan show her the ropes and come back here. I guess I could use a hand with the billing."

CHAPTER TWENTY-NINE

Saturday, October 30

LATE SATURDAY MORNING, Lei toweled off from a shower and rubbed fragrant coconut oil into her skin. Her shoulders were reddened from running on the beach, freckles standing out against her olive skin. She rubbed the oil all over, feeling a little refreshed by cleaning up, but not in the mood for some mysterious date with Alika. She was too keyed up about the undercover op at the papaya farm. She'd already tried to call and cancel and he wouldn't take no for an answer, saying plans were already in motion.

She flicked on some mascara along with some sparkly lip gloss and slipped on the Tahitian pearl earrings her aunt had given her for graduation. The Ni`ihau shell necklace Mac had given her never came off anymore. Instead of a dress, she pulled on narrow black jeans and a black silk tank top, slipping her feet into the new slingbacks.

She heard an unfamiliar thrumming sound and hurried to the window. A black helicopter was approaching, the wind off the props vibrating the air and muting everything but its powerful roar. It wove back and forth as it settled toward the ground, rippling, then flattening the grass in the open area between her house and the Abacans' in prop wash. Lei ran out onto the porch, and her mouth fell open at the sight of Alika behind the controls, face obscured by mirrored sunglasses and flight helmet.

Keiki went apeshit barking, and getting her under control gave Lei a few minutes to regroup and act casual by the time Alika cut the engine and ran out from under the slowing rotors to her gate.

"Surprised?"

"You could tell?" Lei teetered down the porch steps, introduced Keiki to Alika. "You sure know how to make an entrance."

Lei gestured to the Abacans, who'd poured out of their house en masse and clustered on their porch. The oldest Abacan grand-kid, a gangly boy in ragged cutoffs, approached. "Can I see the inside?"

"Eh, howzit," Alika said, giving the kid a fist bump. He must have appeared the ultimate in cool. "Sure."

The other two kids ran over.

"Have fun with that," Lei said. "I've got to go grab my jacket." She left him showing the inside of the helicopter to the kids as she clomped back into the house, shouldering into her jean jacket and picking up the small black handbag she never used. On impulse, she slipped her Glock inside.

"A smart girl's always prepared," she muttered, feeling ambivalent. She fluffed her nonexistent hair in the mirror by the door and tucked the purse under her arm, a little surprised at how much better she felt with the weight of the gun in it. She clip-clopped out to the helicopter.

Mrs. Abacan rounded up the kids as Alika opened the curved Plexiglas passenger side door for her, giving her a courtly boost under the elbow as she stepped onto the strut to get inside. She waited until he got in to give him a good stare.

"You a safe driver? I have trust issues."

"Been certified to fly helicopters since my stint in the air force. I'm a half owner of this little beauty. I wanted to show you more of the island, some things you wouldn't normally see. Put your harness on."

He showed her how to buckle it. The straps pinned her against the molded seat, and she immediately felt claustrophobic. She stuck one hand into her pocket to touch the black stone, sucking a few relaxation breaths.

"This is a Bell 206 Jet Ranger," Alika went on, telling her about the various functions of the dials and knobs in front of them. Lei looked out of the curved window of the Bell and did a few more relaxation breaths. It didn't seem to be working.

"Put your helmet on," Alika said. "It has audio built in." When she made no move to take the bulky plastic headwear, he set it gently on her head, adjusted the strap under her chin. His voice came clearly through the audio.

"You okay? You look a little off."

"Okay." She gave a wan smile and thumbs-up. "Let's just do it."

He reached over, patted her leg, and began their takeoff procedure. Minutes later they rose slowly, Keiki watching from the porch with her ears flattened.

CHAPTER THIRTY

LEI'S ANXIETY began to recede as the glorious topography of Kaua`i opened up beneath her. Fertile Hanalei Valley with its patchwork quilt of taro patches, rugged, lush mountains, cerulean ocean, and plumed waterfalls distracted her with wonder.

Alika made an effort to fly as smoothly as possible, as they followed the dramatic curve of the coast to the Na Pali cliffs. As they hit the ridgeline, the wind swatted at them, causing stomach-dropping bumps until he lifted the collective and took them up and over, spinning off toward the center of the island.

"Where are we going, exactly?" Lei asked.

"Somewhere special. You won't see this any other way."

She took it all in, pressing her forehead against the window. Sheer miles of trackless jungle flowed by without any human stamp. Alika brought them to a wide mesa that overlooked the ocean, marked by a tall green spire. He gently set the chopper down and cut the engine. As the rotors whined down, Lei realized terror had morphed into euphoria, an expanding bubble of joy. She took the headset off and threw her arms around him.

"Wow," she said. "Wow. No wonder the tourists do these helicopter tours. I never understood it before. Thank you."

He tipped her chin up and tried to kiss her, but she didn't have time for that and pulled away, opening her door and hopping out, forgetting she was in heels and promptly landing on her butt in the tussocky grass. He was laughing as he came around the front of the Bell and gave her a hand up.

"Why'd you tell me to wear something nice?" she grumbled. He gestured toward a little cabana that had been set near the edge of the mesa, and Lei tripped again, gasping at the sight. "Oh my God."

He wrapped an arm around her as they made their way over to the little striped tent. A folding table had been set up with a couple of chairs on a Persian carpet; an aluminum bucket held chilled champagne in melting ice, and a big wicker basket hinted of a tasty lunch to come.

"Oh my God," Lei said again. "I don't know what to say."

His smile gleamed with satisfaction. "Speechless. I like it." He pulled her chair out and she sat, taking in the enormous vista. "Champagne?"

"Hell yes. Make it a double."

LEI PROPPED herself on her elbow and fed Alika a grape. He'd thought of everything—not only the folding table, but the carpet with a futon and a pile of colored pillows. They'd been kissing for what seemed like hours, and she knew it was the moment of truth as he looked at her with his half-lidded golden eyes. Waiting for her decision.

She squelched a last blink of doubt. This was what she wanted, who she wanted. He would help her get over Stevens once and for all. She sat up and peeled the silk top off her head, unzipped her jeans and wiggled out of them. She wore her best underwear, a lacy black bra and panties. He pretended to lick his chops, and pulled her toward him by the hips. She laughed as he buried his face in her stomach, growling as he swirled his tongue in her navel. She leaned backward to support herself as he trailed kisses down her abdomen, and her hand landed on the fringe of the carpet.

She found herself holding something that was caught there. He was still kissing her, moving lower down, as she brought the object up in front of her eyes.

A thin gold bracelet.

She pushed his head away, sat up. Turned the bracelet in her hands. It was a classic Hawaiian design with hibiscus flowers and maile leaves around the outside, and inside, in delicate script: For Lisa with love, Alika

She looked up at him. She never would have imagined his face could be so pale. His eyebrows stood out like black slashes. He reached out and took the bracelet from her, and his hand trembled.

"Impossible. Lisa always wore this."

"Unbelievable." Lei grabbed her black tank, hauled it on. Stood up and yanked her pants on, zipped them up. He was still lying there, holding the bracelet. She grabbed her purse, whipped out the Glock, and aimed it at him. "This the rug you rolled her up in to dump her body?"

"What?" He looked stunned, face pale and eyes wide. "No. I didn't kill her. The rug was just sitting in my garage."

She kept the gun on him, began searching the carpet. Lifted the corner.

"Get up." He did. She pushed the lightweight table, moved the chairs. Adrenaline hummed in her ears. Keeping the gun on him, she hauled the rug one-handed out from under the cabana. She flipped it over. In the center, a rusty stain.

"Unbelievable," she said for the second time. "You were gonna make love to me on the rug you used to dump Lisa!"

"I didn't kill her," he said again. His voice was low.

"Tell it down at the station. You're under arrest for the murder of Lisa Nakamoto."

CHAPTER THIRTY-ONE

LEI KEPT the gun on Alika as he piloted them straight to the police station without protest, face bleached and set in the reflected light of the controls. Lei hardly noticed the view, all her attention focused on Alika, watching for any attempt to sabotage their flight.

"I didn't do anything to Lisa," he said, as they descended toward Kapa`a.

"Save it. I should have known not to trust a guy like you."

"Like me?"

"A player. Too good-looking. They'll love you in prison."

A long silence filled with the whine of rotors, the ground coming toward them.

"It wasn't like that. But I don't expect you to believe me."

"I don't believe you," Lei said, pronouncing the end of a relationship.

LEI PACED BACK and forth in the peanut gallery outside the interview room. Her ears buzzed and her stomach roiled. She did relaxation breathing, rubbed the black stone. None of it was helping.

239

The captain sat imperturbably, his fingers laced over his waist, waiting.

Alika sat on a hard metal chair in the interview room, hands cuffed behind him. The room was designed to make suspects uncomfortable: plain windowless walls, a small steel table, shiny expanse of observation mirror, and two chairs for interrogators set at angles to increase their influence.

Fury and Flea came in. The captain had chosen them for their experience and the fact that neither of them knew Alika. Flea went and turned on the camcorder on the wall. Alika's voice came clearly through the speaker. After the preliminaries, Alika spoke first.

"I don't know what she told you, but I didn't do anything to Lisa Nakamoto."

"Yeah, it's a little farfetched that you would," Fury said. Lei went still and then remembered stage one of interrogation—build a connection with the suspect. "Important guy like you, got standing in the community. You wouldn't risk all that for a piece of trash like Lisa."

"Exactly. Not that Lisa was trash—she just liked to party."

"Oh, so you knew her. Socially."

"Yeah, we knew each other since small kid time." His use of the colloquialism made bile rise in Lei's throat. She sat down, pinching the web between her finger and thumb to keep herself in her body.

She felt a hand on her shoulder. Glanced up. Stevens, his hair damp, his eyes intent on the interview. She shrugged his hand off, got up and paced again.

"So you didn't have a relationship with her."

"Well, I wouldn't say that. We were friends." Alika sat as proudly as he could with his hands behind his back, his bulky shoulders bunched. "I would never hurt her. Can I get these cuffs off? I'm not going anywhere."

"Sure." Flea unfolded his height and undid the cuffs as Fury leaned in.

"So what's your theory?"

Alika rubbed his wrists. "Maybe she was into something that was over her head and someone shot her when she tried to get out. That's what I think. I tried to help her, but she paid me back by robbing me."

"So she was endangering your business."

"No, no." Alika shook his head. "Lisa was a good girl. Whatever she did, she did because she was an addict."

"Yeah, but who got her addicted?"

"I heard it was her boyfriend. Name of Hines."

"We got the Hines guy on Oahu. He's saying you're the one who got her into drugs."

"That's a lie!" Righteous anger in the raised voice, flared nostrils and wide eyes. "I cared about her. I tried to help her!"

His conviction gave Lei a quiver of doubt for the first time. Maybe it was too easy, that the rug had been in his garage, the bracelet he'd given Lisa caught in the fringe. It was awfully convenient for someone and awfully stupid of Alika—and he'd never struck her as stupid.

"So she was your girlfriend." Fury was even and relentless, facing Alika from one side of the table, Flea watching inscrutably from the other side, arms folded on his chest.

"Not my girlfriend. A friend. Yes, I cared about her. I was worried about her."

"Friends with benefits," Fury stated.

A single nod from Alika.

Lei's stomach pitched and she pushed out the door, running down the hall to the bathroom, where she vomited up the last dregs of grapes, champagne, and romance.

When she felt a little better, she went back to the gallery. The captain and Stevens were intent on the drama taking place inside.

"Okay, I had a thing with Lisa. An off and on thing. She told me Hines was pressuring her to make meth in the Island Cleaning building; he was threatening her. She didn't know how to get out of it. I knew she was giving in when the break-ins happened; she would never hit my mother's business unless she was desperate."

"So that's why you killed her. Betrayal."

"No! I warned her I was calling the cops, that she wasn't going to get away with it. She begged me not to, said she had to have the money and my insurance would cover it."

"Why did she need money?"

"For the supplies, the distribution. I don't know! I just told her it was over between us, and I was going to the police. And that's when I met Detective Texeira."

"And what a tasty piece of tail she turned out to be." Flea spoke his first words. Both Stevens and Lei recoiled.

"Settle down," the captain said. "Flea's just trying to provoke him."

Sure enough, Alika turned to stare Flea down.

"It wasn't like that."

"I think it was," Fury said. "I think you called in the cops, but with every intention of monitoring every move they made, because money is what you need. It's your real estate business that's going down the tubes. The meth lab was a way to bail out your business, and the burglaries were a way to get some insurance money."

A long pause.

"I'd like my lawyer now," Alika said, sitting back. "I can see where this is going. I'm not saying another word."

And he didn't. Eventually Fury and Flea left after allowing Alika to make his phone call.

"Okay, show's over," Captain Fernandez said. "Stevens, take her home."

"Roger that," Stevens said. He walked beside Lei as she clip-clopped in her pretty shoes down the hall, arms folded tightly over her aching belly. The jean jacket wasn't enough to keep her warm.

They went out to the unmarked Bronco and he beeped it open.

They got on the road. Lei couldn't think of a single thing to say. She leaned her forehead against the window, and that reminded her of the helicopter ride. What an incredibly romantic gesture Alika had made—on a carpet soaked with Lisa Nakamoto's blood. How could he be so arrogant, so stupid?

In her heart she knew the answer—he wouldn't be. He was involved all right, but she didn't think he'd killed Lisa.

"I don't think he did it." Stevens said what she was thinking, like he'd often done in the past.

"I don't either. He's too smart."

"He's involved somehow though. I wouldn't be surprised if the burglary and insurance angle Fury came up with are in the ballpark."

"More will be revealed." Lei blinked, surprised to feel wetness on her cheeks.

"I'm sorry. He seemed like a nice guy."

"Bullshit. You hated him."

He said nothing. They drove on. Lei fell asleep.

She woke up with a gasp. Charlie Kwon was coming down over her, black pupils expanding to block out the light.

Sometimes the worst nightmares were memories.

"You okay?" Stevens looked over as he pulled up to her house. "You up for this FBI thing tonight?"

"I guess I'd better be," she said, getting out of the Bronco. "Thanks for the ride." She didn't let herself look back at him as she went into the little house—the concern in his voice brought tears to her eyes, a thousand tiny pinpricks. She didn't relax until she heard the sound of the Bronco pulling away.

Her phone buzzed at her side; she looked at the number and groaned. Esther Ka`awai. Well, time to get it over with.

"Hello, Esther."

"You arrested my grandson. He never did nothing to Lisa!" The older lady's voice vibrated with outrage.

"I'm sorry, Esther, but it sure looked like he did. He's involved somehow, at the very least." Lei pinched the bridge of her nose, hard.

"We paid the bail. He's out. I hope you're happy."

"I'm not happy, Esther. I liked Alika. In fact, more than liked him." Her voice caught. "I'm just sick about it."

"Well, if you liked him so much, you could believe him. You could give him the benefit of the doubt."

"He lied to me!" Lei exclaimed. "He served me lunch on a rug covered with her blood. I found a bracelet in the fringe that said 'Love Alika' on it! What do you expect me to do?"

A long silence. Esther cleared her throat. "He told me all that, but it sounds worse when you say it."

"Try being there. It started out as such a romantic picnic. I shouldn't be talking to you about this. I can't discuss his case. The other case though—can you give me a list and locations of the heiaus and sacred sites all along the North Shore? It's important."

Another long silence as Esther considered.

"All right," she said. "I'll have it for you tomorrow. Come to my house."

She hung up.

The last thing Lei wanted to do was go out to Esther's house. She felt guilty, angry for feeling guilty, then just sad.

More feelings than she ever liked to have in a day.

LEI PULLED up at the safe house well before time for the cult celebration. The case had to come before anything else, including her upset over Alika. She uncoded the locked gate and knocked on the door.

Marcella opened it. She was in a deerskin vest that ended below her rib cage and a fringed skirt that started mid-hip. The expanse of skin in between showcased a lot of sit-ups—or belly dancing.

"All set for a little orgy crashing," Lei said. "Nice outfit."

"You don't look so bad yourself." The agent gestured to Lei's costume. Lei had on a crocheted bikini top and a pair of short shorts with a peace sign on the butt. Her wig was freshly brushed and tattoos recently touched up. She'd thrown a button-down man's shirt over the ensemble for decency's sake.

"How'd I get the surveillance detail, is what I want to know," grumbled Rogers, cleaning his gun at the table. It was a well-used Glock .40, if the wear on the pebbled grip was anything to go by.

"It's the ladies that get the welcome mat at the cult," Marcella said. "Besides, you don't really blend."

"I'll second that," Lei agreed. In camouflage gear, Rogers was downright intimidating.

Marcella and Rogers had already scouted the farm on foot and from the air and had a surveillance post picked out for him. Two more agents would be out in the surveillance van while the three of them went into the papaya farm.

Lei hid her tiny, clear plastic earpiece behind the black wig's long strands as Marcella did the same. Rogers donned more obvious communication gear, and Agent Morse, the tech expert, checked their equipment one final time.

By the time he was done, the sun had dropped behind the mountain range, and they got into the Camaro and set off for the papaya farm. The white utility van marked "Hawaiian Telcom" followed at a discreet distance.

Marcella pulled over before the gate and let Rogers out of the car. In camo fatigues with a backpack of assorted equipment and weapons, he seemed to disappear as he vaulted the fence and trotted into the rows of papaya trees.

"Sound check, Red One," Marcella said.

"Roger that," Rogers answered. "In my case, it's literal. Red One out."

Lei gave a little snort of laughter. "Ginger here."

"Red Two checking. Okay, we're live." She activated the

recording function of their equipment. Both women were also wearing tiny button cams.

Marcella pulled the Camaro up next to Jazz's VW van. The store owner puffed nervously on a joint, which he stuffed into the ashtray at the sight of them, waving the pungent smoke away.

"Tiger's going to be excited to see you both," he said. "But he's not a gentleman, I'm telling you. Sure you want to do this?"

"We have to get inside, check them out at least. Don't worry. We're not going to draw attention to ourselves."

"Don't know if that's possible, with those outfits." Jazz unlocked the gate and drove the VW through. They followed in the Camaro. He walked back and draped the lock so it appeared shut and then bounced down the potholed road ahead of them, trackless acres of papaya trees stretching away in every direction.

Lei's earpiece crackled. "Red One in position."

"That was quick." Lei remembered from the schematic where Rogers was positioned, halfway up a lone Norfolk pine that marked the edge of the bedraggled lawn around the small cottage squatting in the midst of tall hibiscus bushes. He'd had to traverse the length of the papaya field and climb the tree without being seen. It didn't appear to have been a challenge for him.

They pulled into the yard filled with parked cars in front of a great steel barn. The barn doors were open, people milling around the entrance. Lei couldn't help a glance at the Norfolk pine, but there was nothing to see.

Marcella parked the Camaro and went into acting mode, running around the front and hugging Jazz enthusiastically as he got out of the van.

"Thanks so much for letting me come, Jazz! This is so neat. I've never been on a papaya farm before!"

"Have fun. Just don't drink too much of the stuff in the bowl that comes around." The tips of his ears turned red from what Lei had been privately calling the "Marcella effect." The deerskin costume certainly enhanced it.

Jazz strode into the barn with each of them hanging off an arm.

"Peace and welcome," said the young mother from Polihale with her tanned baby on her hip, swaying to the beat of a drum circle warming up against the far wall. Lei recognized several of the hippies she and Jenkins had met at Polihale; the older couple were preparing something at a table in the back. Lei took a seat beside Jazz, sitting cross-legged as the festivities got started.

Tiger appeared, gleaming with oil, wearing a catlike striped fur loincloth. He glanced at Lei but focused on Marcella, reaching down to take her hand and sit beside her.

"Jazz, who is this lovely sister?"

"Marcella. My new café girl. She's from the Big Island."

"Hi." Marcella smiled, dimple much in evidence. "I like your outfit."

"And I like yours," Tiger said. Lei could swear his canines were longer than they should be. "Welcome to TruthWay."

CHAPTER THIRTY-TWO

THE TIMEKEEPER WOVE through the crowd, letting his body move however it wanted to, spinning and stomping to the timeless rhythms of the drums. He hadn't joined his people in a while, but after repeated trips to the cave to see the Chosen steadily declining, he felt a need to be with others who worshipped what he served.

He was a little high, but not yet fully under the influence of the hallucinogenic brew that would be circulating later. He liked to take it slow, wait and see what experience the Voices had for him. He stomped and spun over to the drum line and picked up his djembe, joining the other musicians in creating the pulsing atmosphere that set the stage for the rhythms of life they celebrated.

His hands beat the stretched skin of their own accord while his eyes roamed. He marked and noticed anyone new. His eye was caught by a particularly fit and uninhibited young woman in a fringed outfit, dancing with Tiger.

Then he noticed the woman sitting off to the side. She was draped in long black hair, but there was something about her peregrine stillness that set her apart.

Now, and when he'd met her.

IN NO TIME, a long feathered pipe was passing as the drums picked up speed. Lei stayed seated as Marcella, Jazz, and Tiger joined the mosh pit of stomping and swaying. She kept looking—she didn't know who she was looking for. Dan? Someone else? She just had an odd, urgent feeling.

Marcella caught her eye, and Lei realized she was drawing attention to herself by staying seated. She got to her feet. A tall shadow appeared at her elbow, and a long finger reached out and touched the necklace at her throat.

"I know you," said Mac Williamson. His big hand took hers, which had suddenly gone numb as her worlds intersected. He drew her off to the side. "What's with the wig?"

"Uh, trying to blend," Lei stuttered. She'd take a leaf from Marcella's book and distract him the old-fashioned way. She shrugged out of the man's shirt. "Dance with me." She dragged him out into the middle of the dancers and put all her panic into swaying and gyrating.

It seemed to be working. He got moving and was surprisingly limber and coordinated. She actually found herself enjoying it as he created space for them to move together and matched her intensity with unique martial arts–like movements.

The drums came to a crescendo, and everyone flopped in a circle as the older couple brought a coconut bowl of mysterious drink around. Mac sat behind her, and she moved into the circle of his long arms, feeling protected.

Marcella crawled over from her spot a few yards distant. "Who's your friend?" She twinkled all her charm at Mac, but Lei could see assessment in her big, dark eyes.

"Mac Williamson. He's all right," Lei said. Her earbud crackled.

"Running background check. Red One out." Lei remembered

one of the tools Rogers carried in his backpack was a laptop with satellite uplink.

The bowl came to them—Cal Haddock, Jazz's brother, handed it to her, and she pretended to drink. The dark liquid left a fizzy aftertaste that numbed her lips.

Tiger moved in on Marcella, nuzzling her neck. Lei wasn't sure how she did it, but somehow Marcella managed to avoid him while appearing to enjoy his attentions. Lei was going to have to learn some of those moves. When the bowl had circulated the room a few times, Tiger stood up and addressed the group, hands outstretched.

"Peace. Truth. Love."

"Peace. Truth. Love," the people chanted back.

"We have some guests today. We want to honor them with a special toast. Lani and Marcella, come up." Lei's scalp prickled with alarm, but she and Marcella stood and faced the cult leader. He took the bowl and raised it high. "Spirits of Truth, bless this bowl. Let it show these sisters the Truth; let them see it reflected in every embrace."

Lei glanced at Marcella out of the corner of her eye as Tiger handed the halved coconut shell, shiny with use, to the agent. Marcella closed her eyes and appeared to drink deep. When she handed the bowl to Lei, it was half empty.

Lei had no such courage. She barely let the liquid touch her lips, and immediately felt the numbness that signaled its effect.

She handed it back to Tiger and he finished it. The crowd cheered, and something about that roar reminded Lei of the blood-thirsty howl of the Colosseum. Her earbud crackled.

"Red One checking thermal imaging. What's going on in there?"

"Marcella drank a lot of the drink," Lei said. The noisy crowd drowned her comment.

"Red Two, what's your game plan?" Rogers's voice was a crack of alarm.

"Authenticity and puking," said Marcella. She bent over and vomited. Some of it splashed on Lei's feet.

"Gross!" Lei exclaimed.

"Red Two—you okay?" Rogers's voice.

"Early training—bulimia," hissed Marcella, staggering realistically. She fell to the ground in a good imitation of a faint, and Lei bent to help her. The drums resumed, and Tiger leaned down.

He hefted Marcella up over his shoulder and put his other arm around Lei, dragging her off the dance floor. The crowd roared again, and Lei looked around wildly for Mac or Jazz.

She couldn't see either of them. Lei was revolted by the garlicky body odor emanating from Tiger's skin. She writhed and tried to break his hold, but he clamped her wrist in a grip that would leave bruises the next day. She felt the walls closing in as he dragged her toward the back door of the barn. Her ears buzzed with incipient dissociation.

She felt Marcella touch her shoulder. The agent held her finger to her lips and winked at Lei. Even with her head dangling upside down over a man's shoulder, Marcella had it together. Lei sucked a few breaths and got her terror under control.

They pushed through a rough wooden door to the outside. Lei stumbled in the long grass as Tiger yanked her forward. "Let me show you how we worship."

He brought them to a tool shed attached to the back of the barn. A single dim bulb hung from the center beam. Several futons lined the floor—this was Tiger's sex lair. Lei could smell it.

She'd come far enough. She flipped her arm, breaking his hold at the same moment Marcella arched up and karate-chopped the side of Tiger's neck. He went limp as a dishrag, crumpling where he stood. Marcella somehow landed on her feet.

"What a shame he passed out," she said, surveying Tiger's sprawled body.

"Ginger, Red Two. You okay?"

"It's handled," Marcella said.

Lei's knees were shaking and her wrist throbbed. All that Tae Kwon Do practice and she still wasn't at all sure she could have escaped from Tiger alone. They picked the cult leader up under the armpits and hauled him into the shed, sliding the door shut. They closed the hasp and stuck a stick through it. "He can still get out. Let's hope it isn't anytime soon," Marcella said. "Let's poke around, see what else we can find."

"Roger that."

"I'm not seeing a connection here so far, just a lot of drugs and sex. I'm also worried that Mac guy will blow your cover."

"He's clean, Red Two," said Rogers. "No priors, not even a parking ticket."

"I don't think Mac knows I'm a detective. I met him socially," Lei said. They trotted to a low nearby outbuilding, another of the metal sheds. Lei rubbed the window—blacked out. A big padlock secured the door.

"Red One. Checking this outbuilding. Anything on the thermal?"

"Heat sources inside but small. Not human."

They circled around and Lei spotted a six-inch circular vent. She reached inside, pushed. Pushed again. They heard the metallic clatter of the grille falling to the floor. Marcella took out a tiny, powerful penlight she carried in a leather pouch at her side and shone it inside. She gave a low whistle between her teeth and handed the penlight to Lei. Lei squinted into the circular opening as she shone the beam around a room. Crock-Pots and trays in rows on several tables, more stacked HEET in boxes, even a giant roll of tiny tear-off ziplock baggies.

"Contents consistent with meth production, Red One," Marcella said.

"Must be how they get their money. None of them seem to have jobs," Lei said. "I wonder if there's any connection to the Nakamoto murder."

"Let's discuss it when the op is over," Marcella said. They

darted back over to the barn and slid along the side of the building, heading toward the house.

"We have movement." The earbud crackled. "Someone's exited the barn. Looks tall enough to be a man. Possibly two."

The women plastered themselves against the side of the wall, hearing stumbling footsteps coming their way.

"Lani?" Jazz's voice.

"Tell him I'm sick so we can leave," Marcella whispered.

Lei stepped out and touched him, and he gave a little shriek of fright.

"Oh my God, Jazz, we barely got away," Lei said, tugging Marcella forward. The agent staggered realistically. "Marcella drank too much of that stuff, and Tiger tried to rape us!"

"I warned you guys—he's dangerous." Jazz sounded genuinely worried as Marcella sagged in Lei's arms.

"TruthWay is not all like that." Mac's deep voice came from the shadows. "I'm sorry you had a bad time."

He walked beside them as they made a beeline toward the Camaro, Jazz bringing up the rear.

"It's okay. I just need to get Marcella home. Tiger passed out before he could do any real damage." Lei supported Marcella toward the Camaro, and Mac opened the door. Lei noticed the carved staff he carried, but she couldn't make out any detail in the dim light. He helped her get Marcella into the car.

"Not all of us are like that," he said again. "Some of us want to show you another way."

"Whatever. I've had enough Truth for one night," Lei said. She got in her side of the Camaro and slammed the door, locking it. Mac's staff tapped on the window. Lei looked up as she turned on the car with keys left under the seat.

"See you soon," Mac said through the glass.

Lei nodded, and the Camaro jumped forward and roared out of the yard.

"Casual; be cool," said Marcella. "Don't blow the cover." She seemed genuinely out of it now, head lolling. "I puked, but some of that shit must have got me."

"Red Two, this is Red One. Meet at rendezvous point."

"Ginger here. She's kind of out of it, and I'm driving. What're the coordinates?"

"Corner of the papaya farm, west side," Rogers barked. He was breathing hard and she could tell he was running.

The evening had started out so under control. Lei looked over at the indomitable Marcella curled up, small and vulnerable in the bucket seat.

CHAPTER THIRTY-THREE

Sunday, October 31

LEI DEBRIEFED with the agents by phone the next morning.

"How are you feeling, Marcella?" Lei had dropped the agents off at the safe house the night before.

"Got a headache, but I'm okay. We've been conferring with the other agents from BAU and reviewing the footage from last night, and we're going to just surveil the cult for now. There's nothing there so far that ties them to the murders. Newsome wants to keep you and me at the Health Guardian to pick up intel in the community and on Jazz, but no more trips to the celebration. Too risky."

"What about the meth lab and Tiger? That man's a rapist, at least."

"We've apprised your captain. He's agreed to hold off on arresting them until we see what shakes out with the investigation. Soon as we know there's no connection, they can move in."

"What about the Nakamoto murder?"

"Thought you had someone in custody."

"I think he was framed."

"That's one for your PD to handle. We have to stay focused on the unsub who's disappearing people. Let me fill you in on the latest so far." The bones found in the cave had yielded their DNA to the grindstone of the FBI's portable lab. Two of the skeletons had been identified through a national missing persons database, and the hand bones in the wall cache belonged to five different unknown donors.

"Unsub?" Lei wasn't familiar with the term.

"Unknown subject."

"Ah. Feds and their lingo."

"Separates the women from the girls."

"Five victims?" Lei shook her head, sipping a second cup of coffee too fast and burning her tongue. "Wow."

"Yeah. The lab is working on those, but it's not a quick process. Becky's been a big help."

"She's good at what she does. Anything else about the bones?"

"The bodies were cut up and each of the pieces burned—but not totally, just the meat burned off. I don't know why the unsub did it that way. He could have eliminated the bones entirely, burnt them to dust so they'd be gone as evidence. Anyway, it's probably part of his pathology—MO to you police types."

"Gotcha. I'm going out to pick up the list of heiau sites from Esther Ka'awai this morning. Stevens needs it to organize the Hanalei Valley cadaver search. I'm not looking forward to it. She was pretty fired up about me arresting her grandson."

"Hey, tough luck on that," Marcella said. Her concern sounded genuine. "I heard you guys were dating."

"Unfortunately, I fell for his charm. Shoulda known better."

"Hey, listen, want some company on the ride out? I wouldn't mind getting eyes on this Esther lady."

Lei hesitated. There was an element of her relationship with Esther that went beyond the case, and in spite of what had happened with Alika, Lei hoped something of that could be salvaged. On the other hand, she welcomed a distraction, a chance to get to know Marcella better.

"Sounds good. Meet me at the Bubba Burger in Hanalei town."

MARCELLA SCOTT SAT beside Lei as she drove the winding two-lane road toward fertile Wainiha Valley where Esther lived. The agent wore a pair of cutoff jeans and a tie-died T-shirt with a marijuana leaf on it. Dream catcher earrings dangled from her ears. Lei wore her shorts and crochet top with a man's shirt.

"Gotta get into the thrift store and pick up some more hippie clothes," Lei said. "These are pretty stinky."

"Yeah. I need some variety, too, for the Health Guardian."

"I think Jazz is the key somehow, but I don't know what the connection is. He seems so sincere in wanting to solve the case." Lei tapped her finger on the steering wheel.

"I've seen that a lot, actually," Marcella said. "The guy who discovers the bomb is the one who set it. The dude who rescues the kid is really the kidnapper. Don't be fooled by his concern last night—he didn't exactly step up to rescue us."

"I know. What I'm really worried about is that...today's Halloween. If the perp is going to do Jay—if he's even still alive—it's going to be today."

"We don't know there's a connection between Halloween—or Samhain—and the disappearances. We have no solid connection there, nothing hard."

"I know, but I can't shake this feeling that time's running out. Jay's family is in town. Kelly, the girlfriend, brought some posters by the Guardian. I feel so bad for her."

"You get used to that feeling. You guys have some undercurrents in this community, that's for sure. Kaua`i looks like such a paradise, but scratch the surface..."

"And you'll find the craziness of any small town." Lei grinned. "Actually, more craziness than most."

"Yeah—no kidding. Kaua`i has a lot of diversity—we've been

working up an area profile on this island, and the fact is that you have almost as many cultures and religions represented per square mile as New York City."

"And throw in isolation, jungle, and economic challenges and sometimes it's a volatile brew."

They bumped up the last bit of road to Esther's pole house. The dogs swarmed the truck, barking as before, and Esther appeared on the upper deck. She called the dogs as Lei and Marcella got out. She watched in regal silence as they negotiated the muddy driveway and rain-soaked stairs. Lei had brought a bag of lychee from the Health Guardian. She held it out to Esther.

"I brought you something."

The older lady took it, peeked inside at the knobbly red fruit. She looked up and her brown eyes softened.

"I love lychee. Who's your friend?"

Lei breathed a tiny sigh of relief. Esther was going to forgive her.

"This is Marcella Scott, FBI."

"Pleased to meet you," Marcella said.

"Welcome." Esther gestured to the open slider. "Come in."

The women slipped their shoes off and followed Esther into the living room. She gestured to the couch. They sat.

"Alika wanted to talk to you, but I told him there was no point. You aren't going to listen to him."

"I can't, Esther, at least until this investigation is over. I just don't have anything to say to him."

"Well." Esther arranged the long, graceful skirt of her flowered muumuu over her knees, and calloused bare feet peeked from beneath the hem. "Never mind that. Here is a list of the heiaus and sacred sites between Hanalei Valley and the end of the road at Ke'e Beach." She handed over a sheet of yellow legal paper. "I also put them on this map as best I could." She handed a folded map of Kaua'i to Marcella. "Show respect. Don't move any rocks."

It was going to be very difficult to look for bones and body parts without moving a few rocks, but there was no point in upsetting Esther about it.

"We'll do our best," Lei said. "Thanks so much for being our consultant and for all your advice. I appreciate all you've done."

"Come visit me sometime on your day off. And I have a final word for you. He's close. Very close. He may know he's being hunted." Esther's wide brow knit, and she gave her head a slight shake, as if trying to hear something just out of range.

"How do you know?" Lei asked. Marcella had gone still, alert as a hawk.

"I just know." Esther closed her eyes, opened them. "I wish I could tell you more."

CHAPTER THIRTY-FOUR

THE WOMEN WERE somber as they took their leave. Marcella unfolded the map and studied it as Lei drove them back to the safe house.

"How reliable is she?" Marcella asked.

"Very respected in the community. She's a spiritual leader and seems to be a bit psychic."

"Tested anything she's said?"

"We verified what she said about the stones and ti leaves with a University of Hawaii professor—it was accurate. She also said the perp has a cave where he cuts up the bodies, and there are four torches. No verification on that, obviously."

"Hm." Marcella turned on her cell phone and ordered an in-depth background workup on Esther and her family.

Lei bit her tongue. Alika's involvement with Lisa Nakamoto had opened the family up to this, not to mention Esther's feedback on the killer.

"So we've finished our background on Jazz," Marcella went on after closing her phone. "Not only does he lack the physical strength to be the killer; he keeps a schedule that would make it almost impossible. He's up at seven a.m. and at that store virtually twelve hours a day."

"I know. I was poking around in his office being his 'assistant' this week and didn't find anything interesting. But the fact remains, he put together that binder. He had the stones from the disappearance sites."

"I agree, but we're just not making anything stick to him directly. He seems to be what he claims, the Guardian of the hippie community who's trying to get some justice for the missing."

"I just wonder, why does he care so much?"

"If we knew that, we might be closer to solving the case."

They arrived at the safe house and Lei let Marcella out. As she opened the door, the agent turned back.

"Maybe we're going about this wrong. Maybe there's something going on with the meth angle, the cult, and Lisa Nakamoto's murder that intersects with this case. So what's happening with the Nakamoto murder and your friend Alika's charges?"

"Not sure. I better call and check on it. Now that we have the heiau sites, maybe the cadaver hunt will turn up something new," Lei said.

"I'll call Stevens and see where that's at. Have a good rest of the day." Marcella slammed the door. She was already on the phone again as she punched in the gate code.

Lei called Fury Furukawa as she drove home.

"Ginger. What's up?"

"I'm calling to see what's going on with Lisa Nakamoto's case."

"Checking on the boyfriend?"

"He's not my boyfriend." Lei gritted her teeth. "I just got some information from his grandmother, Esther Ka`awai, that's important to the missing persons case. I want to see what's happening, make sure we can keep her happy."

"A'right then." He seemed to relent. "It seems Alika's development company has been in financial trouble for a while. He's cashed the insurance checks from the robberies but hasn't replaced what's missing, so fraud looks like a possibility. We interviewed him again with his lawyer present, but he's sticking to his story that he knew Lisa in the biblical sense but didn't kill her and is being framed. Hines is looking like the guy."

"Oh yeah?"

"Guy's gone into full withdrawals. A total tweaker. We've had to book him into the locked psych unit to keep him from killing himself. He's been rambling that he shot Lisa because she was going to blow the whistle on his operation, but none of it's admissible because he's been declared incompetent or some shit by the psychiatrist at the unit." Fury sounded disgusted. "We have to wait for him to get clean enough for a real interview."

"So the murder charges against Alika are falling apart."

"It's looking like that, yeah. The medical examiner came up with a better estimate on time of death, and he's got an alibi for that."

"So is the prosecutor going to drop the charges?"

"Eventually. We're letting him sweat a little, see if anything else breaks."

"Sounds like a plan," Lei said with false enthusiasm.

Alika was innocent. She should have felt better, but somehow she didn't. What if he'd set her up somehow?

"So, remember that tent and stuff he set up on the mesa? We had a pilot fly us up there to pack up the site and look for any more evidence, and we found some interesting trace."

"What do you mean?"

"Evidence of a horse being used for transportation up there. Hoofprints, piles of green crap, you know. We looked around and found some footprints. Bigger than either yours or Alika's. Looks like someone was spying on you guys. There was a broken branch and shoe prints right below the tent in the underbrush."

"Shit," Lei said, an involuntary shiver passing over her. She turned on the truck's heater. "Anything else?"

"You know that crag at the end of the mesa? It's the site of one of the most sacred heiaus on the island. Stevens is going back with techs and the FBI lab guys because it looks like there was human activity not long ago. A fire pit, recent smoke damage on the rocks. Efforts were made to clean it up, but I think someone's been using that heiau. Could be our Cult Killer."

"Who came up with that tag?" Lei asked.

"Don't know, but someone's leaked it to the press and it's all over the place. Where you been?"

"Undercover." Cult Killer—the moniker was horribly catchy. She remembered that lonely finger of stone rising into the sky on the mesa. She had to get up there and check it out. "When're you guys doing that search?"

"We're all supposed to be doing the cadaver search in Hanalei Valley tomorrow, but Stevens and I are trying to get it postponed until we can check this out. Problem is transportation. The captain is worried about the budget and wants the FBI to pay for the helicopters, so we're waiting on their go-ahead."

"If someone's getting up there on horseback, it must be accessible on foot."

"Like I said, the cap wants the Feds to take the lead. Call Agent Scott; she'll know what the story is."

"I just dropped her off. She didn't say anything."

"Doesn't mean she doesn't know anything."

"Shit."

"You been saying that a lot, Ginger. Take it easy. We'll call you when something pops."

"Thanks, Fury. Hang loose." She closed the phone, dropping it on the seat beside her. Fury had decided to be civil, but now Marcella was holding out on her. The agent had taken her information and planned a trip to the mesa without her. The tiny bud of their friendship withered and died on the spot—a feeling like nausea. Following that, a wave of rage.

A junction in the road appeared and Lei whipped a U-turn and headed back to the safe house, turning on the siren and lights. The discordant wail of the siren put noise to what she was feeling. She pulled up and pounded on the door of the safe house. No answer. She called Marcella's cell phone. It went to voice mail.

"Agent Scott, you used me," she said to the empty void of recording. "You just wanted the map with the heiau sites. That was my lead, and I want in on it."

There was still plenty of light, and she knew the source of the intel—Esther. She strode back out to the truck and roared back toward Wainiha. If there was a way on foot to that heiau, Esther would know it. She speed-dialed Jenkins as she roared down the narrow road, leaving a message on yet another voice mail.

"J-Boy—drop whatever you're doing. I need backup. Come meet me at Esther's in Wainiha."

A faded blue Ford truck was parked in Esther's driveway. She parked next to it and jumped out. The dogs backed away as she ran up the stairs to the deck and rapped on the glass slider. She peered in. No one visible. She slid it open, stuck her head in.

"Hello? Esther?"

No answer from the back of the house. She was probably down in her teaching room with whoever was visiting. She padded barefoot across the living room and down the stairs to Esther's inner sanctum. She called again, "Esther?"

The tapa-covered door was closed. She knocked, called louder, "Esther!"

"Come in," came the muffled reply.

CHAPTER THIRTY-FIVE

LEI PUSHED THE DOOR OPEN. Esther was sitting cross-legged on her pillow with her ipu, and seated at her feet was Mac Williamson.

"Oh, hello Mac," Lei said. "I didn't know you knew each other."

"Mac's training. I told you he's my haumana," Esther said. "We were just doing a chant."

Mac held up his ipu, a decorative gourd used for percussion. "Had to grow it, harvest it, dry it, and carve it," he said, indicating the patterns on the surface of the hardened gourd.

"Nice," Lei said. "Listen, I'm sorry to interrupt, but I need that information you gave me and Marcella again. It's important."

Esther set her instrument aside. "What's happened?"

"I can't tell you except that Marcella took the information. She's gone, and I want to check something out at one of the sites."

"Which one?" Mac asked, penetrating brown eyes intent.

"The spire above the mesa."

"I know that site well. There's a trail to it from the back of my land."

"Really? How do you know it?"

"My training." He gestured to Esther, who inclined her head.

"Can you show it to me?" A hasty plan was forming in Lei's mind. Maybe she could join the investigation from below by scouting out the access to the mesa.

"Of course." He uncoiled himself from the floor, and she was struck by the height and power of his frame. She backed up into the doorway.

"Let me make a quick call; then we'll go. Thanks, Esther, and I'm sorry for barging in." She backed away and hotfooted it up the stairs and across the house. She'd left her weapon and cell phone in the glove box of the truck.

She'd gotten sloppy.

She jumped into the cab and locked the doors. No one appeared on the deck.

What if Mac was the guy? He seemed big and strong enough. He lived alone, with access to the heiau and training in ancient Hawaiian rituals. Still, he just didn't feel threatening to her—she'd always felt safe with him.

Her head was saying one thing, her gut another. She took her cell out and dialed Stevens. She left a message.

"Going to the heiau on the mesa with Mac Williamson. He says the trail to the mesa starts on his land. Going to check it out. And I want to talk to you about…"

I love you. I'm sorry I ever looked at anyone else.

The adrenaline of the moment seemed to bring the realization into crystal-clear focus. She'd tried so hard to deny what was right in front of her.

"Stupid melodrama," she said aloud. At least he would know where she'd gone if something happened.

A tap at her window. She looked up and saw Mac, his carved wooden staff in his hand.

"One minute," she said through the closed window. He got into the blue truck, waiting. She pulled her shoulder holster out of the glove box and shrugged into it, putting the man's shirt back on over it. For once she missed the heaviness of her duty belt, with every possible weapon.

Her cell rang.

"J-boy." Finally a live voice! "Where is everybody? No one's picking up their phones."

"The Feds took two helicopters up to the mesa to check out the heiau site up there. I think Stevens and Fury got to go, and there's no phone reception. I'm on my way to meet you." She could hear the scream of the siren in the Subaru. "What's going on?"

"I'm going up to the mesa from a trail below. Can you join me at Mac Williamson's house? He says there's a trail to the mesa from the back of his estate. I want to take a hike from below and meet them up there."

"Why? Can't stand to have something go down without you?"

"Exactly. Apparently there's a horse trail from below. Maybe there's something there the team will want to see."

"Sweets, I'll be there—with bells on." He gave an extra blast of his horn for emphasis. "See you in a few."

Thank God for Jenkins's loyalty and enthusiasm. Lei closed the phone and turned it to vibrate, stuffing it into her overburdened pocket. She rolled her window down.

"I'll follow you," she called to Mac.

He nodded and fired up the Ford.

THE TIMEKEEPER HAD DONNED the tapa malo loincloth and set kukui nut oil torches in the four corners of the central area of the cave. The Chosen hunched in his sleeping bag.

"You're going to kill me." His voice was raspy, and the isolation, fear, and darkness had done their work, because there was also a note of hopelessness in it. The Timekeeper lifted his gnarled, carved kiawe staff and approached the Chosen.

He swung the club at the man's head, and that's when Jay Bennett surged up out of the sleeping bag, dodging out of the way.

The Timekeeper swung again, and this time Jay caught the staff in both hands. Using his forward momentum, the Timekeeper used Jay's leverage, pushing against the staff as he did a sweeping kick, and knocked the man's legs out from under him.

Jay went down hard, his naked body smacking against the stone floor and head snapping back against the rock.

He didn't get up.

The Timekeeper laid out the unconscious body on a plastic tarp, spreading the arms and legs wide according to the rules the ancient Voices had passed down to him. He tenderly removed the collar and washed the Chosen in kukui nut oil, wiping away the excess with a tapa cloth square.

The man who had once been Jay Bennett gleamed in the flickering light, a golden statue, perfect and unblemished. Tumbled yellow hair framed a face like a fallen Nordic god, and in his beauty he seemed eternal to the Timekeeper, the plastic beneath him glimmering like water.

He began to chant, sharpening the knives on the whetstone: a cleaver, scalpel-thin fillet knife, and a handheld meat saw. The rasp of the whetstone punctuated the rhythms of the timeless song.

CHAPTER THIRTY-SIX

LEI WAS IMPRESSED by the beauty and size of the estate as she followed the Ford up a long winding driveway. The spread was nestled between two rain-sculpted mountains with the mesa in the background, a further range of jungled peaks beyond. Blooming oleander hedges bordered a rolling lawn with the gracious main house set like a wedding cake in the center.

"Lotta mowing," she said as she got out of her truck in the gravel turnaround. She was glad she'd put her athletic shoes on that morning.

"Cal does it," Mac said, taking a water bottle out of his truck. "I couldn't keep up a place this size without him. 'Course, I do a lot too. Keeps me in shape."

"I'd love to get the tour sometime, but I'm eager to make it up to the mesa and back before dark."

"Not a problem, though I'm not sure what you're in such a hurry for."

A partial truth was in order.

"Remember Alika? He took me up there on a date, and that's where I found some evidence linking him to a murder. I want to get back up there, see if there's anything else."

"I heard Alika was arrested. Shooting some girl seems out of character."

"I think so too. I'd like to clear his name," Lei improvised.

"He's my brother, you know."

"What?" Lei took a bottle of water out of the truck. She locked it, turning to face Mac, eyes wide. "You're kidding, right?"

"Half brother, I should say. We have the same father."

"So your dad was the guy who wouldn't do right by Alika's mom," Lei said. She patted her cargo pockets to make sure she had her phone, keys, and, of course, the Glock. The shoulder rig already rubbed her bare side.

The band of tension across her chest loosened as Jenkins's Subaru tore up the driveway, light spinning.

"He was already married, thank you very much." Mac seemed indifferent to the approaching vehicle, intent on his story. "When Lehua showed up here pregnant, you can imagine my mother wasn't very happy. She was pregnant with me at the time."

"So did you spend time together growing up?"

"Little as possible. Doesn't mean I want to see him charged with murder."

"I wonder why Alika never told me you were related."

"He has a chip on his shoulder. Even though he's done well for himself, he didn't get all this." Mac gestured to encompass the sweep of the estate.

Jenkins trotted up. He was in chinos and a polo shirt, sweat already marking rings under his arms. "Where's the trailhead? Damn, they're going to be surprised to see us come up from below."

"Mac, this is my partner Jack Jenkins. I guess this is as good a time as any to tell you I'm a cop. I've been working undercover." Lei took her badge out of her pocket and showed it to him.

"I guessed. When you were with that other woman at the papaya farm." He seemed unfazed by her revelation. "Is this hike part of your investigation?"

"Maybe. I think we should be looking for anywhere that…" Lei paused awkwardly. The urgency she'd felt all day, with it being October 31—Samhain—seemed to thrum along her nerves. "Let's go."

They set off across the rolling lawn at a fast clip and passed the last oleander hedge, planted in an overlap so the gap was hidden. A barn and corral were on her left, and she smelled the warm scent of horses.

"We could ride, but I don't think you're dressed for it. You ride?" Mac asked.

"No, and today's not good for my first lesson," Lei said, remembering Fury'd said there was a horse on the mesa. She looked at Mac's feet—they weren't small. Her gut clenched as she wondered what his shoe size was. She dropped behind him a few more feet and signaled Jenkins to keep an eye on Mac. They both loosened their weapons for easy access.

They hurried past the barn to where the trail began in earnest, and soon their conversation was limited to huffing and puffing as it ascended steeply, winding around boulders and trees, switching back every now and again as if to spare them the grade for a few minutes.

Lei's gun rubbed and straps chafed. She finally took the rig off and put it back on outside the shirt, buckling it as they walked.

"Don't know why you need to bring that thing." Mac stopped, leaning against a kukui tree and wiping his forehead with his forearm. "Nothing out here but a few wild pigs."

"Detectives always carry a sidearm," Lei said, snugging up the strap but keeping the snap off the holster. "Nothing personal."

Mac's shoulders relaxed a little as he turned back to the trail. Jenkins raised his brows.

Lei felt the pump of adrenaline waning. It was hard to stay keyed up with afternoon sun beating on her head and birds singing. Mac still carried the carved hardwood staff, using it as a walking stick.

"Nice staff," she said at a level spot in the trail. "What are the carvings?"

"They're petroglyphs. It's actually a narrative of my life. I'll explain it to you sometime."

"I'd like that," she said. The niggling doubt came back—could Mac be the guy? The victims had been hit on the head with something, and it could well have been a wooden staff.

They reached a stream that bisected the path, and Mac jumped from rock to rock, crossing to the other side. Lei looked up the stream to the series of waterfalls that flowed into it. One of the cliffs was bisected by a dark cleft. She remembered Esther's psychic moment a few weeks ago.

"Are there any big caves around here?"

"I don't know about big. Farther up we cross again, and not far from there is one big enough to sleep in."

"I'd like to check it out," Lei said, digging her nails into the pad of her thumb to keep her excitement under control. She picked her way across the stream, Jenkins splashing and cursing behind her.

"Guess we can take a side trip there if you want, but I thought you were in a hurry to get to the mesa."

"No, I'd like to check out the cave," Lei said. "Seems like we have plenty of light for both." Behind Mac's back, Jenkins nodded eagerly.

Mac set off again, and another half mile or so higher, the trail crossed the stream again. A faint path, little more than a goat trail, forked and followed the water upstream, almost obscured by ferns.

They turned onto the side trail and soon reached a cliff. A slit-like, almost invisible opening marked the cave. Mac gestured to the rocky edifice, a trickle of water bouncing down from above, tender maidenhair ferns trembling in its path.

"This is why we have to switch back and forth so much that last mile or so to the mesa. Too many waterfalls."

Lei stood at the edge of the clearing in front of the cave

entrance, assessing. The grass was trampled but recovering. A blackened fire ring marked the center, piles of old horse dung around the area. Robust, pale green kukui nut trees encircled the open space. The stream burbled nearby.

"Someone camped here."

"Yeah. Cal likes to come here, be alone with nature." Mac wiped his forehead with his arm. "You wouldn't happen to have a flashlight?"

"So just the two of you at the estate?" Lei found herself hesitant to approach the cave. The hairs on the back of her neck had begun to quiver, never a good sign. She reached over to touch her weapon, and as she glanced back she saw Jenkins do the same.

"Yeah."

Mac led them forward into the dim space of the cave, a rocky passage that obscured what lay ahead. The smell hit first—musty but sweetish, with a ripeness that clung to the back of the throat.

"Stinks," Mac said. He'd gone farther forward. "Phew."

Lei's eyes had begun to adjust. She thought she saw a reddish gleam of light.

She moved along slowly against the wall. If anyone was going to jump her, this was a great place to do it. The smell, like an animal's lair, made the hair rise all over her body. She kept her hand on the Glock.

"I think we should come back with flashlights." As she stepped around an outcrop, she could see the light of flickering torches in the main cavern. She pulled her gun and heard the snick of Jenkins taking out his weapon behind her.

The stone-floored cave opened into a spacious main cavern. The roof was at least ten feet high, stippled with the pitting of cooling lava that had formed the bubble of space. The floor of the cavern was swept clean but patchy with wetness that had dripped from above. The torches' flame barely held back dense shadows just outside a circle of wavering light.

Reddish torchlight flickered over a long backlit shape hanging in the center of the space. There was something odd about the shape—until Lei's brain finally told her it was a man's body, upside down. His ankles had been lashed with rope and threaded through a hook in the ceiling. A black plastic tarp beneath the figure shone like water in the flickering light.

Mac, ahead of them, gave a cry. "Oh my God!" He ran forward, grabbing the body, hoisting it up. "Help me!"

Lei put her hand back against Jenkins's chest, holding him against the wall. "Is he alive?"

"I don't know! Let's get him down!"

"Whoever put him there might still be here." Lei and Jenkins approached, crouched and scanning. The edges of the room were impenetrably black as they sidled their way to the body, back to back.

"I'll cover you," Lei said, and Jenkins holstered his weapon and seized the lower half of the body, raising the head to waist level. The face was dark with congestion, eyes closed, and mouth duct taped. His hands were bound. Even with dark, engorged features, Lei recognized the distorted face.

"Jay Bennett. This is my missing guy," Lei said.

"He's got rope around his ankles. Lei, can you get my knife? It's on my belt," Jenkins huffed. "This guy is heavy."

One last glance around the cavern, and Lei holstered her weapon, unclipping Jenkins's belt loop and pulling out a wicked-looking combat knife. She reached as high as she could but couldn't touch the looped rope around the man's ankles. "Mac, you try; you're tallest."

She traded places, lifting Jay's inert, slippery body around the waist while Jenkins held up the man's head and shoulders. The body's smell was consistent with being held captive in a cave for a couple of weeks, and Lei took shallow breaths through her mouth, noticing the sheen on Jay's skin, the tang of kukui nut oil.

Mac reached up, sawing at the rope.

Lei barely had time to register movement out of the corner of her eye before Mac hurtled into her with a cry, knocking her into Jenkins. They both lost grip on the slick body, falling to the ground, and Lei heard the clatter of her pistol flying out of the holster. She scrambled onto her hands and knees, crawling backward, trying to see, even as she felt on the ground for the weapon.

CHAPTER THIRTY-SEVEN

A TALL, dark shape, backlit by the torch, swung a staff in a hypnotic arc. Mac was down—still—but Jay Bennett's body swung back and forth, gently spinning.

"Chalcedony. I don't like being called Cal anymore." Voice a light tenor and oddly conversational. "I told you that, Mac."

"Chalcedony. And his brother, Jazz—for jasper." Lei whispered the names of stones found at the disappearance sites. She'd met Jazz's brother in the Health Guardian, and he'd told them who he was every time he took a victim. She inched backward, still feeling for the gun, as Jenkins stood up beside her, his voice booming in the cave.

"Drop your weapon! Police!"

The staff swung, and Lei heard the crack as it connected with Jenkins's weapon, the grunt of pain he gave as it was knocked out of his fingers. Cal followed it, moving in on Jenkins. He stalked forward, the club whirling, just a blur in the dim light—the man obviously had some martial arts training.

Lei's fingers connected with the Glock and she brought it up.

She couldn't see what was happening enough to take a shot—she might hit Jenkins. She heard muffled thuds and grunts as she stood, backed toward the cave opening—she needed the light behind her.

The end of Cal's staff caught Jenkins in the ribs, and she heard the punch of air leaving his lungs as he went down, saw the tumbled legs. As he turned her way, she saw that Cal's bare torso gleamed with kukui nut oil and he wore a tapa-cloth malo.

They must have interrupted his sacrificial ceremony.

"Drop your weapon! Police!" She didn't recognize the scream as her own.

She could see his eyes now, and they were ringed with white. He moved forward, the staff in a ready position at chest height. Light gilded bare, muscled arms as he emerged like a nightmare from the dark.

She pulled the trigger. The report smacked her ears in the confined opening of the cave, deafening her. She'd hit him in the shoulder, and he reeled back but kept coming.

"You think you can stop me. No one can."

She felt more than heard the words, vibrating between them, as he took another step.

She shot him again, this time in the chest. He dropped the club, covering the wound, but kept coming, one hand reaching for her. Those white-ringed eyes filled the horizon, their expanded pupils darkening her vision.

He was almost on her.

She shot him one more time.

He plummeted like a felled tree, landing on her—a weight like a blow. She jumped back with a cry, resisting the urge to empty the clip into him as he hit the ground at her feet. She sucked a breath, holding the gun on him.

He was finally done moving.

She holstered the weapon and ran over to Jenkins. He had a fine red bubble on his lips. It looked black in the dim light.

"Think my ribs are stove in," he said. More blood. More bubbles.

"Just relax. I'm calling for help," she said, thumbing open her phone. No reception. She ran outside the cave. The light hit like a blow. She dialed Stevens because her finger knew that key on the pad—and the helicopter on the mesa was their best way down.

"Lei, we're in the middle of something." Stevens sounded annoyed.

"Send the copter down—J-Boy's injured. Emergency." Adrenaline jittered her voice.

"You're not making sense. Calm down."

"Where are you?" Icy tone, Marcella's voice. The agent must have grabbed the phone. "We heard you were coming up on the trail."

"I shot the suspect—the unsub. He's dead, but Jenkins's injured —badly. Our guide's down too. Jay Bennett's in here, strung up. Don't know if he's alive. Fly down here. We need medical assistance!"

"Texeira, you've got a lot of explaining to do." Lei could hear the accelerating whine of rotors through the phone.

"And I'll do it. Just get here as soon as you can—I think Jay's lung is pierced."

"Repeat, where are you? Need a landmark." Good, they were coming. She took a breath, getting control, and looked around.

"We're about two-thirds of the way to the top. Small clearing by a cliff. I'll be signaling."

"Roger that."

Lei ran back into the cave and knelt beside Jenkins.

"Help's on the way." His breathing was like a kettle on the boil. "I'm going to elevate your feet." She put a rock under them.

"Cold," he muttered.

"You're in shock. Try to relax. They're coming in a helicopter, but I have to go outside to signal. Okay?"

He nodded and closed his eyes, pale as a mushroom. Mac was up, and he was sawing at the rope around Jay's feet. She ran forward and lifted Jay's head and shoulders just in time before his feet hit the plastic tarp. She didn't want to think about what that tarp was there for.

"You okay? Where'd he hit you?" Lei asked.

Mac sawed at the duct tape on the young man's arms.

"Head. Glancing blow or I wouldn't be here anymore. Cal's always been good with his staff."

Lei ripped the duct tape off Jay's mouth, set her ear against his oiled chest. "Still got a heartbeat. Can you get his breathing going? I've got to go signal the helicopter."

"I'll try." Mac tipped Jay's head and blew into his mouth as Lei ran back outside, tearing off the holster and man's shirt. She waved the shirt in the center of the clearing, hearing the percussion of the chopper. Her phone rang and she answered it, still waving.

"Lei, we can't find you." Stevens.

"I can hear you. Down and to the right."

Already her arm ached from waving.

"We see you." Stevens's voice in her ear was a lifeline.

"I love you," she blurted as the helicopter descended.

"Adrenaline talking. We're almost there."

The copter landed, the roar of the rotors overwhelming. Prop wash stung her eyes with a million flying particles. She withdrew into the cave opening.

The copter doors flew back. Marcella was the first out, running to her, hunched beneath the whirling blades. Her eyes widened.

"You hit?"

Lei looked down. Blood splattered her arms and torso. She could only imagine her face.

"The other guy." She pointed to the face-down corpse inside the cave entrance. "Jenkins's inside. He's bad off—I think a broken rib pierced his lung—and Bennett's barely alive."

Marcella, Rogers, and the pilot moved past her. Stevens ran toward her, and she felt her knees wobble for the first time. He folded her in against him, blood and all.

"You hurt?"

"Not my blood," she said into his shirt.

"You did good. You always do good."

"I love you," she mumbled against his shirt. "I really, really do."

"Adrenaline talking," he said again, but he squeezed her so hard her bones creaked.

Marcella reappeared. "Looks like you're right about the rib. He's unconscious. We have to try to keep him as still as possible. But Bennett seems to be coming around."

The whine of another helicopter filled the air; they looked up, but there was nowhere for it to land. Marcella waved it off, talking into her cell phone.

They loaded Jenkins and Bennett into the helicopter, stabilizing them as best they could.

"Who's the dead guy?" Marcella turned to Lei, cell phone still against her ear.

"Cal Haddock. Real name Chalcedony," Lei said. "Brother of Jazz Haddock." Marcella's eyes widened.

"What the hell," she said. "Goddamn it—right there in front of us. Bet Jazz is short for Jasper. Gimme a thumbnail sketch of what happened, so Rogers and I have something to go on."

Lei did so while Marcella unloaded a black crime scene kit out of the copter. She and Rogers snapped on gloves as the pilot warmed up the engine. Marcella opened an evidence bag.

"Weapon in here." Lei took the Glock out of her waistband and dropped it in the bag. Marcella sealed it and put it in the kit. "You'll get it back as soon as we check it for ballistics. You, Mac, and Stevens take Bennett and Jenkins to the hospital. We're securing the scene."

CHAPTER THIRTY-EIGHT

LEI STOOD against the gray backdrop in the interview room, one wall of which was lined with light-absorbent felt. Becky's face was expressionless as she photographed the blood patterns that decorated Lei—front, back, side view, front of arms, back of arms. Lei felt herself sway as the flash burned her eyes.

She closed them, and immediately saw the purple face of barely alive Jay Bennett and Jenkins coughing blood. She opened her eyes and the flash seared them again.

At least it looked like they were both going to live. "Almost done," Becky said. "You can sit now."

Lei sat. Becky got out her evidence collection kit, using sticky pads to collect gunshot residue from her hands and swabs to swipe beneath her nails, take samples of the blood on her face and arms, and a small comb to collect any further trace out of her hair.

"Not much here," Becky said, gently tugging the comb through the short curls on Lei's head. Her mouth was near Lei's ear as she whispered, "I'm sorry. I'm almost done."

"It's okay. You gotta do what you gotta do."

"Now for the clothes. Please remove your outer garments and put them in here." Becky pushed a large paper evidence bag over to Lei. Hoping the surveillance camera was off, Lei shimmied out of the cargo shorts and put them in the bag along with the contents of her pockets and her Ni`ihau shell necklace.

"My top's got trace on it, but I need a shirt," Lei said.

"You get mine." Becky handed her a bright pink tee emblazoned with Mickey Mouse and a pair of sweatpants. "It's either these or prison orange."

"Mickey Mouse it is." Lei took off the crochet bikini top and whipped the T-shirt on as fast as she could. "Thanks."

"Camera's not on, and I have the blinds rotated." Becky read her mind. "Captain said to do everything by the book since this is the FBI's investigation, so I have to leave you in here until one of them gets here to take your statement. Can I bring you anything?"

"Seriously, I could eat my arm I'm so hungry. Can I get food, something to drink?"

"Way ahead of you." Stevens came through the door with a bag from Burger King. The smell of fries, familiar and thick, made Lei light-headed with hunger, and she reached for the bag, stopping when she saw Becky's wide eyes and squinched-up lips. The lab tech handed her a pile of antibacterial wipes from the dispenser by the door.

"You never know where that blood has been," Becky said.

"Oh my God, you're so right." Lei took the wipes and scrubbed her face, neck, and arms, the chill welcome. Becky collected the samples and evidence bags, putting everything on a steel tray.

"See you guys later."

"Bye," Stevens said. He sat next to Lei, opening the Burger King bag as she rubbed her hands with the wipes. Lei noticed the wistful way Becky looked back at him as she closed the door, but Stevens didn't.

Lei bit into her Whopper, closing her eyes in bliss.

"I love you," she said when she could speak. "Now I know I do." She sucked half her root beer down in one long draft.

"Starvation talking," Stevens said, addressing his burger. His dark brows were drawn down. He didn't look at her.

"Becky said the camera's off," Lei said, finishing the last of her meal. It hadn't taken long.

"Oh yeah?" He got up and came back with several more of the wipes. She closed her eyes as he rubbed her face gently, straddling the bench as she sat. He held them up. "You're still a little scary."

A brownish smear of blood marked the wipe and he tossed it into the trash. "You were saying?"

"I love you. And the camera's off."

She moved in on him, sliding her hands up his arms to encircle his neck, pulling him down to her. His lips, when they touched hers, were hesitant, and she teased at them, light kisses until he let his arms come down, wrapping her close, and this time she wasn't sure who was consuming whom and didn't care anymore.

He pushed her back gently, his hands still caressing her arms, hips, wherever he could touch.

"What's all this? Posttraumatic stress? The urge to merge after a near-death experience?"

"That's rude," she said with dignity. "Okay, maybe a little of that, but I left you a message that—um. I realized I loved you."

"That bit about melodrama? I was supposed to get 'I realized I love you' from that?"

"Maybe not." She picked at one of the peeling hippie tats on her wrist. "I'm not good at this part."

"I know." He sighed. "C'mere."

She was wound around him and sitting in his lap when the door opened.

"Sorry to interrupt." Bob Arizumi, Flea's older brother and Lei's union attorney, entered, horn-rims askew. "I hope you didn't tell them anything at the site."

Stevens stayed composed as Lei stood up and straightened the Mickey Mouse tee.

"Just a thumbnail sketch so they could reconstruct the scene."

"You shouldn't have said anything. Let the evidence speak. It always tells a clearer story than the witness."

"I had to tell them something."

"That's why the captain called me. Whenever there's a shooting, you shouldn't say anything to anyone without a representative present."

The door opened again, FBI this time. "How're you holding up? Okay for a few questions?" Marcella asked. She'd had time to clean up from the site and looked beautiful and composed, every smooth, glossy hair in place.

"Ready when you are." Lei kept her voice steady. She felt neither beautiful nor composed.

"My client is just going to make a brief statement. She hasn't even been able to take a shower," Bob said. His intimidation stare didn't appear to be working. Maybe it was the horn-rims. Marcella ignored him, opening the door for another gray-suited agent.

"This is Special Agent LaSota. She's a profiler with the Behavioral Analysis Unit." Lei shook the new agent's hand. The psychologist had a soft grip and hard, dark-olive eyes.

"Detective Stevens, you can watch from the peanut gallery with Captain Fernandez if you wish."

Stevens gave Lei a final kiss, a stamp of intent, and let himself out.

The "brief statement" turned into a long interview. Lei felt completely wrung out when they were done, folding their notebooks, video camera, and tape recorder into Dr. LaSota's square briefcase. Arizumi followed them out, demanding to be kept informed of developments.

The captain entered. Lei had her head down on folded arms by then.

"Lei, you're on administrative leave pending the results of the investigation. I need your badge."

"I gave it to Becky with everything else." Lei blinked gritty eyes. She wasn't crying. She was tired.

"Just a technicality—you know it's procedure. You earned a few days off," Captain Fernandez said, giving her a comforting pat. "You did good."

"I'll take her home," said Stevens, meeting them in the hall. "She's been telling me she loves me all afternoon."

Lei hid her head in Stevens's shoulder as wolf whistles chased them out of the building.

CHAPTER THIRTY-NINE

MAKING love all night after killing a man did strange things to you.

Lei drove the truck toward Esther's house, trying to stay in her body. Her skin felt too thin, every tiny hair like antennae. She could almost hear the roar of blood through the chambers of her heart. Colors were too bright, and she was sensitive and sore in unexpected places.

She was headed out for mandatory post-shooting counseling, and the captain had cleared Esther as a native Hawaiian healer in lieu of traditional therapy. Starting with a new counselor had seemed impossible after all that had gone down, though the sharp-eyed psychologist Dr. LaSota had volunteered to do her debrief.

Lei wasn't that much of a sucker.

She tapped the steering wheel with the fingers of one hand, and even that motion vibrated through her whole body. Her eyes fell on her empty ring finger for the first time in a long time. Surely Stevens wouldn't wreck things by bringing up marriage again.

They'd both been called early that morning—her call had been Fury letting her know both Jenkins and Bennett were going to be okay and that the KPD had raided the papaya farm and busted everyone including Tiger. Stevens's call had been the FBI summoning him to organize a search of the valleys Chalcedony "Cal" Haddock frequented.

"Totally anticlimactic," Lei told Esther a half hour later in the teaching room. "I shoot the guy who did it, but I don't get to be around for any of the proving it. Stevens said he heard the evidence in the cave seemed to be supporting my story and it's looking like a good shoot, but it'll be at least a week until I'm cleared to be back on duty."

Esther sat facing Lei, her legs crossed under a long purple muumuu. She was weaving a lauhala basket, her brown fingers darting sparrows among the strips. Lei sorted the pile of dried material from the hala tree, using a paring knife to peel off the strip of thorns that lined either side of the long swordlike leaves.

"I think you stay in the right place, right now."

A thorn stabbed Lei, and she bit back a curse. "I don't think I'm the type to be good at this."

"You're a Hawaiian woman; you're the right kind," Esther said. "You never learned much about our culture. Shame, that."

"My aunty, she tried," Lei said. "I'm only part Hawaiian, but she told me the legends at bedtime. She taught me how to cook Hawaiian style. For all the good it did."

"Well, now you have a man. You can cook for him."

Lei ducked her head to hide the flame of her blush. Damn the woman. She could see right into her head. "I won't ask how you knew that."

"I'm sad it never worked out with Alika, but you already loved someone else."

"You could have saved me a lot of trouble and told me that back when I asked you about it." Lei ripped a long strip of thorns off with unnecessary force.

"You wouldn't have believed me then. And all I knew was that you had something to learn from each of them."

"I still don't know what that is."

"Think about it. Close your eyes and see each face and tell me."

Lei put the knife and the leaves down. Closed her eyes, breathed in the sweet, musty scent of the dried hala and the richness of coconut oil, and let her mind's eye wander to Alika's face —eyes alight with excitement to show her the helicopter. Golden with passion as he tugged her down beside him on that fateful carpet. She smiled at the same time as tears pricked.

"Alika taught me to take a few risks, enjoy life."

"They cleared him, you know," Esther said. Lei's eyes snapped open to see the kahu picking up a fresh strip of hala, working it into the section in her lap that was ending. "All charges dropped. Even the insurance thing. Only thing he was guilty of was giving Lisa Nakamoto a gold bracelet."

"I'm sorry. I misjudged him." Lei swallowed. "I hope you'll tell him."

"You tell him yourself."

"Ha. Okay. What other bombs you got for me? You way too well informed for a civilian."

"They still consulting with me, now that Alika is cleared. Captain Fernandez, he called me himself to tell me that drug dealer who killed Lisa finally got clean enough to talk. Darrell Hines, he was working with that hippie Tiger to make the meth. They got the cult people working the lab, then Darrell's people at Island Cleaning doing the selling."

"Yeah, Marcella and I saw it firsthand." Lei absorbed this. "That bitch Marcella—I actually liked her, but she just used me."

"Language! This the house of the Lord."

"Sorry. Okay. So why did they tell you all this?"

"Captain wanted my opinion on the cult. Had me talk to that guy Jazz Haddock yesterday, hear all about what the cult believes. Wanted to see how that might relate to the killer. I tol' the captain the cult was just the starting point for what that pupu`le crazy man did."

"Poor Jazz. I wonder how he's taking it that his brother is the Cult Killer."

"Not well, I think." Esther reached for another strip of lauhala and the spine of palm frond that formed the ribs of the basket. "His full name's Jasper. He one sad and tormented man. Especially with the way his sister and mother went make."

"Who died?"

"His little sister. Her name Opal. She died when she only twenty, the mother too. Their house burned down and they never made it out."

"Opal must be the third stone. Cal always left three stones at the place where he took a victim: a chalcedony, a jasper, and an opal." Lei mulled this over. "I think Jazz knew more than he let himself, or he couldn't have come up with the binder."

Lei focused on slitting the leaf she was working on into long strips. Having something useful to do with her hands felt good, keeping her grounded as she sorted through all this new information.

"Your Ni`ihau necklace is missing."

"I had to turn it in. It had trace on it." She wondered if the blood would come off the tiny precious shells. She couldn't wait to get the necklace back; she felt naked without it.

"Mac—he's going be one strong kumu someday—if he can forgive himself for having Cal on his land."

"I think so too. I better get going. I want to go visit Jenkins and Bennett in the hospital now that they're stable." Lei put away the prepared strips of basket material on the shelf against the tapa-covered wall. "Thank you for everything."

"I just doing what God called me to do."

LEI SAT NEXT TO JENKINS. He was awake, but his color was bad. He had an oxygen tank beside the bed and a cannula in his nose, but he was breathing on his own—something the doctor she'd met in the hall said was "very promising."

"How're you feeling?" she asked. He rolled his eyes. "Stupid question, sorry."

Lei rubbed the smooth black stone in her pocket—her hands had become sweaty almost the minute she got into the room. She still hated hospitals.

"I brought you something." She gestured to the bouquet of folded palm-frond roses Esther had made.

"Nice," he croaked. "Manly."

She snorted a laugh. "I didn't make them."

"No surprise."

"I know, right? Esther made them. She sends love."

He closed his eyes as if tired. "Tell me everything."

"Well, they must have interviewed you, right?"

He shook his head.

"Oh crap," Lei said, looking up to see Agent Marcella Scott with her new sidekick, Dr. LaSota, in the doorway. "The FBI's here now. I knew they'd be talking to you, but the timing sucks. I'll have to come back later."

His hand groped across the covers, found hers. "Stay."

"I'm sorry. Detective Texeira's part of the investigation and can't be privy to your interview," Marcella said. Lei had expected as much but still narrowed her eyes at the agent. Marcella was back in FBI gray, glossy curls tamed into a French twist. Only gold snakeskin sandals peeking out from under the slacks gave away her unique style.

"I'll go, but I'd like have a word with you, Agent Scott." Lei patted Jenkins's shoulder. "I'll be back."

She led Marcella out into the hall and turned to face the other woman, hands on her hips.

"You could have thrown me a bone the other day. Told me you were going to the mesa heiau at least. You took my intel and went to make my case without me."

"Who said it was your case? I seem to remember your captain calling in ViCAP to solve it. But if I'd known you would go off half-cocked like that, I'd have kept a much closer eye on you. As it is, you killed the guy. Now we have to go back and try to figure out why he was murdering people instead of just asking him."

"You should have kept me in the loop. We could have worked together and things might have ended differently."

"You're a loose cannon. I suspected as much; now I know beyond the shadow of a doubt." Brown eyes clashed with brown and neither blinked.

"Screw you and the white horse you rode in on."

"Right back atcha. You wouldn't be a bad investigator if you could be a team player."

Lei had no answer to this. Shooting Cal had ended the investigation but left a lot of unanswered questions—ten of them, to be exact. She sucked some relaxation breaths and got a grip on her temper.

"I should have tried harder to get through to someone."

"Damn straight."

"But if I had, Bennett would be dead. As it was, we barely got him down in time, and I don't even want to think about what Cal was going to do to him."

"That's not your responsibility. This was an FBI case, and we involved senior detectives from the local PD, which didn't include you. Keeping you in the dark was nothing personal, and it wasn't my call. I don't owe you shit."

Lei bit back the words—I liked you. I thought you could be a friend. She looked away.

Marcella seemed to read her mind. She tossed that lush, dark head, gave a little toe tap, and the dimple appeared for a second.

"But like I said, if I'd known you better, I'd never have left you out. You'd just come barreling back in, guns blazing." It was as close to an apology as Lei was going to get, and this time they both smiled.

"Okay then. What's it looking like with my shoot?"

"Can't say officially yet," Marcella said. "But it's looking like a good shoot. In fact, I've been talking to the Honolulu field office about you. We think you should apply for the Bureau. You'd be great as a field agent out here, being multiethnic and all."

Lei snorted a laugh in reply.

"Seriously. It's competitive, but I'll put in a good word for you."

"Weren't you just calling me a loose cannon? Saying I needed to learn to be a team player?"

"Well, you are and you do. But you've got good instincts, know how to take initiative, and you're a woman who'd shave her head to go undercover. I think you've got what it takes to be a Federal cop."

"I'm just getting used to being a detective. Just getting used to Kaua'i."

"Don't get too used to it," Marcella said with a wink. "I'll be in touch."

CHAPTER FORTY

LEI STUCK her head into Jay Bennett's room a few doors down. He was sitting up with Kelly wedged into bed beside him. His face looked much better without the plum-dark of congested blood.

"Hi."

"Detective!" Kelly pried herself up, her face flushed. "Oh my God! You did it. You saved Jay!" She ran around and embraced Lei in a welter of bouncing curls and abundant breasts. "I can't thank you enough."

The girl squeezed and wouldn't let go.

Lei found herself hugging her back, blinking hard. "I'm so glad it all worked out."

"You're telling me." Jay's voice sounded rusty. "I thought I was gone; then next thing I know, I'm on a helicopter."

Kelly detached at last, pulled up a chair beside the bed, gesturing to another.

Lei sat. "How are you feeling?"

"Alive. Glad to be."

Kelly grasped Jay's hand. "He was in there for almost two weeks. In the dark, tied up." Her eyes brimmed. "A nightmare."

"A nightmare—that's what it was. I'm just going to think of it that way." His blue eyes were sunken, skin pale and chapped, marked with red rash from the tape. Lei could see gouges around the neckline of the hospital gown where he'd tried to loosen the collar they'd found on the floor of the cave.

"One loose end I'm wondering about. The access code from the mansions was on the back of a Paradise Realty business card in your wallet. Were you involved with those robberies?" Lei gave him her best cop stare.

"No. The hippie group were trying to get me involved with the whole papaya farm meth thing, and wanted me to help with the robbery—several of them were on the Island Cleaning crew to earn cash. Darrell Hines gave me that card—and that's when I took off on my own."

"Jay, you should have told me that!" Kelly frowned.

"I didn't want you to worry. But I think when I bailed Cal decided to grab me. He was involved with the papaya farm thing. I had a lot of time to think about it, and I must have been a loose end as well as a—I don't know what. I always knew he was going to kill me in the end, I just didn't know why or how."

"Tell me about Cal Haddock. No one's told me much about the case since I shot him." Lei shouldn't be asking, but she couldn't help it.

"He wouldn't say much. He'd come in, bring me water, empty the slop bucket. I tried to get him to talk to me, see me as a person, but he hardly wanted to look at me. I made a run for it one time." Jay rubbed his head ruefully. "He was pretty quick, took me down and dragged me back in. No water for two days, no light, and this." He turned his head so Lei could see the lobe of his ear was gone, a scab marking its location. "That was my punishment."

"Unbelievable," Lei said. "It's amazing you're sane."

"Thinking of Kelly. That's what kept me sane." Jay kissed the girl's hand, looking into Kelly's changeable brown eyes. "I found what I was looking for when I went on my walkabout—and she was right in front of me the whole time. I'm just lucky enough to have a second chance. Thank you, Detective, for that."

"You're welcome," Lei murmured. The young couple barely noticed as she slipped out.

LEI PULLED in to the Health Guardian on her way home. The store enfolded her with now-familiar scents, and she pushed aside the clashing curtain of beads to look into the back office.

"Jazz?"

Jazz Haddock looked up from his desk. His chambray eyes were sunk deep in folds of shadow, his mouth a pursed line. "What are you doing here?"

"I probably shouldn't be talking to you." Lei closed the inner door, sat down on the couch, rubbed the black stone as she looked at him. "But I had to. Are they done interviewing?"

"Those FBI assholes all but stuck bamboo shoots under my fingernails, but I couldn't tell them what I didn't know."

"That it was your brother. I know."

"And you shot him."

"I had to. He was going to kill us, kill Bennett, if I didn't. I'm sorry it went down that way, believe me."

He put his head back against the seat, closed his eyes. She noticed he hadn't braided his long gray hair, and it straggled over his shoulders.

"He went off the deep end after our mother and sister died—had a schizophrenic break. I brought him here to heal, thought he'd find peace in manual labor out in nature. Took him to TruthWay to help him find some spiritual comfort. Can't believe it all ended this way."

"Did you ever suspect?"

"I knew he wasn't well. I knew he wasn't taking his meds. What I can't forgive myself for is the stones—I should have put it together. Jasper. Chalcedony. Opal." He hung his head into his hands. "I think on some level he wanted me to figure it out and stop him. But I never did. I won't tell anyone but you, but I think on some level I must have known. That's why I made the binder."

"It's over now," Lei said. There was nothing else to say. "The binder really helped solidify the investigation. You tried."

"I tried. It wasn't enough. Too many died." They sat in silence for a long moment.

"I wanted to say—it was good working with you. Might stop by for a smoothie now and again. Wanted you to know... I'm sorry." Lei stood up.

"I know you are. Me too." He lifted his head and his chambray eyes were shadowed with sorrow. "See you around, Lei."

STEVENS SAT beside her on the top step of her back porch in nothing but his boxers. They sipped morning coffee and watched the river. Keiki wriggled on her back in the grass, flailing her paws and grunting with the joy of a good roll. Lei leaned her head on Stevens's shoulder.

"It's nice to see that robe again. I'm rather fond of it." His hand reached into the collar, rubbed her bare neck.

"I love you, you know."

"You keep saying that."

"I keep meaning it. But you haven't said it back."

"And I won't."

"Why?"

"You know why—it makes you freak. So I'll just do crazy shit like this." He held out his right arm. The inner muscle of his forearm was tattooed with a tiny purple heart encircling Lei. They'd been too busy doing other things for her to notice it.

"Oh my God. A purple heart." She laughed. "When did you do that? You must've been drunk."

"As a skunk. I was crying in my beer the day I saw those roses, and J-Boy hauled me down to the tattoo guy before I knew what hit me. He's been trying to get us back together."

"I'll have to get him back. Give Anuhea his home address or something."

"Or something."

"You know, Marcella asked me to apply for the Bureau."

"Aw, shit. Wonder what kind of work they have in Quantico for aging detectives like me."

Lei punched him in the arm. She was distracted by the purple heart again.

"Cutest little tattoo I've ever seen. We're not going anywhere. It's ridiculous." She traced the heart with her forefinger.

"I may add more as necessary—but don't worry, I won't tell you I love you."

"Cross your heart." She traced an X over the tiny tattoo.

"I won't ask you to marry me either."

"Excellent." She kissed the little tattoo, trailed more kisses up the bulge of his biceps and along his collarbone as she climbed into his lap. His arms wrapped around her and his voice was rough in her ear.

"You know, promises are made to be broken."

Turn the page for a sneak peek of book three of the Paradise Crime Mysteries, *Black Jasmine!*

SNEAK PEEK

BLACK JASMINE, PARADISE CRIME MYSTERIES BOOK 3

The first tent was camouflage patterned, a still, hunkered shape in the green gloom.

"Maui Police Department. Anybody home? Come out and talk to us, please," Lei said.

A zipper opened in a slow parabola, and a thin young woman wearing stained jeans, her hair in dreadlocks, crawled out, accompanied by a draft of garlic and urine. She sat in a camp chair beside the tent opening, eyes flashing defiance.

"Yeah?"

"Did you hear the crash last night?" Pono asked.

"No."

"You sure about that? It must have been pretty loud. Shoots, you're lucky the car didn't run through your tent here on the way off the cliff." Lei played bad cop, her favorite role.

"I'm a heavy sleeper."

"Could be you had some help with that." Lei nudged an empty Jim Beam bottle near her foot.

"I said no. I never heard nothing." The woman folded scrawny arms across her chest.

"C'mon. We're not saying you had anything to do with it.

Someone died, though, and we're trying to at least establish when it might have happened," Pono said, conciliatory, warm as honey in summer.

"I told you, I was sleeping."

Lei'd had it. She pulled a pair of rubber gloves out of her back pocket, snapped them on, and reached for the zipper of the tent. "Did you hear my partner tell you someone died? I'm guessing there were some illegal substances in here, helping you sleep that heavy."

"Hey, stay out of my tent!" The woman scrambled up. "Yeah. I heard it, around two a.m. I know because the kid woke up, was crying."

Kid? They both leaned forward, and in the gloom of the tent they could see the faint gleam of a toddler's face through the screen insert of the door, wide dewdrop eyes tracking them like a tiny wild thing in its den. The urine smell must have been diapers.

"Tell us more, or I'll take that kid straight to Child Welfare," Lei said. A familiar rage swept over her with white-hot power. There was nothing she hated more than child abuse and neglect. She wanted to grab the baby and run away with it—to somewhere light and clean, where there was no drinking, drugs, or danger.

"You're right, Lei. We could do that." Pono redirected his gaze to the homeless woman. "Or we could get you into the shelter."

Lei shrugged. "Guess it's up to her, what we do with the kid."

"Fuck you, cop. It's not against the law to be homeless, and I never did nothing wrong. I take good care of my baby." The young mother snarled. On second glance, she probably wasn't out of her teens, and her eyes welled with furious, terrified tears.

"Watch your mouth. I'm taking that baby." Lei reached for her handcuffs.

Pono stepped in.

"I'm sure you take good care of your baby. Just tell us what you heard." His big, warm hand landed on Lei's arm, both restraining and anchoring her.

"Just heard the crash. And you're right; it was loud."

Lei sucked in some relaxation breaths, realizing she'd been too aggressive. But she was still going to call Child Welfare. This tent in the bushes was no place for a baby. Maybe the call would help get the girl some services, a real place to live.

The young mom didn't have anything else for them. No, she hadn't come out of the tent. She didn't go out late at night with the baby. She hadn't seen anything until that morning when she'd gone out to look at fire trucks and the commotion on the bluff. What did she think? Someone drove their car off the edge—it wasn't the first time there was a suicide out here. Which was true, Lei remembered. There had also been some suspicious overdoses, and prior to this, a missing woman and a teenager beaten to death, both cases unsolved.

Pauwela Lighthouse was not a homeless camp for the faint of heart or those with any other options.

They worked their way from tent to tent, hearing much the same story, a big crash at around two a.m. Lei wondered aloud where the campers got their water, and one obliging toothless denizen showed them the former pineapple field irrigation system that had been breached. Water was brought into the central camp area under the biggest ironwood tree via a series of screwed-together garden hoses.

They went to one last tent, a little bigger and set apart from the others, where an imposing Hawaiian woman sat at a table made from an upright cable spool. She was sorting long, sword-shaped hala leaves, which hung, drying, from a line under the tarp outside her tent. Lei wondered what a dignified woman like this was doing at the seedy camp. Usually Hawaiians took each one another in; it was shame to the family for a relative to be in need.

The woman looked up at their approach. Long iron-gray hair was wound into a bun and pierced by a bamboo chopstick, and she wore a drab muumuu and had rubber slippers on her swollen feet. Her eyes were dark, inscrutable wells.

"What you cops stay looking for?"

Lei held up her badge. "Eh, Aunty. Know anything about the crash last night?" She called the woman by the title of respect used in Hawaii by younger people to elders.

The woman picked up a long piece of hala, pandanus used to make basketry, hats, and floor coverings. She worked the long leaf with her fingers, expertly shredding off a row of spines that edged the length of the leaf with a thickened thumbnail.

"I saw someone leaving after the car went off."

"What? I mean, you sure, Aunty?" Lei's attention sharpened.

Dark eyes glanced up, a tightening of contempt at the corners. "I know what I saw."

"What's your name, Aunty?" Pono had his notepad out.

"Ramona Haulani."

"Well, Ms. Haulani, tell us more."

"I don't sleep so good." The woman shredded the stripped hala leaf into half-inch sections, each about eighteen inches long. The thumbnail appeared to work as well as any paring knife. "I was awake, and I heard the car drive up to the edge. I came out of my tent." Ramona gestured. From the door of her tent, she had a clear view of the bluff where the car had gone over.

"I wanted to see what was going on. I knew it was late, the hour of no-good."

Lei considered asking about that but decided it was more important to keep the woman talking.

"Then, after the engine was off and it had been sitting awhile, it rolled forward and went off the edge." Lei and Pono darted a glance at each other. This scenario didn't sound like a teenager driving off the cliff in a suicide.

"It was loud." It must have been; everyone had mentioned that. "Then I saw a little light, just a flash, like one of those mainland lightning bugs. It would go on and off, moving away from where the car went over."

"Did you see anything else? Who was holding the light?" Lei

tried not to rush her.

"No. It was dark, hardly a moon even. I saw the light—flash, flash—moving down the road." She gestured back toward the main road. "I thought it must be someone walking, using a small-kine flashlight."

They pumped her for more information, but that was basically all she had. She hadn't talked about what she has seen to anyone, and Pono encouraged her to keep quiet.

"I can keep a secret."

Ramona picked up another hala leaf, slit the edge. The older woman's nail must have been sharpened, the way it cut through the plant material with a zipping sound that reminded Lei of the body bag closing. Lei found her hand in her pocket again, rubbing the black stone.

"Why you stay out here, Aunty?" Pono asked.

"I nevah like the family tell me my business. I do what I like," Ramona Haulani said, and the darkness behind her brown eyes hinted at secrets. They thanked her and hiked back to the truck.

Lei drove them to the station while Pono wrote up notes on his laptop. She was still entertained by the sight of his big sausage fingers flying nimbly over the keys. Sunset slanted across the dash, and her stomach rumbled again. Those pretzels hadn't lasted long.

"We'll have to meet with the lieutenant in the morning," Pono said, still typing. "She's going to want to get up to speed, stat."

"I know—but I don't have to like it." Lei and the lieutenant weren't fans of each other. "I'm not thinking suicide anymore."

"It'll be interesting to meet with the ME and go over the autopsy report. Somebody walking away from the wreck looks bad. More paperwork." Pono liked to grumble about that, but they both knew he was better at it.

Her phone vibrated in her pocket and she flipped it open. "Hey, Stevens."

"When you getting home? Dinner's almost ready."

"Half hour."

"'K, then. Love you."

"Likewise." Lei closed the phone.

Pono looked up. "How's loverboy?"

"Hungry. He's almost got dinner ready."

"When you guys going to get married?" Pono never tired of trying to get others into his own debatable domestic bliss. He and Tiare had stopped at two kids, something Lei considered a good thing, but the struggle to make ends meet with a family wasn't something she was in a hurry to duplicate.

"Mind your business." Lei dropped Pono at the station lot, where his lifted purple truck was parked.

"See you tomorrow, Sweets." The ironic nickname her Kaua'i partner, Jenkins, had dubbed her with had been bequeathed to Pono. She'd finally given up fighting it.

"Too soon, bruddah."

I stretch out on my four-hundred-thread-count Egyptian cotton sheets and flick on the flat-screen TV to the news, looking for something about the crash. I sip my evening cosmopolitan, waiting through school budget crises and a whale watch gone awry. It's been another long, productive day managing the company, doing what I love. I'm lucky—or no, that isn't right. I've made my own luck, starting a long time ago when I stole that name that felt so much more a fit than the one I'd been born with.

Finally, a grainy video, obviously someone's cell phone—a fire truck hoisting up a yellow metal mesh body stabilizer on a wind-blown bluff. A cluster of uniforms wrestle the basket to the ground beside the fire truck as a voice-over begins.

"Tragedy struck on Maui when an unidentified young girl in a car went off the cliff at Pauwela Lighthouse. Authorities are still determining if the crash was an accident. Neither of the seasoned detectives assigned to the case were available for comment."

Just a quick blip. The "seasoned detectives" will have the devil of a time finding out who the mysterious dead girl is. I've made sure of that. I close my eyes to savor the high from the night before. I felt like I could fly, soaring like an owl over the moonless nightscape. That high. God, it was something. Maybe that was it—I felt like God, granting life, taking it away.

I need to do a little research. I take out one of the prepackaged burner phones that I keep around for such moments and dial a number I've memorized—my contact at MPD. He doesn't know who I am, but he likes the deposits I make every time I need him. That, and I have a few choice photos that ensure cooperation.

I get info on Texeira and Kaihale, detectives on the case, and tell him to keep me informed. I boot up my Apple Air, thin as a wallet. In moments, I'm online, pulling up everything I can find on Pono Kaihale.

*There isn't much. Until recently, he'd been a regular patrol officer on the Big Island. After he was promoted to detective, he moved to Maui. He looks like a tiki god come to life in his departmental photo. Buzz-cut hair, wide brown face with a bristling mustache, even wider neck. Typical **moke** cop.*

Leilani Texeira is another story. A slender, athletic-looking woman with a lot of curly hair, she has tilted almond eyes, a smatter of freckles, and a full mouth. That mouth, cut wide and set hard, shows attitude.

Texeira's got a face that's more than pretty; it's hard to forget. I feel a little frisson of unease as I read about the Cult Killer case on Kaua`i—biggest case the sleepy island had ever seen, and Texeira was in the middle of it all the way to the end. I look at her photo again. Attitude is right. I'd better monitor things closely, and that means more payments to the mole, more hassles.

That stupid little redhead is still costing me money and I hate that. I never let anyone beat me at anything. I can't stand losing. But she's already dead, so I can't take anything more out of her, goddamn it. I need something to take my mind off things. I punch in a number on the bedside phone.

"Kimo. Send up some merchandise. I'm in the mood for dark meat."

I mix up the drink in a highball glass—a potent cocktail of Rohypnol and Viagra that guarantees me a good time. For this one, I go light on the roofies and heavy on the Viagra—might as well teach him something he'll remember. When Kimo pushes the merchandise in the door, I hand him the drink with a smile.

He's not sure what to think, doesn't know what's coming, so he drinks it after I clink his glass with mine...and pretty soon he's just what I need to get the kinks out. I like the way my beautiful white skin, so silky, looks against his mocha hide. I like the taste of a little blood, spread around like finger paint. It's a good session.

When Kimo picks him up, my sheets are messy so I have the maid come change them while I take the SIM card out of the phone, stick it in a chunk of apple, and grind it up in the disposal. I toss the plastic phone body into the recycle bin.

I go back into the bedroom. It's white and pristine once again, creamy drapes hiding the door to my bondage room, toys cleaned off and put away. I pay that maid well to not be seen and not be heard.

I take a shower, but now my shoulders are sore from the work-out. I use my regular cell to call the masseuse to come work the knots out, which he does rather nicely. Finally, oiled, perfumed, and pleasantly tired, I turn off the crystal bedside lamp and gaze out the sliders to the night sky reflecting off the black sea.

It's taken all that to get me to the state of relaxation I was in before I heard the name Lei Texeira.

She owes me for that.

Download *Black Jasmine* and continue reading now!

ACKNOWLEDGMENTS

Aloha dear Readers!

I grew up on Kaua`i, and it was a special joy and treat to write about my hometown, Hanalei, where I enjoyed many of the activities Lei does and more—surfing, sailing, diving, paddling, and jogging on the beach at Hanalei Bay. In developing Torch Ginger, I made a list of some of my favorite places (such as the Blue Cave) and figured out how to work them into the story. Some events that seem far-fetched, like the annual flooding, are in fact, true.

That said, a lot of other things are made up. I stayed away from actual buildings/addresses, instead inventing them entirely—such as the Kapa`a Police Station (which in real life is a sort of kiosk at the beach park.) The estate Mac owns is imaginary—as is the heiau on the plateau. And while there is a beautiful hotel in Princeville, it does not have an underwater bar with a disco ball, alas. Perhaps they should consider it on their next remodel!

Special thanks to two women knowledgeable about Hawaiiana who read the manuscript to help me avoid glaring mistakes in the cultural practices mentioned in the book: teacher Josalind Akoi and Hawaiian Immersion teacher Leina`ala Kenolio Vedder both read the manuscript and gave me feedback on language, the character of

Esther Ka`awai (entirely fictional, but based on my experience of certain powerful women imbued with mana`o) and other aspects. I apologize in advance for any mistakes—I meant no disrespect. My intention with my books has been to educate a wider audience about Hawaii (and its culture) through an entertaining read.

I continue to thank my detective reader Jay Allen, without whose law enforcement tips Lei would be lost, and beta readers Linda Lafragiola, Bonny Ponting, Julie Wallace, Noelle Pierce and Holly Robinson. You guys helped me rein in the galloping story, and my amazing editor Kristen Weber helped me forge it into a sequel worthy to follow Blood Orchids.

I also want to acknowledge Dr. Rex Couch, retired Medical Examiner for Kaua`i. Until his death, Dr. Couch provided valuable feedback on the bodies in my books. Dear Dr. Rex, you will always be missed...

Now on to the next one!

If you liked the story, *please leave a review*. It's the best thanks you can give any author!

Much aloha,

FREE BOOKS

Join my mystery and romance lists and receive free, full-length, award-winning novels *Torch Ginger* & *Somewhere on St. Thomas*.

tobyneal.net/TNNews

TOBY'S BOOKSHELF

PARADISE CRIME SERIES

Paradise Crime Mysteries
Blood Orchids
Torch Ginger
Black Jasmine
Broken Ferns
Twisted Vine
Shattered Palms
Dark Lava
Fire Beach
Rip Tides
Bone Hook
Red Rain
Bitter Feast

Paradise Crime Mystery
Special Agent Marcella Scott
Stolen in Paradise

Paradies Crime Suspense Mysteries
Unsound

Paradise Crime Thrillers
Wired In
Wired Rogue
Wired Hard
Wired Dark
Wired Dawn
Wired Justice
Wired Secret
Wired Fear
Wired Courage
Wired Truth

ROMANCES

The Somewhere Series
Somewhere on St. Thomas
Somewhere in the City
Somewhere in California

Standalone
Somewhere on Maui

Co-Authored Romance Thrillers
The Scorch Series
Scorch Road
Cinder Road
Smoke Road
Burnt Road
Flame Road
Smolder Road

YOUNG ADULT

Standalone
Island Fire

NONFICTION

Memoir
Freckled

ABOUT THE AUTHOR

Kirkus Reviews calls Neal's writing, *"persistently riveting. Masterly."*

Award-winning, USA Today bestselling social worker turned author Toby Neal grew up on the island of Kaua`i in Hawaii. Neal is a mental health therapist, a career that has informed the depth and complexity of the characters in her stories. Neal's mysteries and thrillers explore the crimes and issues of Hawaii from the bottom of the ocean to the top of volcanoes. Fans call her stories, *"Immersive, addicting, and the next best thing to being there."*

Neal also pens romance, romantic thrillers, and writes memoir/nonfiction under TW Neal.

Visit tobyneal.net for more ways to stay in touch!
or
Join my Facebook readers group, *Friends Who Like Toby Neal Books,* for special giveaways and perks.

Made in the USA
San Bernardino, CA
06 February 2020

64102834R00202